ALSO BY KIMBERLY MULLINS

Notebook Mysteries Series

Divided Lives (aka K.R. Mullins)

1897 A Mark Sutherland Adventure

Lights, Camera, Murder!!!

THE FAMILY BUSINESS

THE
FAMILY
BUSINESS

KIMBERLY MULLINS

To Jonathan and Joshua I am loving our lives together.
To Claudia who means so much to me.

PROLOGUE

The door splintered and boards flew toward all parts of the room, one hitting her on the shoulder. The police entered, guns drawn and aimed at the only person in the room.

"Freeze!" one of the officers shouted.

She disregarded the request, picked up her whisky, and drank it quickly. She could feel the pain radiating down her arm. "Did you need something, boys?"

"You're being taken in for violating the Volstead Act," he told her. He waved to one of his men to take her into custody.

PART I

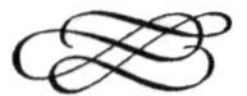

CHAPTER 1

hicago, 1896

The young man gathered up his books and tied them with a string. Running steps sounded on the wood floors in the foyer, and small hands yanked on his jacket. He looked down and saw a small face with dark hair falling in the little boy's eyes.

"Benji, what's up?" he asked the boy.

"Can I tag along with you, Patrick?"

Patrick kneeled in front of the boy and pushed his hair off his forehead. "I thought you were going to hang out here today."

Benji cocked his head toward the sitting room and sighed. "They're fighting again."

Patrick listened to the girls in the next room and acknowledged the observation. "Yeah, they don't get along, do they?"

"Like oil and water, is what Emma says," said Benji, crossing his arms over his chest, mimicking Emma's stance.

"Yeah," Patrick laughingly agreed. He thought about his errands; he enjoyed the boys' company and understood his wish to get away from the fighting. "I'm going to the library. Want to come with me?"

Benji's head nodded up and down. "Yes, please." He ran back into the sitting room to get his jacket and hat, then returned to Patrick and took his hand.

"Go tell them you'll be with me," Patrick said.

"No," the boy muttered, scuffing his feet. "I don't wanna."

"I'll go with you," Patrick offered. "Will that work?"

"Yeah, I guess."

The two walked to the sitting room. Opening the door, Patrick yelled into the room, "HEY!" Benji buried his head in Patrick's leg.

The two girls stopped screaming at each other and turned slowly toward him. He held up his hands. "Don't start on me."

"Well, what is it?" Lottie asked her brother, ready to get back to her fight.

"I'm taking Benji with me."

Jemma spoke up. "Have fun." She turned back and grabbed Lottie's hair. Lottie did the same, and their fight resumed.

Patrick looked at Benji. They both shrugged and headed out the door.

"Thanks!" Benji looked at his hero.

"I'm here whenever you need me," said Patrick, ruffing up the small boy's hair.

"Me too." He grinned.

CHAPTER 2

 *hicago, 1918*

"Ben, John's looking for you," Clay said as he stood next to the table.

Ben didn't look over at the man. "Thanks." He put down his cards and pushed his chair back. Groans sounded across the table.

"Don't fold!" ordered a man across from him.

"Yeah, let's finish the game," complained another. The stakes were high, and the money was piled in the middle of the table.

"Well, if you want to tell John that..." Ben said, starting to pick up his cards again. "I'll stay if you want me to let him know it was you."

The two men looked at one another and then back at him. The first man stuttered, "No, you go. We're fine."

Ben stood up and, with his back to the men, he grinned at Clay. They walked to John's office. Clay went in to tell him Ben was there and came out a few moments later. "You can go in now."

Patrick walked by Clay and, as he reached for the doorknob, said, "Stay away from Jemma."

"I don't know what you're talking about."

"I know about Edna, and if you don't want things to get messy, break it off with Jemma."

He nodded. "I'm marrying Edna this weekend."

Ben was satisfied with that answer and entered John's office. He stopped short in surprise. It wasn't just John; there were three other people in the room. His father, Lottie, and Patrick's wife, Jean. He ran over to Jean, kneeling next to her. "Is Patrick okay?" His mind was racing. Patrick had joined the Army during the Great War, and letters between the two had been sparse.

She started to cry. Ben wiped his eyes, struggling to find the next question.

"Before everyone's in tears, Patrick's alive," John said in a loud, clear voice. "Now, everyone, we need to plan." He looked at Ben and said, "You're integral to this."

"John, I'm still not sure," Ben's father started.

John turned his gaze to him, his voice low and gravelly. "Charles."

Charles stopped; he understood the hierarchy in the room. He sat back down without further argument.

John turned to Ben. "Take a seat." Ben moved over to take a chair near his father and waited. "I had a request from Jeremy and Emma to help out in this situation," John told the four of them.

"And me," said Jean, wiping her tears.

His face softened into a smile as he looked in her direction. "Yes." Their families had been close since Patrick's aunt and uncle had saved Jemma and brought her home to them. When

Jean married Patrick, she was included in his protection. *Whether they wanted it or not*, he thought.

"Ben, we'll need you to accompany Jean overseas."

"To see Patrick?"

"To bring him home," John replied. He continued to fill them in on the plan.

That evening, as Ben packed his bag, he could see Charles standing in the open doorway. He seemed to be bracing himself for the upcoming conversation with his son.

Ben didn't look up from his bag; he continued to roll up his shirts. "It won't work, Dad. I'm going."

Charles sighed and walked into the room. "There's still fighting ongoing with Germany."

"I'm going," Ben repeated, his tone ending the topic.

"Then you'll need these." Charles walked over to him and held out a stack of tickets. "You'll travel on the *S.S. Kroonland* from Hoboken, New Jersey."

Ben turned to take them from him. "That ship sounds familiar," he said, looking down at the various train and ship tickets.

"It should. It was the ship that was struck by a torpedo. It was slightly damaged, recommissioned quickly, and was armed for defense during the war, and I think continues to be. It's now being used as a troop ship to get Army and Navy personnel home."

"It's a military ship? How were Jean and I able to get tickets?"

"Your grandfather has contacts," Charles said simply.

"France?" asked Ben, looking at the tickets. "Isn't Patrick in England?"

"There's another ticket. You'll transfer there and continue to England. All of your transportation has been arranged to get you and Jean to Patrick." He put a hand on his son's shoulder. "You don't have to do this."

Ben slipped the tickets into his pocket and slammed his bag closed. He picked it up and said, "Yes, I do. He's family."

CHAPTER 3

 *ngland, 1918*

Ben and Jean traveled by train and then by ship until they finally stood outside the hospital ward Patrick had been assigned to.

A man leaning on crutches nearby asked, "Are you here for someone in that ward?"

"Yeah," Ben told him. Jean stayed silent, staring at those closed doors.

"Those guys were lucky to survive; they were at Saint Mihiel."

Ben looked at Jean, her eyes were wide. They didn't know where Patrick had been hurt, but they'd heard about the fighting at Saint-Mihiel. That was the site of the first independent American-led offensive to break the stalemate with Germany. Saint-Mihiel was a town surrounded by German soldiers. The mostly American unit caught the Germans in a withdrawal and were able to take advantage and push forward. There was a cost; forty-five hundred lives were lost there.

"Oh, Ben!" Jean shuddered.

"Hey, it's okay," Ben told her. "He made it through; we have to concentrate on that."

She nodded, trying to fight back her tears.

Ben looked at the man and asked, "Is that where you…"

"Where I lost my leg? You can ask. It's not a secret." He cracked a grin. "No, I got run over by a Jeep. Never got to see any action." The smile faded. "I was lucky." He used the crutches to move away from them.

Jean leaned on Ben's shoulder. "Lucky? The man's lost a leg, and he says 'lucky'. Oh, Ben, why did he have to go?"

"You know Patrick and Frank felt a strong obligation to defend our country," he said, hugging her close.

"And now Frank is missing, and Patrick has come back injured."

"He is back with us; that is what we have to concentrate on."

"Ben, I'm scared. Patrick lost his hand; how do I react?"

They stared at the double doors. He held her hand tightly. "It's Patrick; the hand doesn't matter." He hugged her close again and said, "Do you need some time? I can go in first."

"No, I should… He's my husband."

"Let me."

She nodded slowly and reluctantly moved to a chair across the hall and sat down. The trip and what was ahead of them were weighing on her mind.

A nurse opened one of the doors, wearing a scarlet cape over a gray dress with white cuffs and a white muslin cap. She stepped out and said, "You can come in."

Ben looked over at Jean, and she nodded. He turned to the nurse and said, "After you."

"Won't she be coming into the ward?" the nurse asked in a low voice.

"She just needs a minute."

"Then she should take it."

She held the door, and he followed her, walking past men lying in beds lined up side-by-side, four rows deep. The men were in various stages of treatment. Some had wrapped arms or legs, and others had missing limbs. Ben saw nurses moving bed-to-bed, offering ministrations.

The nurse he was following stopped and pointed to a bed a few feet from them.

Ben grabbed a chair and dragged it over to sit next to the restless man in the hospital bed. He leaned over and asked, "Can I tag along?"

The body stilled, and his eyes popped open. "Benji! You're here!"

"I am. We've been sent to get you home."

"We! Does that mean…" Patrick looked around wildly.

"It does," Ben started to explain.

"Patrick! I'm here," Jean said, coming up beside him.

Patrick reached out with both his arms, forgetting the missing hand. Jean didn't care and went into his arms. Ben stepped back to give them their privacy.

"How are the kids?" Patrick murmured.

"Lottie and your parents are with them," she said into his chest.

"Has Frank made it home?" Frank was his best friend and his captain on the police force. She looked at Ben and then back at Patrick. "He's missing."

"Missing? What does that mean?"

"Not confirmed dead," Ben replied bluntly.

Patrick nodded. "There's still a chance then. Does Annabeth know?"

"She's over here searching for him. I've sent notes to let her know we're here."

"Good. I want to help her any way we can," he said. He teared up again. "God, I'm so happy to see you."

A man in a white coat walked over to the bed, his head down. He stopped, looked up, and asked, "Should I come back?"

Patrick and Jean pulled apart, both wiping their eyes. Patrick spoke. "No, please. Do you have it with you?"

"What does he have in that box?" Jean asked. Ben walked over to them and had the same question.

"My new hand," Patrick said, his voice matter of fact.

Ben looked on with interest as the box was opened. It was indeed a hand, made out of wood, with a place to slide onto Patrick's stump and a shoulder strap to fasten it.

"Did you make this for Patrick?" Jean asked tentatively, reaching out to it.

"No, these are mass-produced now. We need these men to get back to normal life as fast as possible." The man took the hand out. "All right, Patrick, sit up and slip out of your shirt."

Patrick did as he asked; he was so thin that his bones stood out. Jean stayed steady and didn't look away. This was her Patrick, and she'd be there for him no matter what. They watched as the prosthetic was fitted to Patrick's arm.

"Fit is good, but for now, you'll have to wait to wear it for a few weeks."

Patrick nodded, looked at the hand. "It doesn't do much," he said.

"Not yet, but there are a lot of changes coming. I'd just say this is your first, not your last."

After the man took some measurements, he told them, "I'll make the changes and bring this back to you."

"Will the hand fit when Patrick gains weight?" asked Jean.

"Planning on fattening me up?" Patrick teased her.

"I am. That is my number one goal."

The man responded with, "I will make the necessary changes."

"Thank you," said Patrick. Jean and Ben echoed him.

The man put the hand back into its box. He nodded to them and walked away.

A few moments later, a doctor walked up, and Jean asked, "When can we take him home?"

"That's something we need to talk about," the doctor replied. "And you are?"

"I'm his wife Jean, and this is Ben. We're Patrick's family."

The doctor nodded. "I'm Dr. Harris. Patrick can't be moved anytime soon. It will be at least six months."

"Will you both stay?" Patrick asked them.

There was no hesitation; they said at the same time, "Of course, we will."

Patrick released the breath he didn't know he was holding.

John had planned for this contingency and had set up a place for Jean and Ben to stay. He'd keep to his promise; Ben would be there as long as Patrick needed him.

At the therapy session, working with his new hand a few months later, Jean and Ben sat watching the doctor and Patrick.

Dr. Harris looked at Jean. "Jean, I want to show you some exercises you can do with Patrick. Can you come with me?"

"Is that okay?" she asked Patrick.

He nodded and smiled. He kept smiling until Jean left the room. Ben said, "You can let go now."

Patrick's smile dropped off his face. "It hurts so much." He reached with his still intact hand to where the limb no longer was.

"You don't have to be brave for her."

Tears welled up in Patrick's eyes. "I don't know how else to act."

"Why not just be yourself?" asked Jean from the doorway. Patrick sniffed and tried to wipe his eyes.

Ben stood. "I think I need to give you both some time alone."

PART II

CHAPTER 4

hicago, 1919

"What're you doing? Go on in," Ben said from behind Jemma as he gave her a nudge toward the tall, imposing closed doors of John's office.

She planted her feet and said, "Don't rush me, Ben."

"Jemma, if you want to do this, you need to stand up to him."

"I will," she said defensively. She looked back at her brother. "You know this includes you also."

"Hey, I'm ready for the confrontation. Why're you stalling? Scared of his reaction to our ideas?"

She straightened her shoulders. "No, it's time to take the company in another direction. We're ready."

"Then why're you waiting?"

Still, she hesitated. "Will he think we're trying to take over?"

"Aren't we?"

She grunted. "John can't be in charge forever."

Ben leaned against the wall and pulled his hat over his forehead. "You nervous about telling him you want to be the head gangster?"

She shot him a dirty look.

The door opened, and a distinguished man with a full head of gray hair stepped out. Mel looked at the duo and asked, "You were saying something about John?"

Jemma had known the man since she was a child. He never kept anything from John and had always been his second in command. She stared at him without saying anything.

When an answer wasn't forthcoming, he said, "He'll see you now."

Jemma walked past him through the open door. "Mel," she acknowledged.

He looked at Ben and said, "You're next," looking pointedly at Ben's hat.

Ben snatched it off his head and waved it at Mel. "After you."

He quirked an eyebrow and turned to enter the office.

Jemma stopped inside the room and got a good view of John Harden. Even at seventy, he had a commanding presence. He was a tall, broad shouldered man with his grey-streaked hair perfectly combed and his dark blue suit pressed.

"Ready to talk?" he asked his granddaughter, staring at her intently.

She raised her chin. "Yes."

He walked to his desk while the two stood and watched him. "Sit," he commanded. They took the chairs in front of the desk. Mel moved to stand behind him, his literal right-hand man.

Ben started. "Johnny Torrio looks to be making moves that we need to watch. He's buying up small businesses and restaurants all over Chicago."

John slammed his fist down on the desk. "Can't he stay with his damn whore houses? I control the gambling in Chicago!"

"Times are changing," Jemma commented.

"What do you mean by that?" John asked, narrowing his eyes at her.

"I think that these moves show that the direction isn't gambling joints," she pointed out in a firm voice. "Gambling will take a back seat to alcohol. Prohibition will be where we make our money."

"You have some ideas on how to get our stake in this enterprise?" he asked, glancing from one to the other.

"Yes, we do the same as Torrio, but I'm thinking bigger. We buy up all of the bars in the area to expand into the alcohol trade."

"We also look for businesses where we can have larger backrooms and ways for people to get in and out secretly," Ben added.

"Do you think an expansion like that's a good investment at this stage?" John asked with a frown.

"I think it's the perfect time," Jemma said. "People will drink regardless of the law, and we can provide them with what they want."

"We think they'll drink more when the alcohol's limited," said Ben.

"Supply and demand," John murmured. He stood up, walked to the large windows, and stared out. "We have other worries right now; the Irish North Side Gang and South Side Italian Chicago Outfit are gearing up for an all-out war."

"Will we be involved?" Jemma asked. She began shuffling her plans around in her mind to stay in Chicago to support John.

John shook his head and didn't turn around.

Ben spoke up. "I hear some big names are coming in from New York and Florida; it's going to get bloody around here."

"You think I can't handle them?" John asked, still looking out the window.

Jemma shot Ben a glance. He shrugged.

John turned back to them. "You have something else to

discuss?" he asked Jemma idly, sitting back in his chair. "Maybe you want to take over my position with the company?"

Jemma raised her chin. "One day," she acknowledged. "Just not today."

John's mouth quirked up briefly, then he said abruptly, "Show me the properties you're thinking of."

She opened her file and handed the list to him. He reviewed the file. "Changes," he murmured thoughtfully. He closed the file and handed it back to her. "Get on that. Take our accountant and an architect with you."

Mel spoke up. "An expansion will put us on Torrio's list."

"You think we aren't already on it?" John asked his friend.

"And if a war starts?"

"We evaluate possible losses at that time." With that, he waved his hand in dismissal at Jemma and Ben. He looked up from his desk and saw they hadn't moved. "You're still here?"

She nodded. "We have more to discuss about expanding our operations."

"Isn't that what we just decided?"

"That's for Chicago; now we need to talk about New York. The places there will have entertainment, food, and alcohol," she stated boldly.

"Gawd, next, you're going to want dance floors," John sneered.

"That's right, we're thinking big."

"Not just New York," Ben filled in. "We want to expand further, maybe to California. The men building the city there will want drinks. We can set up our network from East to West."

Jemma said, "Ben can handle the California expansion, and I'll take New York."

John sat back and looked from one to the other. "You've been working on this for some time?" His tone implied *without* him.

"John, we know we can do it. It's time for us to take a bigger role in the business."

He sat back, the spring squeaking in the chair. "Oh, I know you can. I'm not sure I'll let you."

"Why not?" she asked in a steady voice.

"Yeah," said Ben, sitting up straighter, "why not?"

Mel stepped forward in a silent warning.

John waved him off. He stared at the duo without speaking, thinking of the future.

Jemma broke the silence. "John, I'm redundant here. You're here. Ben can help support the expansion and then move to California."

He looked over at Ben. "Can you handle the expansion here and in California?"

"I can get the properties purchased here and in California," he confirmed.

John looked at Jemma. "You have this all worked out. What're your plans for me?" Jemma looked at Ben and then back to John, not voicing her thoughts. He sighed and lay his head back on his chair. "You know, I hadn't expected to be running things forever."

"Dad and Mom had other interests," murmured Jemma.

"I know, they started to pull back when you were kidnapped; it was too much for them. They only wanted a private life after that." He looked at them. "Now I have you and Ben."

"You do, and you need to let us control the operations in New York and California," she said firmly.

He sat forward, any weakness lost. "Fine. You'll control those operations, but remember you have a responsibility to the family. We have to operate as one. Do we understand that?"

"Yes," they both responded.

"Hmm," he said, taking out a cigar from his right desk drawer. Jemma got out a match and moved to his side of the desk to light it for him. He sat back, and they watched the smoke rise.

"All right, you move ahead with the plan. New York first. But," he cautioned, "you'll need to keep the books and send the family a cut."

"Of course."

"I'll have the bank set up an account for you to have full access of in New York. You'll need that to purchase the properties."

"I thought to rent initially."

"No, buying's best. This is about getting a foothold in New York and then California. We'll also want specific modifications to those properties."

"Thanks, Grandpa," she said, kissing him on the head.

"Get going," he said gruffly. "You have work to do."

They left the room. He smiled softly. "Family." He glanced over at Mel, his face hardening. "Mel, look into Torrio. I want to know where he's overstepping."

"Should I put out a warning?"

"No, for now, we watch. We'll make a move when there's cause."

Mel nodded. "I'll check with my contacts."

John nodded and moved back to look at the windows. It had taken a while to build up his presence there, and Johnny Torrio or anyone else wouldn't take him down.

CHAPTER 5

*N*ew York, 2019

"No," Jemma said to the man with her. She pointed to the low ceilings in the tiny dark space. "This is just too small. I need something that I can expand."

"It'll also need a large back room," murmured Ben.

"And several exits," she murmured back.

"What kind of money are we talking about?" the man asked baldly.

Jemma and Ben were keeping their Chicago connections quiet. She gave him a long stare and finally said, "Max, there's enough for an entire city block. Cash."

Max paled considerably. With a shaky hand, he tore the pages out of his book and crumpled them up. "Then we start again with a new list." He walked to the door, then turned to them. "Follow me."

Ben stopped her. "We should also look at a few smaller places for storage in case we're raided."

"You're right." She looked around and crinkled up her nose. "Just not this one."

He noted the mold and the sagging ceilings. "Agreed."

They walked out and found Max waiting by his Model T touring car. He held the door open for them. Once they were inside, he walked to the driver's seat. He drove quickly, dodging other cars and horse-drawn carriages, going further into Manhattan. The buildings went by, and when they stopped, they were at 86 Bedford Street between Grove and Barrow in the West Village.

"Greenwich," Jemma said with a twisted smile. Brother and sister leaned over to gaze out the window at the structure, her attention wholly on the building in front of them. Her mind swirled with plans. "Is the whole building available?" she asked Max.

"Anything is, for a price," reported Max.

"There must be holdouts. People not wanting to sell out," said Ben in a low voice.

"That's what I was thinking," she responded in the same tone.

Max got out and walked around to open their door. They exited more slowly, looking at the three-story building. It was what she'd requested, and it took up the city block. She walked up and touched the brick; it was red with a thick black line running down the length of the building.

She turned to Max. "Where does it exit?"

"On 86th street," he said. "There's multiple exits."

She nodded. "We'll need the whole thing. No half-ways about this project."

Max started to smile broadly and covered it with a loud cough. "This way." He pointed to the doors in the center of the building. They walked over and saw that glass windows framed the entrance.

"These will have to go," she said, studying the view.

Max protested. "But the windows will cost more to remove and will reduce the value of the building."

Jemma didn't bother to respond.

Max stopped. It wasn't his business to question their use of the property. He cleared his throat and asked, "Ready to go in?"

"Hmm," Jemma said and followed the man inside. The space was a little tight, with only a long bar and a row of tables and chairs across from it. It was a long, deep space that appeared to be well taken care of. "It has possibilities."

"The bar could be saved," Ben said, running his hand over the dark finish.

A man walked over to them, wiping a glass with a white towel. "Nice, isn't it?"

"It is," Ben agreed, bending down to examine the intricate craftsmanship. "Are you the bartender here?"

"I am the owner. My father carved it out, and I finished it. It's the heart of the place." He noticed Max standing behind them and stiffened. "What're you doing here? I told you I wasn't interested."

Jemma raised a brow at Max.

Max muttered, "Don't worry. I'll work it out." He went down to the end of the bar and waved to the man to follow him.

The bartender moved toward him with a scowl on his face.

"What do you think?" Ben asked Jemma in a low voice.

"If the rest of the building is in the same shape as this space, this is the one I want," she said firmly.

"He might not sell," he said, watching the duo's body language. Max put his hand on the other man's shoulder, and he shoved it off.

"Max," Jemma called, "can we see the rest of the building?"

"Yes, of course." He turned back to the bartender, whose face was dark red and set in a scowl. They had a low-intensity confrontation. Whatever he said to the man had them moving together toward Jemma and Ben.

"I'm Charlie Hudson. What do you want with the building?" he asked bluntly, directing his question at Ben.

Max said, "Charlie, give them a chance."

"Shut up, Max. I'm handling this." He turned back to them and demanded, "Well?"

"I'm opening a business, and I'll need a lot of space," Jemma told him, ignoring the surprised look he sent her.

"She wants the whole building," said Max.

Charlie's eyes widened. He took out his polishing rag and absently started to wipe down the bar. "I had a lot of plans for my business. I don't like the government saying what I do is wrong or illegal." Jemma looked at Max. "You have other locations to show us?"

Max pressed his lips tight, not willing to accept that this wasn't it. He nodded and said gruffly, "All right, we can go now."

Charlie watched them open the door, then called out, "What can you offer?"

"We'll need to see the rest of the building," Jemma told him.

"Follow me." They started toward the back. He opened the door, and Ben and Max went past him into the room. Charlie put his arm in front of her to block her path. "Are you in charge?"

She kept her face expressionless and stared up at him. "I am."

"What business are you thinking of having here?"

"I'm not ready to share that now."

"Maybe I'm not ready to let you through," he countered.

She walked even with him and elbowed him in his large stomach. The breath left him with a woosh, and he moved his arm down. She ignored him and entered the room, with Max grabbing Charlie's arm as he attempted to follow her.

Jemma looked around the large storage space. "Is there an exit?" She'd found what she wanted, though. Now, what did the rest of the building look like?

"Yeah, just out there," Max called as Charlie glared from his place at the door, his arm wrapped around his middle.

Jemma nodded at Ben, and he went to check it out. When he returned, he said, "It exits onto the back street."

She turned to Max. "Can we see the other areas of the building?"

"Yes, of course. Come with me."

They followed him to the front of the bar, leaving Charlie in the back. Once they were outside, they entered a large door to the right. The rest of the building contained empty shells of space. The more she saw, the more she thought, *It's the right choice.*

"That guy, Charlie," commented Ben, "he's not the most personable."

"There were plans for Charlie to expand and make his bar bigger than it is now," Max explained. "And he's rather bitter about the new laws coming out."

"He looked like he didn't want to sell."

Max looked over at the man and back at them. "We can work it out. He'll see it's the best way forward."

"Give us a minute," Jemma suggested to him.

"Of course, I'll meet you outside."

When she and Ben were alone, she looked around and said, "We'll need a lawyer to make sure everything's done legally and an architect to make the changes to our specifications."

Ben's gaze followed hers. "We are in Greenwich Village," he reminded her.

"So we are," she murmured. Ben waited. "Yes, I know that you're thinking of Lottie."

"You know she's a good lawyer and someone we can trust," her brother reasoned.

"We'll see. I was also thinking about Ellis; he should be able to recommend an architect."

He pushed her. "We can go see Lottie tomorrow, or we can look around at more buildings."

"No," she said and went to the door. She pushed it open and called to Max, "This is it. Draw up the papers. We will give you our attorney's name to finalize."

"Whose name will you give him?" muttered Ben.

"Lottie," she said, her mouth set.

"We need to see her first, to make sure she'll be okay with this."

"We will," she said through gritted teeth. He sent her a side look. "We will," she said again.

Max waited for them to finish and called, "Send me the address." He got into his car and drove off with a wave.

As they watched him leave, Ben looked over at Jemma. "Where to now?"

"There's no reason to delay things. Let's go see Lottie now."

He raised his eyebrows but didn't say anything as he followed her outside.

Jemma raised her hand and hailed a cab. It pulled up, and they got into the vehicle. "To 841 Broadway," she told the driver.

"Where'd you get her address?" asked Ben.

"John," she said with no further explanation.

"Hmm. Didn't you attempt to pull out her hair last time you were together?"

"She had me in a headlock. I had to do something," she said, her voice huffy.

"You don't get along."

"That's not fair," she argued. "We got along very well when we were little."

"No," he corrected, "you used to fight even in the early days."

"Yeah, we did." She smiled slightly. "I wonder if she's up for another one."

"Jemma, we need her. Try not to attack her."

She looked ready to explode. She finally sighed and relaxed her jaw. "Fine. Business first."

The cab driver pulled to the side of the road and looked over his shoulder. "We're here."

Ben handed him the money, and they got out onto the busy sidewalk. He looked up and saw a sign that read 'Lottie Flannigan, Attorney at Law' hanging there. He turned to her Jemma. "Ready to go in?"

She straightened her shoulders and nodded.

He walked to the door and opened it. The large room had two desks, one on each side of the room. All the walls were filled with thick books. There was no one there to greet them. They wandered around the room until Jemma came upon a set of frames. She reached up and tapped the diploma. "Looks like the real deal."

"It is," came a voice from across the room.

Jemma turned slowly. "Lottie."

"Jemma." The tone sounded the same from both women.

"Before an all-out fight starts, can I greet Lottie first?" Ben asked.

Lottie's tight lips moved to form a wide smile. "Hello, Benji," she said and held out her arms. He went over and hugged her tightly. "It's truly a pleasure to see you."

"Enough of the mushy stuff already," said Jemma. Her voice showed her disgust.

"Always straight to the point, huh, Jemma? Okay then, why are you here?" She moved to her desk and sat down.

"This is too open," Jemma told her, looking around.

Lottie raised her eyebrows. *That kind of meeting,* she thought. "I can work something out. Just a second." She went back into the room she'd just left.

She returned with a blond man who looked to be about Lottie's age. "No, I don't mind. I can finish the paperwork at my desk," the man said. He didn't look their way as he took the pile of documents to the desk on the far left of the room.

"That's Chris, my partner." They nodded at him. Lottie said, "Follow me." She opened the door to the conference room.

Jemma and Ben followed. Ben closed the door behind them. Lottie said without turning around, "I wouldn't do that, Jemma."

Jemma slowly lowered the hand she'd extended toward Lottie's hair. "Sorry, reflex."

Ben shot her a look and mouthed, "Be good."

"I'll try," she mouthed back.

Lottie moved to the far side of the long table and sat. "You need legal help? Any dead bodies I need to be aware of?"

"Not yet," Jemma said, scowling.

Lottie raised her brow. "No reason to get uptight."

Ben reminded her, "Jemma, this is your operation."

Lottie waited for her to begin.

"We're setting up a business here," she explained.

"Hmmph."

"I'm setting up a *business* here," she said forcefully.

"What type?" Lottie asked.

"A club."

Lottie laughed suddenly. "Your timing's a bit off, isn't it?"

"Not really. We're counting on the Volstead Act going through." Volstead would usher in the prohibition of alcohol and make it a federal crime.

Lottie sobered suddenly. She tapped her pencil on the paper in front of her.

"Fine, you don't want to help us," Jemma said. She stood and pushed her chair back, knocking it to the ground. Ben stood up reluctantly to follow her.

"Where're you going?" Lottie asked, sitting back in her chair.

"You don't want to help us," Jemma repeated through gritted teeth.

"Did I say that?" she said with no inflection in her voice.

Jemma continued to stand, but Ben dropped back down in his chair. "Sit down, Jemma, and tell Lottie what your plans are."

Jemma hesitated and then moved to turn her chair upright and sat down. Lottie waited expectantly. "We're looking at the building near here that backs onto 86th Street."

"The whole building?" Lottie asked, taking notes.

"Yes."

She tapped her pencil again. "I know that building; it has multiple owners."

"Yes, we met one of them today."

"Was it Charlie Hudson?"

"How did you know?" Ben asked her.

"Others have tried to get that location; he usually shuts them down."

"We've spoken with him," confirmed Jemma.

"He said he'd sign?"

"Not yet," Jemma admitted, "but he looks like he might need the money."

"How much are you thinking?"

"Let's just say, I want to make him an offer he can't refuse."

"Is this being funded by John?" asked Lottie.

"It's the family business."

"I know the two other owners want out before the new law comes into effect; they'll sell. I'll work with Charlie." Lottie studied her notes and looked up abruptly. "How do you plan to stay open after the law comes into place?"

"There'll be secret entrances and hidden exits."

"You'll need a carpenter and an architect."

"Will you keep this quiet?"

"You mean will I help you hide your secret club where alcohol will be sold illegally?" Lottie asked her bluntly.

Jemma looked at Ben, and he shrugged. She turned back to Lottie. "Yes."

Lottie sat back. "I don't like this law. I think it's not only unfair to a great many people, but it also limits our liberty."

"You'll help?" Jemma asked.

"I'll organize the purchase of the property. And I'll recommend some people to do the work you'll need."

"You sound like you've already done this type of counseling," Ben said.

"Let's just say my client base has changed. Who's your agent here in New York?"

"Max Payne."

She nodded. "He's a good man, but don't tell him the purpose of the building; the fewer people who know, the better off you'll be."

"Agreed," said Jemma. "We also want to keep John's name out of this."

"So, this'll be your operation? You'll be the Lady Boss?"

"Yes."

"I like that idea."

"See, I told you. You can get along," Ben teased them. "Lottie, are you still able to work in California?"

She frowned. "Are you planning to expand there, too? Same as here?"

"Yes, I'm moving there to set up operations."

"Let's get things organized here first before you head out there."

Ben nodded. "That works for me. I need to set up operations in Chicago before I can move to California."

Jemma looked at her watch. "We need to go see the suppliers." She looked at Lottie. "The bank's been set up." She reached into her purse and pulled out a card to hand to her. "We want this worked out by the end of the week."

"You don't ask for much, do you?" Lottie told her, taking the card.

"No, I trust you can get the job done. Do you have contact information for the carpenter and architect?"

"It's the same person; I have his information." Lottie flipped pages in her notebook and wrote quickly, handing it to her.

"Jojo?" Jemma read aloud.

"Yes, he's talented and knows this kind of work."

"Is he trustworthy?"

"Extremely. He's worked with Grandpa Ellis in Chicago, and he's doing similar work in the area."

"We'll contact him."

"How long will you be in town?"

"I'll be staying in a hotel until the construction starts."

Lottie nodded. "Where are you thinking of living on a more permanent basis?"

"I was thinking the second floor of the same building as the business."

"Good idea, you'll be able to keep an eye on operations. Make sure that you have a separate entrance; you don't want the business in your personal space."

Jemma frowned a bit; she hadn't thought about that. "That's a good idea," she said begrudgingly.

"I do have them occasionally," Lottie commented dryly.

Ben went over to hug her. "Thanks, Lottie. I'll contact you about the timing in California."

She hugged him back and smiled brightly. "I won't mind a trip; it'll give me a chance to see Patrick and Jean."

"I love Jean and Merle's movies," Jemma commented, nodding to the movie posters featured on the walls.

"Me too. Going with Ben will give me the opportunity to watch them being made."

"How is Patrick?" asked Jemma.

"Better," Lottie said, wiping her eyes quickly. "He was in a lot of pain initially, but that seems to have settled. Jean hit it head-on and wouldn't let him go under." She turned to Ben and said, "Thank you for going with her to get him home."

Ben nodded but didn't say anything. It had been a hard time.

Jemma cleared her throat. Patrick had always felt like her older brother. "I'll send him a letter soon."

Unexpectedly, Lottie's face softened, and she went over to Jemma. She took her hand and said, "He's mentioned that you'd continued writing to him when he was away and when he returned."

"Yeah, well, he is family."

"He is. *We* are."

That comment surprised Jemma, but she stayed silent. Lottie released Jemma's hand and went over to take Ben's arm to walk him out. "California's exciting. Get Patrick to take you to the studio when you get there."

"Remember, this is business," Jemma reminded her.

"Oh, don't worry. I'll be charging for these services," Lottie acknowledged.

"We know," Jemma replied. "We pay our bills." With that, she waved to Ben and exited the office.

Lottie watched the duo leave. She followed them out and leaned against the doorway. The office was empty of clients, and Chris was buried in his books. He looked over at her and asked, "Anyone I know?"

"Not unless you've been to Chicago."

"Are they well known in Chicago?"

"More like infamous," she said and walked to her desk.

He frowned. "Our client base is changing."

She sat at her desk and laid her head back on the chair. "Yes, I think we have exciting times ahead of us."

CHAPTER 6

"She could've turned us down," Ben told his sister.

Jemma pulled out a cigarette and tapped it on her hand. She put it to her lips and lit the end, staring ahead onto the busy city street. Cars were rushing by, and people were pushing past them on the sidewalk. "Yes, I'm surprised she agreed."

"Why do you always want to attack her?"

She rounded on him and said defensively, "It isn't always me. Sometimes she starts it."

"Why?"

"We just don't get along, okay?"

He shrugged. "Okay."

"Don't we have another appointment?" she asked, wanting a change of topic.

"Yeah, the supplier is next."

She dropped her cigarette and ground it onto the pavement with her high heel. "Let's go."

Ben hailed a cab, and they were driven quickly to a small, rundown restaurant. They got out, and when Ben was paying,

Jemma looked around. "No worries about being seen here," she said, sarcasm coloring her tone.

"The whole point is to get this going with no one the wiser," he reminded her as the taxi drove off.

"Hmm, I just hope it's clean," she said in a low voice and followed him in. The man at the counter didn't say much when he picked up the menus and guided them into the darkened room to their table. Once they were seated, he left them abruptly. "They can't afford to have the lights on?" she asked, looking around.

"Give it a chance," he suggested.

"Is anything edible here?" she asked, tilting the menu to try to catch some light.

A rather round man wearing an apron answered her. "Everything is good here, and if you don't want to try it, you can leave."

She looked up from the menu and growled, "Prove it. Bring me your favorite dishes."

He glared at her and stomped off with a grumble.

"You just make friends wherever you go, don't you?" her brother commented.

"I'm not here to make friends." She looked around and asked, "Do you see our man anywhere?"

"I was told he was small and dark," Ben said, looking around, too.

"He'll fit in here," she muttered, glaring.

"I think that's him," said Ben, nodding toward the door.

Her gaze followed his. The man at the door met Ben's description: a short, rough-looking man in a wool jacket and a dark hat, not over 5'5".

Ben raised a hand, and the man acknowledged the signal. He moved over to their table.

"Joey?" asked Ben, standing.

"Yes, and you're Ben and Jemma?" Joey asked, holding out his hand.

Ben shook it, and Jemma nodded at him. "Why don't you sit?"

Joey followed their lead and sat down. He waited a minute, then said, "All right, you got me here. Now talk."

Jemma looked around without answering.

"We're safe here," he told her.

Jemma reached for her bag and pulled out a notebook. "We plan on opening a club. We'll need good liquor, quality product, and beer."

"You came to the right person. I can get it in, but we'll need to start now."

"How can you get it here?" asked Ben.

"We have multiple ships. We'll have the paperwork and pick up the drums overseas. Our major sources will be from Canada and Mexico. The mother ships will take on the booze."

"What address will be listed in the paperwork?" Jemma inquired.

"They're falsified so that workers won't question our orders." He continued, "We'll set up rendezvous points in international waters. Usually about three nautical miles out."

"How do we pick up our deliveries if you can't get in closer than three miles?" Jemma asked.

"You'll need to get some high-speed contact boats and a remote location to move them into."

"Do you have a recommendation where I can get these?" *There're so many details,* she thought.

"Yes, I have contracts I trust."

"What's the timing for the deliveries?" Ben asked him.

"We'll only move these at night. You'll meet the mother ships and then ferry the liquor ashore."

"We'll also want bottles. Wine and champagne," Jemma told him.

"That can be arranged."

"We'll need to get those storage locations purchased sooner rather than later," Jemma said, looking at Ben.

"That's a good idea," Joey agreed.

The first man came back to their table with a line of waiters loaded down with food. As they set it on the table, he asked, "Joey, are they with you?"

"Yeah, George, we're getting some business done."

Jemma looked at the food that was set in front of them. "Well, it looks edible," she allowed.

George huffed.

Joey grinned and picked up his fork. "Try it," he invited. "You'll like it."

Jemma slowly picked up her fork and tried the dish directly in front of her.

Ben said with a mouth full of food, "This is amazing."

George pointed to a pasta dish. "Try that one."

Ben didn't hesitate and reached for the recommended dish. He scooped it onto his plate and took a bite. "Yum."

Jemma continued to eat the various dishes in silence.

George waved the servers away, but he stayed at their table waiting for Jemma's reaction. "Well?" he demanded.

Joey said in a low voice, "George, cut it out. They're customers."

"No," Jemma said, slowly putting down her napkin, "I'll respond." She looked at George. "I have an idea to share with George. Why don't you sit down?"

George stuttered and turned to Joey for direction.

"Sit," he commanded.

He sat.

Jemma leaned forward. "Now, gentlemen, I have some plans to review with you."

CHAPTER 7

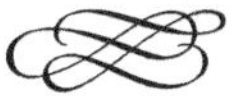

*B*ack at their hotel, Jemma and Ben sat together in the living room of their suite.

"Are you good with things here?" Ben asked.

She looked up from her notes. "I am now that we have the real estate and supplies settled. I'll stay here at a hotel until we can get the building ready. Will you use the same business model in California?"

He stroked his chin. "I want to look around and see how California's reacting to this."

She reached out her hand to him. "I wish we could stay in the same area."

He took her hand and teased, "We want world domination, don't we?"

"Yes," she confirmed.

"Then I take one part of the country and you the other."

"With John in the middle."

"Yes, and John wants Chicago to be set up first." He dropped her hand and walked over to his stack of papers. "I have the properties we looked at in Chicago. I'll make my move when I return." He turned to her with a frown. "Jemma, seriously, you'll need to find someone here you can trust."

"I have you," she protested.

"I won't be here," he pointed out.

"John always said, we have to manage this as a family business," she reminded him.

"That hasn't always worked out for him," he retorted.

"Yes, his sister, Candace," said Jemma. "She was rather evil."

"She shouldn't have involved children in her illegal activities. John wasn't close to her, and that situation was untenable."

"Yeah, from what I hear, Great Grandma Coreen caused that situation."

"John and Candace fought for her attention," he agreed.

"Our family's such a mix and one that John didn't expect."

"Events have changed our lives and brought us our family," he said. "Sis, you need someone like Mel in your life. John trusts him and relies on him with everything to do with the business. He's family. You need someone like that here like that."

"Do you have a Mel in California?"

"Patrick's there," he said simply.

"He used to be a police officer, so be careful there. The family business must survive, and we need teams of people we trust."

CHAPTER 8

he next morning

Jemma opened her bedroom door and entered the living room. She pulled her robe closed over her nightgown and tied it. "Up already?" she called over to Ben. He sat near the large windows with a pile of newspapers in his lap.

"Coffee's over there," he said and didn't look up.

"Have you ordered breakfast yet?" she asked with a wide yawn.

"Yeah, it's on its way."

"Anything interesting in the paper?" she asked, pouring coffee into a white cup.

He lowered the papers and tapped them.

She walked over to get a closer at the article: 'California Wine and the Impact of Prohibition'. "Wine? We have that coming, and most of our inventory will be the hard stuff."

"Here and in Chicago, that's true, but I'm reading about California. Did you know there are more than a thousand wineries there?"

"I didn't," she admitted. "I guess we'll have to rethink the inventory allocations."

"Production," he said, "that's what I'm thinking about."

"What do you mean?"

"What if I get in on the side that's making that inventory?"

"Ben, that could be a problem; we'd planned to sell the product, not be producers."

"I'm thinking about churches. The sacramental wine will still be made."

"Is that going to be enough to support a business?" Jemma scoffed.

"Maybe, maybe not," he said, "but I do want to look into it before I start putting money into any properties. We know New York and Chicago. California's a different element."

"It's all that sun they get there; it bakes the brains."

"Could well be. Can I contact you here if I need you?"

She walked over, slowly stirring her coffee. "Of course. I can be reached here. I have some other ideas I need to evaluate."

"Other than the main club?"

"Yes, I'll also move forward with the additional locations."

"Sure, for storage."

"That and an eventual expansion."

"Thinking ahead?" he asked.

"If we don't take the locations, others will," she reasoned.

"You think this'll be that big?"

"I do. I think it'll set us up for life." A knock sounded on the door. "The food's here," she said.

"Okay then," he said, rubbing his hands together. "Let's eat and then you can see me off on the train."

"Where will you stay once you get to California?"

He glanced over at her. "A hotel probably."

"Have you contacted Patrick and Jean?"

"I've wired them that I was coming out for business. They said they'll meet me at the station when I let them know the dates."

"Do you have a car lined up?"

"Jean's brother-in-law is in the car business. I'll get with him."

She nodded. "Call me once you get settled."

"I will," he promised, drinking his coffee quickly

"Wine, huh?" she mused.

"Yeah."

"Add me to your list of buyers."

He grinned. "That I'll do."

Later that morning, the taxi dropped them off at the station. "Wait here for me," Jemma said to the driver.

She and Ben walked through the station and out to the tracks. The train drew up in a cloud of steam.

She suddenly gripped his hand.

"Hey, what's this?" Ben asked, concern dropping his voice.

"I just feel we're all being pulled apart."

"We're family and will always be there for one another," he promised.

"You're right," she said, releasing his hand and smoothing out his lapel.

"Just remember, you're the boss lady here. Set things up the way you want them. And find someone you trust."

"I will."

"Last call!" yelled the conductor.

"You'd better hurry." She watched as he ran for the train.

He climbed the steps and turned back, "Bye, Sis!"

Jemma waved and watched Ben disappear onto the train.

CHAPTER 9

hicago

"John, the locations have been purchased and set up," Ben said. "The architects have drawn up plans, and we expect them to be completed before the end of the year. We'll use the same supplier as Jemma and move the alcohol over land to us."

"This looks well thought out," John replied, reviewing the written plans at his desk.

"I'm leaving it in good hands. You and Mel," Ben told him, nodding to the tall, silent man by the door.

"Tell Patrick and Jean hello for us," John said.

"We'll expect a visit from you and Mel soon."

John didn't look at Mel. "We'll see if we can."

Ben grinned at his grandfather. "I'll set everything up."

"Keep us involved and get us some of that wine."

"I will," he promised. Ben grabbed his hat and left the office.

Mel slowly shut the door. "He's worked hard, and the bars are well underway."

"Any movement from Torrio?"

"He seems to be doing the same thing we are, getting things set up."

CHAPTER 10

alifornia

Seven to ten days, Ben thought. *So much better than the four and a half months it would've taken before the transcontinental railroad opened up.* He boarded the train and went to his private room. He had more newspapers and a list of realtor names. *Time to plan,* he thought.

The week rolled by slowly, and when the final whistle blew, the loud voice calling for the California stop was a relief. Ben closed his bag with a click and folded his coat over his arm. It was much warmer than he was used to. He made his way down the narrow hallways and waited for his turn to step off the train.

"Ben!" He heard a familiar voice call out, and as he stepped down, he turned his head toward it. It was Patrick! He raised his free hand and waved with a wide smile on his face. There'd been letters and many phone calls between the two since they'd returned home. He had missed him.

Patrick didn't appear to be a man with a handicap. At first

glance, you wouldn't have noticed his hand was carved out of wood. Ben did know and held out his left hand to shake Patrick's warmly.

"Finally, we got you here," Patrick enthused.

"I did promise when we were in London," Ben reminded him.

"Yes. I'm glad you're finally here." Patrick looked down. "Is this your only bag?"

"Yeah."

"Traveling light?"

"I'm thinking of staying here permanently. I can buy what I need as I go."

Patrick smiled at that and bent down to grab the bag with his prosthetic limb.

Ben knew better than to argue. He watched as Patrick reached under his shirt. He had his hand on the handle of the bag; his prosthetic fingers moved and locked to pick up the bag. "Well, come on, let's get you home."

They moved to a shiny new car. "Nice," Ben said, running his hand over the hood.

"Jean's new toy. She likes fast cars," Patrick told him, putting Ben's bag in the backseat.

"Still," his friend teased. "We saw a movie of hers last week. I think the car went off a cliff?"

Patrick nodded. "That was all her. She wants everyone to know that it's a woman doing the stunts."

"She didn't get hurt?"

"No, no, the stunts are well planned out. But that isn't her latest interest."

"It's not? What else could there be? Trains, cars, and motor-cycles." Ben ticked them off on his fingers.

"You'll see," Patrick said. "Hey, want to come watch her latest film being made?"

"Count me in. I heard you're working at the studio."

"I am."

"What job?"

"Something I'd wanted to do for a while," Patrick confirmed. "That hand I came home with, it didn't have the dexterity I needed." He'd put his hand on the steering wheel and secured it to steer the car.

"The early hands were basic," Ben agreed. "Remember that doctor in England…"

"The one who decided I couldn't leave until I learned to use that first hand?" Patrick laughed. "I still talk to him. I was so happy to see you and Jean that day. It felt like I'd been away from home for so long."

"I was happy that John thought of it." Their families were different in many ways, but their bonds were strong. Ben looked around at the buildings and streets they were passing. "You passed the hotel."

"No hotel. You're family. You'll stay with us," Patrick told him firmly.

"Hmm, we may need to talk about that."

"Later."

"I'm not going to argue. How many kids do you have now?"

"Just the same as last time," Patrick countered, "three."

They pulled slowly into the long driveway that led to a nice, large home. "Another craftsman?" asked Ben.

"Jean likes them. And we're still near Merle and her family."

"You have more land," Ben observed, looking around at the vast green space. At that moment, what seemed to be more than three kids ran out of the house to meet them. "I thought you said just three?" asked Ben.

"Yeah, looks like Merle's kids are over as well."

"You guys having a party?"

"Everyone wants to see you."

The car rolled to a stop, and they got out. "Ben! Ben!" called several voices.

He hadn't been around much since he'd accompanied Patrick and Jean home. He was happy for the welcome. "Hey, gang. Let's see if I remember everyone. Line up." They hurriedly got in line, and he counted each one, placing a hand over their heads. "Sophie, Elizabeth, Tim."

Merle's kids were a little harder, but he guessed right when he said, "Hazel and Phineas."

"You're right!" Sophie called.

The sun was beating down on them, and he reached up to loosen his necktie.

Patrick noticed and said, "Let's go into the house. There's some lemonade." He started walking toward it.

"Please," Ben said gratefully, following him.

"Papa," called Elizabeth. "I think that's Mama." Her finger pointed behind them.

Ben turned to where she was pointing. He didn't see a car, but he did hear a buzzing sound around them.

"No, look up," she told him, waving wildly toward the sky. "It's Mama!"

Ben followed her direction and saw an airplane. "Close, isn't it?"

"You ain't seen nothing yet," Patrick said, walking back to them. The airplane didn't just fly over them; it tilted its wings toward them and seemed to be landing almost on top of them!

"Wow, does that pilot know what they're doing?" Ben stepped back involuntarily.

"Not to worry, she does," Patrick said calmly.

Ben shook his head in disbelief. "Is that Jean?" he asked incredulously.

"Her new hobby," Patrick confirmed. Watching her land and coming to a stop, they could hear her laughing in the distance.

"Can I go see Mama?" Tim asked, dancing with excitement.

"Yes. Stay clear of the plane until Mama tells you it's okay," Patrick directed.

"Sure is exciting around here," commented Ben.

"Yes, this business changes all the time."

"Change... Yes, that's why I'm here."

While Tim ran to the plane, he turned to Ben. "Let's get you inside. Kids! Back inside," he said.

They entered the home, which was grand, but also lived in. Kids' shoes lined the front room, and games and toys were scattered about the living room to their right. "Try not to trip on anything," he told Ben.

"I won't. You mentioned something about lemonade?" He was parched from the hot weather.

"In the kitchen."

The kids scattered as soon as they went inside. Patrick used his lever to open up his hand and put the bag on the ground. "Sophie, take that up to Ben's room."

"Okay," the girl said and grabbed it before Ben could stop her.

He just shook his head and watched her go upstairs with it.

Patrick grabbed Ben's shoulder. "Come on, we should have a few minutes to talk."

He went to the back of the house. Patrick pushed the door open to a large kitchen. He went to the cabinet to get glasses and lemonade. "You said you're coming for business. Not John's type, I hope."

"Not gambling," Ben confirmed. "But something you might think is about the same level."

Patrick frowned. "What is it?"

"Prohibition's coming."

"Yeah, word is California won't have state laws, just the federal. We've been stocking up." He pointed to the pile of boxes in the corner.

"The law does encourage that," Ben said, looking at the pile.

"What kind of business would involve you with the Volstead Act?"

"I have some ideas; all will involve alcohol in some way."

"In what way?"

"I'm thinking of getting into the production side."

"At a time when alcohol's illegal."

"Do you think people will stop drinking just because they're told not to?"

"Not based on how we've behaved. Are you sure this is the best business for you?"

Ben thought of the crowded, happy house. "I won't be able to stay here, you know."

At that moment, the door swung open, and Jean entered with two children hanging on her. She kissed their heads and said, "Off with you now." As they ran off, she yelled after them, "Don't get into trouble! Dinner will be soon." She walked over to Ben and hugged him. "Good to see you."

Patrick had gotten up and poured Jean a glass of wine. Jean sat back and lifted the glass for a long drink. "So, tell me. Are you visiting or moving here? Want to be in the movie business now?" she teased.

Patrick looked at her. "He's here to work."

"I guess I could get you into the movies. What do you want to do? Stunt work?"

Ben laughed suddenly and said, "I'll leave the stunts to you."

"Then what?" she asked, confused.

"What's coming up?" countered Patrick, nodding toward her wine glass.

"Prohibition? You'll have to explain that to me."

The two men stayed silent.

"You're staying with us, so you might as well tell me now. I'll get everything out of you eventually."

"Well, I was just telling Patrick that I plan to stay in a hotel."

Patrick sat forward. "No, you don't have to. We have a lot of catching up to do."

"No, I think it's better for everyone if I stay at the hotel."

Ben started to talk, but Jean interrupted. "You don't want us to get involved?"

"It's not just that. I'll be conducting business with some, let's say, unsavory people, and they'll be in and out. You don't want that here."

Patrick frowned. "You want to look like a tough guy. Is that it? You want to be like John."

Jean tapped his arm. "Don't."

"No, it's okay," Ben reassured her. "I get where you're going. I do want to be a successful businessman, and part of that's developing a reputation. Maybe a hard reputation." He looked over at Patrick and said, "John may not be your favorite person, but he was there when you needed him."

Patrick put his glass down, stood, and walked over to the large window overlooking the yard.

Ben started to stand, but Jean shook her head. She took her glass and sat back. Ben followed her lead. Jean looked at him. "Tell us what you're thinking for your business."

Ben picked up his glass and tapped it with his finger. "Wine."

"Wine?" she asked, holding up her glass.

"I've been studying the business and want to speak to growers here."

"What're you thinking?"

"I think there might be ways to work in the wine business during this time."

Patrick turned back to them and asked, "Legally?"

"Mostly," Ben confirmed.

"Patrick, sit down," Jean told her husband. She turned back to Ben. "We're against prohibition."

"Yes, I've seen your inventory." He smiled.

She took a sip and said, "We do enjoy our wine."

"You said *mostly*," Patrick said again, not willing to let the topic go.

"As you mentioned, I am John's grandson, so I'll also be setting up bars and maybe some small clubs around town."

"I've heard that everything will move underground," Jean said.

Patrick sighed and sank down in his chair. "Me too."

Jean looked at Ben. "You know it won't be the local police regulating it here. It'll be federal."

Ben sat forward. "There'll be money, a lot of it. Life-changing money."

Jean looked at Patrick with a raised eyebrow. She turned back to Ben. "Are you suggesting we invest with you?"

"I'm not suggesting anything. It's just an opportunity I want to make you aware of," he said with a shrug. "I have all of the backing I need."

"John again," said Patrick in exasperation.

"My money's tied up in this, too," Ben stated.

"Is this what Jemma's up to in New York?"

He frowned. "You heard about that?"

"Lottie called and said there were business opportunities in New York that Jemma was buying into," Patrick responded.

"She's in the process of buying up different properties. Her work model will be a little different. She's planning on opening a nightclub and other bars," Ben confirmed

Jean asked, "Where will you start?"

"I'm meeting a realtor tomorrow to start touring vineyards."

"Be aware, they're a prickly bunch," commented Jean.

"How so?" Ben needed to know everything he could about this business.

She laughed. "You'll see as you meet them."

The door slammed open, and several children stood in the doorway. "Moooommmm, we're starvin'. What's for dinner?"

The adults laughed, and Patrick said, "How 'bout burgers?"

"Yay!" the kids cheered.

"Now, out! While we work on it," Jean told them. She

retrieved an apron and put it on while Patrick retrieved some hamburger patties from the icebox. "Ben, will you come to the set? We're filming an interesting film later this week."

"He can drive in with me," Patrick told her.

"What day?" Ben asked.

"Thursday, I think," she said, grabbing a stack of plates and silverware. "At least, that's what's on the schedule." She pointed toward a tall cabinet and ordered, "Ben, grab the tray there and the glasses from that cabinet."

He retrieved the tray and added the glasses to it.

"Can you manage the lemonade?" she asked.

"I can." As they walked out, hands fully loaded, he asked Patrick, "Do you go to the set often?"

"It wouldn't work without him," Jean commented wryly, holding the door open for them. The sound of kids laughing and talking reached them.

"Why?" he asked with a frown, following them to the covered area that housed the tables, chairs, and barbecue. They set their things down and Patrick moved to stoke the charcoal on the grill.

"I'm the crank-camera man," he said over his shoulder.

"I didn't know! When did that start?"

"When I got the new hand earlier this year, it gave me more options."

"He has an eye for details," Jean said. "He was able to see what others didn't during a key scene late last year."

"It wasn't that much," Patrick demurred.

"It was," she corrected him.

"I started to apprentice with Harry Fischbeck on the movie *Of Wives and Men*. He taught me how to turn a camera crank with this," he said, holding up his wood hand.

"You also met Grace Davidson on that picture," his wife reminded him.

"I know that name. She's an actress," said Ben.

"She is, and she has an interest in cameras. She worked as a crank in 1915 and 16."

"She worked with me after her scenes were finished."

"Hold it. A woman camera operator?" Ben sputtered.

"Women are allowed in business, you know," Jena huffed with a twisted mouth. "There's many more: Gladys Brockwell, Angela Murray Gibson, just to name a few."

"Sorry about that, you just caught me by surprise," Ben confessed.

"She gets a little sensitive on the subject," Patrick told him.

"Yeah, I do," Jean admitted. "Too many people assume my stunts are done by a man in a wig. It gets frustrating." She smiled at Patrick. "Anyway, he worked hard and has graduated to being a crank on my films."

"Someone has to keep a watch on you," he reminded her.

"No one better," she said and blew him a kiss.

"I can't wait to see you in action." Ben turned to Jean and asked, "How long have you been flying?"

"About six months."

Patrick checked the burgers and went to the table to pour himself a lemonade. "She waited for me to be ready. I didn't want her doing anything dangerous when we got back from England," Patrick explained.

She put her hand on his arm and squeezed. "I took some time off. We're in a better place now."

"It was amazing to see you land," said Ben.

"You haven't seen anything yet," Patrick said.

"Are there planes in your movies?"

"Not quite yet. There've been some industrial films. When they do, I have hopes I'll wing walk in a future picture."

Ben stroked his chin and said contemplatively, "I can't wait for that!"

They laughed, and Patrick called out, "Dinner!"

The kids ran up like a small herd of elephants and Jean gave them their orders. "Girls and boys, run inside and get the fruit trays and potato salad."

"And the napkins!" called Patrick from the grill.

"What about dessert?" Tim asked cheekily.

Patrick grabbed him in a bear hug. "After dinner. Now go help bring things out here."

Everyone followed directions, and the group sat at a large table, passing around trays of food. It was loud, and when they finished, there was a chocolate cake shared with everyone.

The sun had gone down, and silence descended on the group. A woman's voice called from the house. "Any left for us?"

"Come over, Merle!" Jean called to her sister.

Jesse and Merle appeared; Phineas and Hazel ran over to them. "You go play a bit more. I want to chat," Merle directed her children.

Jesse and Merle walked over to Ben. "It's good to see you." Merle hugged him.

Jesse shook his hand. "Is there anything left?" he asked. He took off his hat; it'd been a long day.

"There is. I have some warming on the grill," Patrick replied.

They ate and talked well into the evening.

Eventually, Ben stood and stretched. "I hate to say it, but I need to call it a night."

"You're sure you won't stay with us?" Jean asked again.

"I'll be able to stay for longer visits once the businesses have been set up."

"I'll go get your bag," Patrick said.

"Thanks!"

"It was good to see you again," Merle told him.

Ben looked at Jesse. "I'm in the market for a car."

He nodded. "Let me know what you're thinking, and I'll have it delivered."

"I'll get the information over to you," he confirmed.

"Ready?" Patrick called from the back door of the house.

"I am. I'll see you all again soon," he called out to everyone. He joined Patrick and walked out to the car.

On the drive, Patrick commented, "I would've liked you to stay with us."

"We will see each other. I just need to get the business set up."

"I have some of my own money. I'd like to give it to you as an investment."

"Even though you don't want to be involved in something illegal?" Ben asked lightly.

"We don't agree with the law. I trust you. You're family, and I want to be part of your new business."

"You're sure?"

"I am. It also allows me to keep tabs on your activities."

"I'll schedule my meetings and keep you updated on the steps."

"Thanks. And, brother, we're happy to have you here."

"Thanks." Ben grinned. He started to get out of the car and then leaned back in. "Remember, I'm the boss here."

"Yes, sir, I'll do that," Patrick replied with mock seriousness.

Ben got out and sauntered up the steps to the hotel. As he got close to the entrance, he slowed his pace and popped up his jacket collar. He appeared to be a different man.

Patrick shook his head at the reminder of who and what he was related to in Chicago. He turned the car toward home.

Ben approached the door and waited for the doorman to open it for him. When he entered, the doorman snapped his fingers at a bellhop standing nearby. The bellhop approached quickly and said, "I'll take your bag." Ben handed it to him. "You can follow me, sir."

"Thank you."

They crossed the grand carpeted lobby. Crystal chandeliers hung from the ceiling.

"Sir," the front desk agent at the desk greeted him.

"Yes, I have a reservation."

"Name, please." The agent opened a large book in front of him.

"Ben Harden."

The agent's eyes widened in surprise. He knew that name. He stuttered a bit when he asked, "Where are you coming from?"

Ben answered, "New York." He'd made a trip to check in with Jemma before leaving for California. The agent quietly exhaled in relief at the news. "But I'm from Chicago." That bit of news knocked the air out of him.

Ben had expected that reaction. His grandfather's reach stretched from coast to coast. Jemma preferred to use a pseudonym, but he didn't mind having people know who he was. In this situation, it would get him in the door.

"I'll have your bags taken up," the agent stuttered.

"No need, I'll take it from here." He nodded at the bellhop to leave the bag. "May I have my key?"

"Yes, of course." The agent handed Ben the key. "Please sign the guest book." Ben signed and started to walk off toward the elevator. An assistant handed the agent a stack of letters. He looked down. "Sir," he called. Ben turned and saw the agent walking quickly over to him. "You had these waiting for you."

Ben took the letters and put them into his jacket pocket without looking at them. He nodded at the man and made his way to the elevator. It was waiting for him.

The elevator operator asked, "Floor?"

"Eight, please."

They stayed silent until the door opened on the requested floor. The operator nodded, and Ben made his way to the door indicated on the key.

He opened the door to the suite. The space was spacious and inviting, featuring a blue couch, side chairs, and a desk. He walked over to the desk and removed the letters from his pocket. The realtor would meet with him tomorrow morning to review properties. He shuffled the letters. One was a note from the bank; the money was in place for projects when he was ready. Lottie had sent him a note and said she was on her way. He smiled when he saw the last letter; it was from his mama and papa.

He moved to the bedroom and sat down on the bed with a genuine laugh. "Traveling again," he murmured as he read through the letter. Papa wanted to paint as much of the world as he could reach. The next stop for them was Ireland. Though he and Jemma were their children, they'd ended up more like their grandfather.

Their parents hadn't shared their interests; they'd been left in John's care for their education and training.

He closed the letter and walked to look out the window at the growing city.

Things will begin tomorrow, he thought.

CHAPTER 11

The next morning, he responded to a knock on his door. "Mr. O'Neil," he greeted a tall, thin man.

"Please call me Terry, Mr. Harden."

The two men shook hands.

"Come in, and you can call me Ben."

They moved to the couches, and Terry pulled out a notebook. "I have several properties that you'll want to review." He handed over a sheet of paper with the list

Ben looked it over. "I also want to tour some wineries."

"Were you looking to buy some wine while you're here?"

"Something like that."

Terry frowned. "Is there another interest you have with them?" He wasn't going to mention that it might be the wrong time to buy into the wine business.

"A partnership is what I'm looking for."

The realtor shook his head. "The wineries here are formed by families; they don't want outsiders."

"They'll want me," Ben said flatly.

"But, sir, we don't have an invitation. What will we tell them?"

"Tell them I want to hear about their wine."

Terry rubbed his neck. "That may work; they do like to talk about how they make their product."

"You have some in mind?"

"Yes," Terry said slowly. "I know of three for sure."

"Then what're we waiting for?" Ben said, standing.

The realtor let out a long sigh. "I thought this would be easy."

"Oh, it will be," Ben assured him.

"And the other properties?" Terry asked hopefully.

"Once we start looking at the wineries, we can go see those also."

Terry brightened. "Oh, that's good news." He eagerly led the way to the elevator and then downstairs. "My car is outside."

Ben didn't turn, but he could feel the glances his way. Word had gotten out who he was, and that was what he wanted. He followed at a slower pace. Once he was outside, Terry was waving toward his car. "Over here."

They were soon on their way. "I thought we'd head out to the furthest winery and make our way back here."

Ben nodded. "What can I expect?"

"A healthy sense of 'they know what they have and how to keep it'. They can be quite snobbish. Each owner thinks their strain is the only one worth drinking."

CHAPTER 12

The first and second locations weren't what Ben was looking for; he needed more land for his plans. The next two had the land he wanted. They pulled to the side of the dusty road and got out to talk.

"That's all the ones I know of who might be willing to talk," Terry said.

Ben took off his hat and wiped a handkerchief across his sweaty forehead. "Is it always this hot?"

"It is. Are you sure you want to be in the wine business?"

"I do," Ben said firmly.

"Would you like to see some of the local spaces now?"

"That's a good idea." They got back into the vehicle and drove to town.

"There's a lot of new construction here," Ben commented at the second location.

"Yes," Terry agreed, "it's a young city and growing every day with the movie business."

"That'll make things easier," Ben murmured.

Terry looked at him contemplatively. "If you tell me your business, I might be able to provide a more fitting property."

Ben looked over with raised eyebrows. "It's family business; I can't share right now."

"Right, right, I understand," the realtor stuttered and started to point out features of the current building.

Later, they walked out of the last space. "I'll take the four properties you showed me today, and I want the second two vineyards we toured."

"To lease." Terry nodded as he made notes.

"No," Ben corrected, "to buy."

"They may not be available," Terry cautioned.

"They will be. Make the offers."

"Yes, of course."

"I'll also need some storage locations, more out of the way."

"Fine, fine. I'll get those lined up."

Ben strode to the car, Terry struggling to keep up. The realtor was out of breath when he got behind the wheel.

CHAPTER 13

$\mathcal{E}$arly the next morning, Ben was reading the paper and sipping his coffee. Terry had called and said he'd be there to review contracts that morning.

A knock sounded at the door. He walked over, carrying his paper, and absently opened the door. Without looking, he turned away and waved toward the coffee. "Help yourself."

"I prefer juice," came a husky, feminine voice. That was NOT Terry.

Ben whipped around to face her. It was a young woman of, possibly, Spanish descent. "Who're you?"

She sauntered to the couches, her skirt swirling around her ankles, and sat down. "I'm Marisol Valdez."

He tilted his head and frowned at her. The Valdez winery had been considered but removed from the list. Terry had been sure they wouldn't be welcome.

"Join me. We need to talk," she said.

He was used to strong women with Lottie and Jemma in his life. He sat across from her. What did he have to lose?

Marisol seemed surprised he'd followed her direction and

eyed him for a long moment. He continued to watch her, waiting. "I have a proposition for you."

"What do you know about me?" he asked.

"That you're looking to invest in wineries at a very confusing time."

"Prohibition," he supplied.

"Yes," she said. "We are producing a product that will soon be illegal."

"Except for sacramental wine."

"Ah, I see you've done your research. Yes, but that alone won't support our business."

"Then why come to me as an investor?" She opened her mouth, and he stopped her. "Unless you want to be in the illegal wine business?"

"I think there's another way," she said, reaching into her bag for a notebook. She tore out a page and handed it to him.

Ben took the paper and glanced down at it. He didn't know what to expect, but a recipe wasn't it. "Are you giving me your wine recipe?" he asked, confused.

"No, that's the recipe we'll include when we sell our grapes to the public."

"I don't get it."

"Read the caution statement at the bottom," she directed.

He read on and started to laugh. "These are instructions on how NOT to make wine. He read it aloud, 'Do not store the grape juice in a jug. Do not put away in a dark area for twenty-one days, because this could accidentally turn into wine. To prevent fermentation, add 1/10% Benzoate of Soda.'" He sat back and smiled. "Very clever."

"Section 29 of the Volstead Act allows for 200 gallons of non-intoxicating liquors and juices."

"And how were you thinking we could work together?"

"You have the money. We need more land."

"You have a vineyard; isn't it big enough for this purpose?"

"We make an award-winning wine. My papa won't want to jeopardize that. I hear you've offered on several vineyards."

"How do you know that?" Ben asked. His voice went deep. *Terry*, he thought.

"Some of our neighbors have been talking. You've offered to buy a couple that border our winery."

Ben walked to the desk and pulled out maps of the area. He moved them to the dining room table and spread them out. "Show me where your vineyard's located."

Marisol walked over, ran her hand over it, and stopped. She pointed. "It's here."

"This is the land I've offered to buy." He ran his hand down the map.

"Thousands of acres, already planted with vines. They're inferior grapes," she told him.

"What will you provide in this deal?"

"The name, facilities, and management to make the grapes available to customers. We're grape growers; we know the business."

"You said the grapes on those vineyards are inferior."

"That'll work better for this venture. Inferior grapes can be grown faster. That way, we keep the vines at our winery untouched."

"Why are the vines so important? Aren't all grapes the same?"

"The wine we make is special, and it'd take up to eight years to regrow what we have now."

"Hmm," he said, thinking. There'd be people with a lot of money who'd still want quality wine. That'd include California, Chicago, and New York.

"Then do you agree we should be in a partnership?" Marisol stated, watching him.

"Tsk tsk, I need to see the place first. Who's the owner?"

"My father's the owner and the head of the family."

"And is he willing to go into business with me?"

Marisol moved to a chair and sat down. She laid her head back and said, "Well, that's the big question."

"Have you mentioned your plans to him?"

"No, he won't listen to me. He's hardheaded, and the idea must come from him."

"And just how do you expect to have that happen?" Ben asked, exasperated.

"You'll have to figure that out."

"No pressure, then. And your role in the negotiations?"

"I'll be on your side."

He looked at her for a long moment and said, "Okay, I'll be there with my realtor tomorrow."

She stood. "Be ready for a fight."

CHAPTER 14

Terry sat with his notebook open in Ben's hotel room.

"That one!" he exclaimed, his eyes wide.

"That one," Ben said firmly. "It borders the vineyards that I've offered for."

"I told you he doesn't want to sell," the realtor complained, gripping the page of his notebook.

"That one," Ben repeated. "And I want to go today."

"I'm not sure we should just show up without notice," Terry said and crumpled the page in his notebook.

"Are you worried about our welcome?" Ben asked, standing to get some coffee.

"I am. This man doesn't give tours!" Terry said, now tearing the page from his notebook. He looked down at it, wondering what'd happened. "There's nothing I can say to stop you?"

"No."

"Fine," the realtor said, slamming his notebook closed. "We might as well go now."

Ben took a long drink and set his cup down. He went over to pick up his jacket and hat. Terry nodded and followed him out of the room. Terry was muttering all the way down.

Once in the car, after they'd been driving a long while, Ben asked, "How long until we get to this one?" He pushed up his hat in the hot, dusty car.

"We're here. We've been on their land for a while now."

"So much land," Ben said, looking around at the seemingly vast landscape.

"And some of the best grapes. This is El Dorado County. It's California's third-largest wine-producing area. It had the first Bordeaux style winery in the USA. Their Inglenook wines won gold medals at the World's Fair in Paris in 1889."

They'll have reasons to want to stay in business, Ben thought.

"The Valdez family makes some of the best wine, but he isn't interested in investors," Terry told him.

"Doesn't he need the money?"

"He thinks he's going to be fine, that this will all resolve itself."

Ben laughed; he understood the man's reasoning. "I can't wait to discuss this topic with him."

They pulled up to the main house, which sat on the far side of the vines. It was a white two-story house and well taken care of. Terry pointed out the buildings around the property.

"Over there, behind the house, there are the wine-making barns, storage, and fermentation rooms."

"You know about the wine business," Ben said with a raised eyebrow.

"It's California. The two main movers are movies and wine," Terry replied. They got out of the car, dust hanging in the air around them. "I did forget to tell you about the daughter," Terry said.

"Stop right there." Marisol stood in front of them, her skirt swirling as she stepped out with a rifle. She had the weapon pointed at him. "Tell me your business or get off my property."

"Daughter?" Ben asked. *Is this her being on my side?* he wondered to himself.

"That's her," Terry pointed out.

"Thanks a lot," Ben muttered under his breath. He turned his attention to the girl. "Morning, ma'am. I'm here to see Angelo Valdez."

"He doesn't have any appointments today."

"He'll want to meet with me."

"I don't think so," she said as she put her finger on the trigger and cocked the rifle.

"Marisol! For God's sake! Be careful," Terry pleaded with her.

"Terry, is that you?" Marisol squinted in the bright sunlight. She lowered the weapon. "Why didn't you say so? Well, come on in." She moved the rifle to her shoulder and waved them inside. "Papa, Terry's here and brought a stranger with him."

"Not so strange," Ben murmured, taking off his hat and following her into the house.

ew York

The building was coming together. Jemma walked around the large expanse, admiring the brickwork. They'd boarded up the front of the building, and the construction and reasons for the business would be kept quiet. The club would be known by word of mouth rather than through physical advertising.

She approached the large door and tapped it lightly. The spy hole was opened, and eyes appeared.

"Hey, boss," the man said and opened the heavy door to let her into the club. "Working late hours this afternoon?"

"Hello, Casper. Yeah, they're finishing up my place upstairs," she explained. "I should be able to move in soon."

"That way you won't have to go back and forth to the hotel."

"Finally." She could hear saws and hammers echoing into the entryway. "It's a little loud today."

"I'm good with it; I just stay far away from them." He picked up his book and went back to his chair by the door.

She followed the noise into the large main room of the club. Jojo saw her enter and walked over. "Hi, boss. Any notes?"

"Not yet. Have you worked on the secret compartments in the bar?"

"Yes, come see it." They walked across the large dance floor to the carved ornate bar. Jojo opened the small door and held it open for her to access the inside of the bar. The shelves lined the area under the entire length. They were set up to hold an assortment of bottles. He pressed a button, flipping the bar shelves upside down. "The bottles will smash directly into the sewer," he explained.

She sighed. "Better than having them found, I guess." She examined the location of the button. "I'd hate to lose any alcohol accidentally."

"It's just a failsafe," he assured her. "And the button has to be pressed hard to work."

"I'll want this in our small locations also."

"We won't be using this anytime soon?"

"No, but we'll look at expanding at some point."

"I'll work on that," he said, making notes.

She lowered her voice and asked, "Any progress on the other project?"

"Yeah," he said in a hushed voice. "It's a little slow; I only work on it at night."

"Good man," she commented. "I'll be here tonight; I'd like to see it for myself."

"Of course."

The hammers and saws finally drove Jemma to her office. Slowly, the noise died down. She glanced down at her watch and saw that it was now evening. She put down her pen and closed her books. *Dinner would be good now.*

A knock sounded at the door. She called, "Come in." She wasn't surprised to see Jojo standing there. "Come on in, Jojo."

"You have company, boss."

Jemma stood, laying her hands on her desk. "Did you let them in?" she asked. Casper would've gone home for the evening, and Jojo was the only one still here working.

"I did."

"Go back to what you were doing, Jojo. I'll handle this." Lottie's voice could be heard coming from behind him.

"Thanks," he muttered to Lottie and headed back to his work.

"Lottie, was I expecting you?" Jemma asked, sliding the closed books into a drawer on her right. She locked it and turned her attention back to Lottie.

"Jojo thought you might want to see me."

"He's right. There're some things we need to confirm."

Lottie bent down and picked up a basket she'd set by her feet.

"What's that?" Jemma asked.

"Food. I hear you don't get out much."

"No, I don't, and I appreciate your thinking of it." She moved to the long table to the side of the room, and Lottie followed. They worked together to clear the long oblong table and unload the food. "There's too much for just us," she protested.

"I included Jojo in my count," Lottie replied.

"Call him in," Jemma invited.

Lottie opened the door and called out, "Jojo!"

He walked in with a grin. "I'd hoped to be invited to the soiree."

"Sit, and eat," ordered Jemma.

"Gladly." He started to fill his plate. His nights were long, getting all of the hidden passages, rooms, and other secret compartments ready. With the addition of Jemma's notes from earlier, there would be at least four other locations that would need similar arrangements.

Lottie and Jemma followed his example. The three ate

silently. Once done, Jojo stretched and said, "Thanks, Lottie. Got to get back to work."

"Good to see you. Any word on Frank?"

His smile faded. "Ma's still overseas; she won't accept that he's gone."

"Did they ever find his body?"

"No, not yet. From what I understand, there are many unidentified bodies, and Ma wants to see all of them."

"I'm sorry. I miss him."

"I hate that she's over there without me."

"She has Patrick's contact there assisting her?"

"She does, but I'd like to be there with her. For when they find him." He wiped his eyes and said, "I'm going back to work."

Lottie nodded. He shut the door behind him, leaving them alone.

"I shouldn't have asked about it," she said, throwing down her napkin on the table.

"No, I think he needs to talk about it."

"Does he have hope that Frank will be found?"

"I think he did initially. With every letter he received from Annabeth, he thought it'd be good news. But with each letter, it's been draining for him. Has Patrick said anything to you?"

"He's been sending money for Abigail to continue her search. He's holding out hope that Frank will be found."

"I'm surprised he didn't go himself."

"He wanted to," she admitted, "but he has a lot of responsibilities in California."

"That can't have been easy for him."

"It wasn't," Lottie admitted. "Look at this," she chided, "we're getting along. Who would've thought?" She smiled at Jemma.

"Not me, certainly."

Both went silent at that comment. Lottie cocked her head at Jemma. "Why do we fight? Even as adults?"

"You don't remember what started it?" Jemma asked idly,

tapping the table with her right hand, her fingernails clicking on the tabletop.

"No, I can't say I do."

"It was so long ago."

"Well, tell me!"

"We were little, playing on the floor at the boarding house. I was five or six; you were a little older. I had a doll that Jeremy and Emma had brought for me from France. You wanted it."

"I remember that one. Didn't she have long black hair?"

"And blue eyes. You do remember," Jemma accused lightly.

"I remember the doll."

"It really wasn't the doll. It was what you said to me when you snatched it away."

Lottie frowned and stayed silent.

"You said that it wasn't from *Aunt* Emma and *Uncle* Jeremy. That I wasn't family at all, just a gangster's spawn."

"I said all that?" She shook her head and said, "I was the brat, Jemma, and I was desperately jealous of you."

Jemma's mouth fell open. "Me? But you had them all there with you. All the time."

"Yes, but you and Ben were cherished and always considered part of the family. And even though you two weren't their own kids, Emma and Jeremy loved you both just as much as they loved Henrietta. Look, when I said that, I was wrong. And since I'm the main catalyst of this, I'll be the one to step up and offer an apology." Lottie stood and held out her hand.

Jemma stared at it and laughed, a low husky sound. She only hesitated for a moment; she reached out and clasped her hand. "Ben and Patrick will faint away when they hear."

Lottie laughed. "Then it's worth it."

"How is Hen?" Jemma asked.

"She and Danny are working on having another kid."

"Is she still getting arrested as much?"

"Not as much since she became a mom," Lottie admitted. "But if I know her, she's planning something around Volstead."

Jemma smiled. "Now that we've kissed and made up, would you like to see the progress?"

"I would." They walked down the hall and out into the main room, where the large dance floor was coming together. "There's been a lot of progress."

Jemma pointed toward the back of the dance floor. "A stage will be built, and the bands will set up there. The dressing rooms are behind the stage."

Lottie nodded. "The dance floor's big," she said, walking down onto it.

Jemma gestured around her. "Tables will surround the area."

"And the lighting?"

"There'll be two types. They'll be brighter during the day and darker at night."

"Show me the kitchen and the back rooms," said Lottie.

"Sure, follow me." They walked toward the back. The work was ongoing, and the hidden room was open.

Jojo called out to them. "There are a few high windows in the back that need to be removed."

"Are they secure?" Lottie asked him.

"They're high up, so it shouldn't be an issue. I'll take care of that tomorrow," he said and added it to his notes.

"Can you show them to me?" Lottie asked.

"They're back here," said Jemma.

Jemma and Lottie went further into the storage area, and she pointed to the high windows. Lottie followed her finger and saw a leg with stockings and red heels sticking through the window.

"Not high enough apparently," Lottie replied laconically, staring at the scene in front of her.

"Jojo!" Jemma called out, not taking her eyes off the leg, "Close up and come out here."

"What do we have here?" Jojo said as he joined them.

"Not sure yet," said Jemma. The person had stuck her second leg through the window and was swinging them back and forth, trying to find purchase.

"It appears to be a girl," Lottie stated.

"Sure, got nice legs," Jojo said appreciatively.

"Yeah, we got that. What we don't have is why," Jemma huffed. "Hey, girlie, what're you doing there?"

"What?" called the girl, her head not yet visible. "Oh, I just thought I might drop in."

"Cheeky. Well, come ahead," Jemma called back. "We might as well meet you."

The girl started to drop down, and Jojo went to catch her. He caught the attractive girl in his arms.

"Oh, thanks." She smiled.

"Anytime." He grinned back and continued to hold her.

A redhead, observed Jemma. "Jojo, put her down. We need some answers."

He did so reluctantly and moved away. "I'm going to go back to work."

"Main area for now, please," requested Jemma, not taking her eyes off the girl. He got her silent message and moved out of the room.

Jemma and Lottie stood silently watching the girl. She was young, probably in her late teens or early twenties. "What were you trying to accomplish with that stunt?" Jemma demanded.

"I need a job," she said boldly, her chin lifting.

"And this is how you apply? You couldn't have come in the front like everyone else?" Jemma asked, exasperated.

"I know what you're doing here," the girl said boldly. "I've been watching you."

"So, threats to your future employer? Extraordinary girl," Lottie said with a slanted eye at Jemma.

"Who did you hear the information from?" Jemma demanded.

"I could just tell, you know? There're no windows, well, except those," she allowed. The girl looked around with interest. "So, can I see the main area?"

"Sure, why not," Jemma said sarcastically.

The girl didn't get the sarcasm and ran by them. Lottie shrugged. They followed at a slower pace, Lottie with raised eyebrows; Jemma's face was pensive.

The girl spun around in a circle on the dance floor. "Wow, this space is big enough for tables, a band, and dancers. And look at this beautiful bar," she exclaimed as she ran over to it.

Jojo was working on the wood display shelves on the wall; she grinned at him. He returned it.

"Excitable, isn't she?" murmured Lottie.

"Yeah. Okay, girl, what kind of job are you thinking of for yourself?" Jemma asked.

"Not just me, my brother also," she said, running past them to look at where the band would sit.

"Your brother, too? Cheeky little thing, are you? And where is he? Digging a tunnel as an entry point?" Jemma asked.

"Oh no, he's outside in the back waiting for me to get him."

"Jojo, go get him," Jemma said in an exasperated voice.

"Be right back, boss," he said as he jogged off.

"Now, what jobs do you want?" asked Jemma, getting to the point.

"I'd like to be a manager," the girl said boldly.

"I've already filled that one," Jemma told her.

Lottie whipped her head around. "With who?"

"Later." Jemma looked back at the girl. "And your brother?"

"Oh, he's strong and can do most any job you have," the girl assured her.

At that moment, Jojo pulled a young man through the back door and locked it back up. "In there," he directed.

The young man moved quickly and stopped short of his sister. He whispered, "Are we in trouble?"

"Not yet," Jemma answered. She looked at both of them for a long minute. "All right, you're hired."

Lottie pulled Jemma's arm and led her a couple of steps away. "Are you crazy? You're going to hire them just like that? They just broke in here."

"Who else is qualified to work for me? People who get in, no matter the obstacles. I need people like that." Jemma turned back to the brother and sister. "You'll start tomorrow morning."

The duo grabbed each other's hands. "Yay! Thank you!" the girl bubbled.

"At least get their names," Lottie told Jemma.

"What're your names?" responded Jemma without looking at her.

The girl stepped forward, pulling her brother with her. "Lauren and Darren O'Brian."

"Irish. I should've guessed," Jemma said, looking again at their hair.

Lauren narrowed her eyes and raised clenched fists. "You got something against the Irish, lady?" she growled.

"Careful with those fists, young lady." Jemma laughed, "No, I have nothing against the Irish. My family's from there. I was commenting on the red hair."

Lauren put a hand up to her hair. "Oh." Then she smiled and said, "Okay."

"Go home, get some rest. Be here at nine am," Jemma told them. They started to leave, when Jemma stopped them. "And Lauren."

"Yes," Lauren said, turning back to them.

"Use the door, next time, please."

Her face turned red, "I will. I promise."

They left, and Jojo shut the door behind them. Lottie stood and looked at Jemma.

Jemma raised her eyebrows. "My business, Lottie."

"Yes, you're right," she allowed. "How do you know you can trust them?"

"How do you know you can trust anybody?" Jemma asked. She sighed. "They need the work, and I'm going to give them a chance."

"You're going to need a large staff."

"Yes."

"You said you've hired a manager."

"Did I?" she asked, noncommittally.

"Jemma!"

"Okay, okay. I hired Charlie."

"Why?"

"That's a good question," Jemma replied.

"And?"

"He knows the New York bar scene."

"You know he can't be trusted."

"I know, but I also need to know where he is and what he's up to."

"And making him your manager will do that?"

"I believe it will. I'll be able to keep tabs on him."

"I think it's a mistake."

"It may end up that way," Jemma agreed.

"What about the other positions?"

"I have a list of jobs. I'll use Lauren and Darren to start asking around."

"You're right, it's not like you're going to be able to advertise in the paper."

The clock chimed the late hour. Jemma glanced at it. "Jojo, why don't you stop for now? Go home and get some rest."

"Let me clean up some and lock down the spaces." He gathered up his tools and his bag and moved to the back room.

Lottie was still there.

"Isn't Lissette waiting for you?" Jemma asked her.

"Yes, she is. I should probably head home. What about you?"

"I need to add more notes to my books. I'll be going soon."

"Back to the hotel?"

"Just for a little while longer."

"I'll stop by in a few days."

"What for?"

"Not sure," Lottie admitted. "We're family, in spite of what I said in the past, so I want to be here for you."

"Did Ben tell you to do this?"

"Ben? No, it's my idea. I'll be leaving for California soon after that."

"Ben mentioned he's found some vineyards and other properties."

"Yeah, I'm also going to evaluate the wine venture he's considering." She checked her watch. "I'd best be heading home."

"Okay then, have a good evening." Jemma walked her to the door and braced it closed after she left.

Jojo called over, "Boss, I'm headed out also. Want me to walk you home?"

"No, I'll be fine."

CHAPTER 16

*L*ottie drove her motorcycle home. It was late, and the streets were quiet. She pulled to a stop and walked the motorcycle into the small garage beneath her and Lissette's multilevel brownstone. The house was dark and quiet. She made her way up the stairs and entered the dark bedroom.

"How's Jemma?" Lissette's voice came from the bed.

"You still awake?"

Lissette sat up. "I sleep better when you're here."

Lottie sat on the edge of the bed to pull off her boots.

"How's Jemma?" Lissette repeated, sitting up and moving to sit next to her.

"She seems fine."

"You sound worried."

"She's alone, and it's dangerous here."

"She's chosen a different path than you, one that eventually leads to breaking the law. What're you going to do about it?"

"Be there if she needs me," Lottie admitted.

"You can turn on the lights," Lissette said.

"A small one," Lottie said and reached over to turn on the side table light.

"Eek!" Lissette screeched.

"What? What is it?" Lottie asked her, looking frantically around the room.

"Why is that in here?" Lissette pointed to the chair nearest the bed.

"What?" Lottie asked, still looking around.

"That!" Lissette pointed to the black-haired doll with dark blue eyes.

"Oh, her. I thought I'd keep her in here," Lottie said innocently.

"I don't know why you brought that from your parents' house last time we were there."

"Hmm, just thought I might need it," she murmured, reaching out to touch the doll's hair.

"Cover it up or something then. It's creepy."

Lottie snickered, turned out the light, and crawled into bed to snuggle with her love.

CHAPTER 17

 *alifornia*

"We won't sell," the man said, his arms crossed over his chest. He stood in the doorway, effectively blocking the entrance into the house. A younger man stood near him, watching.

Unexpectedly, Marisol spoke up. "Papa, we need to hear him out."

He didn't respond, but he also stayed silent. Marisol nodded at Ben to continue.

"Sir, I'm not here to steal your business. I've been studying the wine business in California, and I'm looking for a partnership."

"That makes you an expert," Marisol's father derided.

"Can we move this inside?" Ben asked. They hadn't made it to the porch, and the sun continued to beat down on them.

"Can't stand the heat?" the man chided.

"I can stand the heat just fine; I thought you'd like to speak in private."

"Fine, let's move inside." He waved to his daughter. "Girl, put that gun away!"

"Yes, Papa."

Her father turned into the house. She motioned for Ben to follow. They entered the house. It had been designed for the area, and it was much more pleasant inside than outside. Ben breathed in the cooler air, relieved to be out of the sun. The group started to follow when Marisol's father stopped and said to the man next to him. "RL, we'll call you if needed."

"Angelo, you don't want me here?" RL asked with a deep frown.

"No, it's family business."

RL grabbed his hat and slammed the door as he stormed out of the house.

Ben glanced over at Marisol. She shook her head and turned her gaze to her father. Ben turned to Terry. "I have this. Why don't you stay out here."

"But, but…" the realtor stuttered.

Ben's persona changed; his face hardened, and he seemed darker. Terry saw it and stopped talking.

"Terry, you come with me," a woman said. "I'll feed you."

"Bella, that would be lovely," he said and held out his elbow to her. She took it, and they headed to the back of the house.

The small group entered a large room full of books. Marisol shut the double doors and moved to the couch. She laid the rifle on the floor in front of her. Ben took a seat near her.

Angelo stood in the middle of the room with his arms crossed. "What are you proposing?" he challenged.

"I've offered to purchase the wineries bordering your property."

"A few acres won't do anything for you in this industry," Angelo scoffed.

"It's more than a few," Ben said.

"How much more?"

"45,000 acres."

"You purchased the two wineries?" Angelo moved to a large leather chair and sat down. "Why do you need so much? Prohibition is coming. People are talking about pulling out their vines and replacing them with flowers! Bah!"

Ben hid a smile and said, "They are. I was able to buy them because the owners wanted out."

"Their wines are inferior to mine; it won't work as a partnership."

"We'll see."

Angelo shook his head and pounded his fist on the desk. "Your reasoning makes little sense. Why invest money when we won't be allowed to make a product?"

"I have an idea, but we need to move quickly to be ready."

Angelo frowned and nodded for him to continue.

"Smuggled wines will make a fortune for producers during the upcoming Prohibition. If it's done right," Ben quantified.

"Illegal operations," Angelo muttered. "They're making my family business a dirty thing. It's to be celebrated and drunk with appreciation."

"I have an idea about how to make the process legal. At least part of it."

Angelo sat forward, listening intently.

"The Volstead Act says that wine is illegal, but grape juice isn't. Section 29 enables people to make two hundred gallons of 'non-intoxicating cider and fruit juice, as long as it's made at home for family use consumption.'"

"How does that help the wine business?" Angelo asked, exasperated. "The money is in the alcohol. This makes no sense."

"You're right," Ben allowed. "The idea is that we sell it as grape juice *but* add a warning about how not to accidentally make it into wine."

"Explain yourself."

"It's like a warning, Papa," Marisol explained. "It would tell that the grape juice is for non-alcoholic drinking only."

Angelo mulled that over. "Which would actually instruct them on how to make wine. That might allow us to stay in business," he muttered as he stood and walked to the window. The vines were stretched out in front of him. *My beautiful wine.* He shook his head at the thought. He sighed and asked, "How would they be moved?"

"The grapes? I have rail transportation that'll move them all over the country."

"That would be limited," Angelo said, still staring outside.

"Why?" Ben had thought it through: the space needed, the pickup, and delivery.

"Rot. The grapes won't make the trip, especially into the other climates you're suggesting. Even wine bottles have to be treated carefully in different environmental conditions."

Ben frowned. He hadn't thought about this.

"Papa, what about a concentrate?" Marisol asked.

He shook his head. "It's still a liquid, and we don't have the facilities. Making a concentrate also removes much of the wine flavor. We wouldn't want our names associated with a bad-tasting product. Our wine is too good for this process. I'd rather shut down than let that happen."

Marisol chewed her bottom lip and looked at her papa.

"Okay..." Ben was thinking through this new information. "Angelo, you mentioned the vineyards I purchased have a lower quality grape?"

"They do. I wouldn't want them associated with our name."

"How about we use the grapes from the other vineyards for this project?"

"The process will still take additional facilities."

"That's where I come in. I can provide the money for anything that might be needed."

"I'm not sure," Angelo admitted. "Can we handle such a large process?"

"What would you rather do?" Marisol asked her father.

"I could tear it all out and grow orchids," Angelo said.

"Do you know anything about orchids?" asked Ben.

"I don't," he admitted.

"Papa, these vines are too important. It's important to our family; it's our heritage."

"I know. Everything we've worked for will be wiped out. You know we won awards in Paris at the World's Fair?" Angelo picked up a picture from his desk and took it over for Ben to view.

"I'd heard about that," Ben told him.

"It was a special day," Marisol remembered.

"It looks like it." Angelo and Bella were in the picture with the judges; everyone was grinning broadly.

"Look, we'll brand the concentrate under a different name. Create a new company where the wine and the concentrate are separate. We can work that out," Ben allowed.

"So, Papa, we'll work with Mr. Harden?" Marisol asked.

He looked over and said sadly, "It seems there's little choice."

"I think you'll find, Angelo, that it'll be a beneficial relationship for both of us," Ben tried to assure him.

"We shall see. We know nothing about this process. Where do we start?"

At that moment, Bella entered with a tray carrying glasses of iced tea. She set it down on the table. Then she moved to give her husband a kiss on the cheek.

Marisol said, "The main question is how to ship the grapes. I still think concentration would be best, but it'd have to be sealed in jars."

Bella listened to the conversation and asked, "Why not dry out the concentrate and form it into bricks?" All three people went silent and looked at her. "It would be rather easy, I think.

We mash the grapes, boil the juice, and evaporate it to a gelatinous form. We could pour that and dry it in trays, then cut it into bricks."

"Would that work?" Ben asked.

"It should."

"We should test," Marisol replied.

"How soon could you test?" asked Ben.

"Today," Bella responded. "It will take a few hours to boil the grape juice to a concentrate. We'll have to dry inside; there's too much dust outside. That should be ready in a day or two."

"I'll help," Marisol told her mother.

"Not my good grapes!" Angelo protested.

"We have grapes that were rejected," Marisol interrupted. "This will just test the process to make sure it can be done."

He nodded grudgingly.

"Then we test," said Ben firmly. "After we finish here, I want to get the other winery purchases finalized. My lawyer should be in town today, and we can start setting up contracts."

"What happens to our wine here?" Angelo asked as he moved back to the window.

"You continue to make it. I have some contacts with churches in Chicago. We can set up contracts showing that the wine produced will be used for sacramental wine. We'll also be shipping your supply via car to Chicago and New York."

"Bootlegging," Angelo said. This time, his voice sounded like he was considering it. "You might consider talking to George Remus. I hear he's setting up routes."

"Papa!" said Marisol, shocked.

"I've been listening to other wine growers; they're starting to work with him."

"I know of him, and I'll consider it," Ben said, "but the more we can control the process ourselves, the more money we'll make. There are already shipments of wines being set up from overseas; we don't want to lose that business either."

"And when will this end?" Angelo asked.

"That's the big question; we have to be ready any outcome."

"Will it end, Papa?"

"All things do eventually," Angelo told her.

"Before we start, can Marisol show me around the vineyard? I've some production questions."

"Yes, yes," Angleo said. He was distracted by the changes that were being presented to him.

"We have our tasks," Ben told the group. "Bella and Marisol will conduct the test for the concentrate, and I'll move things forward to purchase the other wineries."

"And me?" asked Angelo, his voice mocking. "Do you have a task for me?"

"You need to get a letter organized to the churches in Chicago, along with several bottles. I'll have them delivered to them."

"I can do that."

"How about that tour?" Ben asked Marisol.

"Of course, come with me," she said, walking toward the door. Bella raised her eyebrows, but didn't comment. Ben followed and caught up to her. She was striding quickly to the barns, around the back of the house.

Marisol pointed to the building. "That's where we start."

"Is it?" he asked, still following.

She moved faster, unsure why he made her nervous all of a sudden. She opened the door of the barn and walked through it. He closed the door behind him, and she felt the walls closing in. She moved quickly over to the first mechanical device.

She turned to him. "This is the destemmer. It removes the stems from the grapes."

"Makes sense," Ben said, all his focus on her. He moved closer. She backed away and went to the next device.

"And what does this one do?" he asked, continuing to follow her.

"This is for fermentation. The liquid is heated and then moved into these drums," she said, backing into them.

"You're running out of room, you know," he said idly.

She ignored him and continued the tour. "Then, after maturation, we move to bottles." And at that point, she backed into the bottles and into a wall.

He approached and braced his hand over her head and leaned into her. "I have another question."

"You want to know how long the wine stays in the drums before we move them?" Her voice peaked high.

"No," he said and lowered his head down to hers. Marisol threw her arms around him and pulled him closer. He lowered his hand to her back and kissed her. "Now that's the kind of research I was hoping for," he murmured and continued to kiss her.

They heard a door slam, and they broke apart.

"What was that?" he asked.

"No idea. Where were we?"

A little while later, they entered the kitchen.

"Why don't you wash up?" suggested Bella. Ben moved over to the sink to wash his hands. "And you, you've got a little smudge on your lips, girlie," she said to Marisol, handing her a cloth napkin.

Marisol took it and wiped her mouth vigorously. "Thanks, Mama."

Two field workers walked into the room carrying baskets. "You can put those there," Bella directed them. The workers set the baskets of grapes next to the sink.

"Thank you."

They nodded and left through the door they'd entered.

"Not Papa's good grapes," Marisol teased her mother.

"No, I wouldn't do that. Let's move them over to the large metal strainers."

"What're we looking for?" asked Ben.

"We're treating them the same as we would good wine. We remove the stems, inspect for bruises, make sure they're ripe with no mold, and wash the dirt off."

"Next, we'll crush the grapes with potato mashers," Marisol told him.

"Why don't we use the equipment in the barn?"

"This is just a small test. We don't want to turn on all the big machines for these few grapes. Plus, it'll be easier to control here," Bella explained. They worked steadily, crushing the grapes in deep bowls.

"Marisol, grab that other bowl there. The larger one," her mother said. Marisol put down her masher and got a larger bowl. "Drape the muslin over the bowl and pour each of your bowls slowly into the cloth."

Marisol and Ben each poured their bowls into the cloth-covered bowl. Once they'd been poured, Bella gathered the edges and squeezed the wet muslin ball.

"Take the liquid to the pot on the stove." Ben carried it over to the stove and poured it into the large pot. Bella laid the ball down and moved to the stove to bring the grape juice to a boil. She watched it closely to keep the pot at a simmer, reduced by half.

"What does this create?" Ben asked.

"A thick syrup," said Marisol.

"Spices or sugar can be added later, if we want more flavor in other batches," Bella told him.

Ben checked his watch. "I need to leave now; I have to pick someone up at the train station."

"Thanks for the help, Ben," Marisol said and blushed.

"Anytime." He grinned at her as he strolled out.

"Didn't the two of you just meet today?" Bella said.

Marisol busied herself cleaning the kitchen. "I don't know what you're talking about, Mama."

Bella walked over to her. "I saw the instructions for the grape juice."

"So?"

"I know your handwriting."

"It was my idea," Marisol admitted.

"Why not come to us?"

"We need the money, an investor, and I knew Papa would fight the idea. I heard Ben was in town touring wineries."

"You're right."

"Will you tell Papa?"

"About which part? That it was your idea for the bricks or that you were kissing Ben on your tour?"

Marisol sighed. "Either, I guess."

"Not for now."

CHAPTER 18

The whistle blew, and the train came to a stop. Lottie took her bag from the top shelf and put her red-brimmed hat on her head. She stepped off and heard her name being called. She turned toward it and saw Ben walking over to her.

"Welcome to California!" Ben smiled.

"Thank you. Did you wear the lipstick for me?" she asked, touching his cheek.

He looked startled and took out a handkerchief to wipe his face. "Did I get it?"

"Yes, anyone I know?"

"You'll meet her soon."

She let the subject drop. "Do you have lots of work for me?"

"We have a plan."

"Oh, so it's *we* now. You have been busy."

"I have several deals going through that I need you to review."

"Have you found a way to make it legal?"

"Mostly," he said with a grin. "We've found a loophole in the law."

"Oooo, a test of Volstead." Lottie grinned and rubbed her hands together. "I can't wait."

In his room, she was looking through the contracts. "Are you sure you don't want to rest first?" he asked.

"After all that time on the train? No. Terry's done a good job getting the offers organized and at a good price."

"Most of the owners want out, the sooner the better."

She put the papers down. "Everything looks in order."

"The other contracts are there for the bar locations."

She looked through them. "These seem to be in order, too."

"They're new construction, so I'll need to build them out."

"Check with Patrick. He knows carpenters in the movie business."

"I'll do that."

"You mentioned a partner?"

"I hadn't planned on one," he admitted with a small laugh. "Then a small whirlwind entered my life."

"Who would that be?" she asked curiously.

A knock sounded at the door. "That should be her now," Ben said.

"Do you want me to make myself scarce?"

"No, of course not."

Lottie sat back to watch the show. She knew the impression of her being alone in a hotel room might give to a girl in a new relationship. Ben was a bit naïve.

He went to the door, and as expected, Marisol was waiting. Her dress was colorful and cut longer than those of girls her age. "Ben," she said, and started to hug him. Over his shoulder, she spotted Lottie. She immediately stepped back and said, "I think I'm interrupting something." She turned to run, but Ben grabbed her sleeve.

"Wait," he said. "I want to introduce you to someone."

"Who is she?" She hesitated. "Is she your girlfriend?" Her eyes went wide. "Is she your wife?"

"Wife? No!"

"Well, why not Benji?" Lottie teased. "Am I not good enough to be your wife?"

"Lottie! Stop it!" Ben growled, struggling to keep Marisol in the room. "Tell her!"

Lottie stood and strolled over. "Oh, all right. I'm Ben's lawyer, not his wife and not his girlfriend."

Marisol stopped struggling and asked, "You're not?"

"Nope. We are family, though, just not romantic. Especially not with this muttonhead." Lottie chuckled.

Marisol looked at the attractive woman and said, "Family. Good. I like that."

CHAPTER 19

The car rattled over the bumps in the road. "Nice car,"
Lottie commented.

"Thanks, I just got it from Jesse."

"Marisol's lovely. Is there something serious there?" They'd
eaten lunch together, then she'd gone home.

"I feel like I'm falling fast," he admitted.

"Wow, that hasn't happened before."

"No, she's special."

She continued to watch the trees and dusty roads. "How
long until we get there?"

"We are there."

"Wow, the land here just goes on and on."

"It does. We'll start seeing the vines soon."

She nodded and watched for them. They turned, and the
vineyard came into view. "Are your two other vineyards just as
big?"

"Yes."

"Hmm," she said, sitting back. "That's a lot of money on the
front end."

"I think we'll make it back five to sevenfold."

"And you've taken Patrick as an investor?"

"I have."

"Got room for me and Lissette?"

He nodded. "I think there's plenty to go around."

"Let me know how much; I'll draw up an additional document for me and Patrick."

"That'll be fine."

They drove by the vines, and she spotted a house in the distance. "Is that it?"

"It is," he confirmed.

Lottie reached in the back and pulled her satchel into the front seat.

He drove up in a cloud of dust; it seemed to follow them to the house. He stopped and took the keys out of the ignition. "It's pretty here," she commented, "but hot."

"It is. I do miss the cooler temperatures," he confessed, loosening his tie.

A fist pounded at her window. She jumped and asked, "What the hell was that?"

"A who, not a what." Marisol had mentioned that Angelo felt it was time RL left. "I'll put a stop to this."

"No, don't get out."

The fist pounded again.

Lottie's eyes were wide. "What do we do?"

Before Ben could do anything, Angelo came out of the house with a shotgun leveled on his shoulder. "RL! Get out! Now!"

"No, I want him! It's his fault! He messed up my plans." RL continued to pound on the window.

Angelo stood sternly at the head of the steps; his gun aimed at RL. "RL, you're fired. Get off my property."

"Stay here," Ben told Lottie. She nodded, watching the man outside her window. Ben got out and pulled a gun from his jacket. He pointed it at RL. "I think you were given a message to leave."

"You!" RL pointed and stuttered. "You're trying to replace me in everything! I'm more family than you! I won't go until Marisol tells me to."

"RL," Marisol called to him, walking from behind Angelo.

"Marisol, I knew you'd be here for me. Come away with me. We can be married."

"Why you!" Angelo stormed. "I'll tear you apart." He started to charge down the stairs, but Marisol stopped him, holding his arm.

"No, Papa, I have this," she said in a low voice. "RL, you need to leave now."

"No! That's them telling you to say that. It's me you want."

"No, RL, it never was. I never wanted you; you know that. It's time you left."

When he stepped forward, Ben cocked his gun. "Not a step further."

RL grabbed his hat off his head and threw it on the ground. He turned and stalked off to his truck.

"Marisol, get Bob to make sure he gets off the property," Angelo ordered.

"Yes, Papa." She ran down the steps and around the house. As she passed Ben, she mouthed, "I'm sorry."

Ben watched the dirt kick up behind RL's truck, and then another car came racing by the house and down the road.

Marisol rejoined them. "Papa, I never promised him anything."

"I know, girl. Go help your mama in the kitchen. I have business with this man."

She looked over at Ben and nodded before heading back inside.

Ben slipped the gun back into his pocket. He tapped the

window and waved to Lottie. She cautiously opened the door and got out.

"Well, that was exciting."

"Yeah," Ben said, wondering if the man was actually gone.

"You two come inside," Angelo told them. "We have business to discuss."

CHAPTER 20

"Marisol, help with the trays," Bella called to her daughter.

Marisol ran over and helped move the test trays to the large tables. Once the trays were where Bella wanted them, she looked at Marisol. "Is RL finally gone?"

"I didn't encourage him, Mama."

"Did I say you did?"

"No, you didn't."

Bella cocked her head and said, "Tell me about this young man."

"I don't know any more than you do, Mama." Marisol hesitated as she avoided her mother's eyes to check to see if the concentrate was close to dry.

"He's a good-looking young man," Bella observed.

"Yes, he is."

"Take it slow, Marisol," her mother cautioned. "Love, real love, takes time."

"Yes, Mama." Marisol stopped what she was doing and turned to her mother. "Mama, didn't you and Papa marry the day you met?"

"Bah, that was a different time."

Was it though? Marisol wondered.

"They are drying nicely," Bella noted, touching them lightly. "What now?"

"We wait and continue checking them. We may have to change the size of the pans for better drying times." Marisol turned to leave the kitchen. "And where are you going?" Bella asked her.

She turned back slowly. "I thought I might see if our guests need anything."

"If they need anything, they'll let us know."

"Humph," she muttered and went to sit on a stool, watching her mother pull out ingredients to start making pies.

"Marisol," Angelo called.

"They called, Mama," her voice singsong.

"Oh, you." Bella threw a towel at her. "Go see what he wants."

Marisol dodged the towel, patted her hair, and smoothed her skirt.

"You look lovely," Bella told her.

"Thank you, Mama," she said and headed out. She went to the study and found the three drinking wine and talking.

"Marisol, come in," Angelo said. "We were talking about who'd oversee the grape concentrate part of the new business."

"Did you want a list of people from me?" she asked, confused.

"No," Ben said, "you'll work with me to manage the new business."

With Ben, she thought. She kept her gaze steady and directed at Angelo. "I'd like that."

"Good, that's solved. Though I'll need you here until I can replace RL."

"Louis is ready," she replied. "He knows the job."

"Work with him over the next few weeks, and then we can transition you to your new role."

CHAPTER 21

A few days later, Ben, Angelo, Bella, and Marisol walked around and examined the material in the pans.

"Now that they're dry, we can cut them into bricks and wrap them for shipping," Bella said.

"Should we test the fermentation process? It should be about twenty-one days. We need to know what the juice tastes like when turned into wine," Angelo said, wrinkling his nose at the dried concentrate.

Ben considered that and said, "Yes, in the meantime, Marisol and I'll choose a place to put the new building to house the production of the bricks."

"I'll get them into bottles today with water and store them in the pantry," confirmed Bella.

"Where will the building be located?" Angelo asked.

"We'll add the building to the other two vineyards. That way, we keep the process separate. Lottie's finished up the legal paperwork. We own the land."

"We?" Marisol asked.

"Yes, *we*. Lottie and I want us to be true partners, my family and yours. And we think that the bricks will make us all rich," said Ben.

"What size are you thinking?" she asked.

Angelo grabbed a piece of paper to mark out the areas. "We will need areas big enough for vats and areas for pouring the thickened juice into trays for drying." Bella moved over, and everyone had input on moving walls and even the height of the roof to help with production.

"Don't forget we'll need a packaging area near the drying," Marisol said.

Angelo nodded and added space to the drawing. "And storage."

"Yes." Ben stared at the completed drawing and asked, "Can't some of this be automated?"

"The cutting of the bricks would be one that we could automate," suggested Angelo. "I have some vendors who work in production plants; they may have some ideas."

"I'll take these with me, I am supposed to meet my carpenter today to review the bars I have in town," Ben said.

Angelo nodded. "Bring the final design to me, and we'll make sure we're ordering the right equipment."

"We also need to think about hiring people to work in that building," Marisol commented. "And I have ideas for the wrappers."

"Draw up the design," Ben told her, "and we can meet with the printers. I'll also have Lottie evaluate the instructions to make sure it's all legal."

"Do we have time for all of this to get done?" Bella wondered. "Picking season is coming up in a few months."

"Yes," Marisol assured her. "We've inspected the vines and they're well-managed. The staffing has stayed on. The picking season will be hectic, but we'll do well."

"We'll need to get an advertisement out for people to work in our new factory," Ben said.

"I'll draft it and get it posted," said Marisol.

"Things are coming together," Ben said, looking at the notes. "Marisol, would you like to go over to the other vineyard to look at possible building locations?"

Marisol fought back a smile. "That will be nice." She ran over to her mother and whispered, "I'll be back to help with dinner."

She raised an eyebrow and said in a low voice, "Watch yourself, little girl."

"Are you ready, Marisol?" asked Ben.

Angelo started to raise his hand to stop them. "They shouldn't be allowed to be alone."

"No," Bella said, "she's a part of this business. Let her go."

He turned to her. "Is it a mistake?"

"The partnership or letting them be alone together?"

He sighed. "We are taking so many chances."

"We need to move forward to survive."

"Yes," he said and took her into his arms.

CHAPTER 22

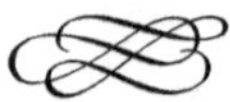

Marisol followed Ben out to his car, and he held the door open for her. He closed the door and then went around to get into the driver's seat. He started the car and drove them through the vineyard and out onto the main road.

"Where do the pickers come from?" he asked.

"From local Mexican and Filipino communities in the area."

He drove for a few minutes and pulled the car over to the side of the road.

"Is something wrong?" she asked, looking worried.

"Just this," he said and pulled her to him.

"This is what I was waiting for!" She laughed.

"No, I just haven't had a chance to talk to you."

"You had a chance to talk at the barn," she pointed out.

"I had other things on my mind," he said and lowered his lips to hers. "How did I get you all to myself today?" he murmured after he lifted his head and laid his forehead on hers.

"It was Mama," she said, running her fingers through his thick hair.

"I thought she was on my side." He grinned. He moved back

to his seat and started to drive to the neighboring vineyard. They pulled onto the property. "The house is empty now; the current owners have taken the money and left for Spain."

She nodded as they pulled to a stop in front of the house. "Will you live here?"

"Yes. I'll move out of the hotel in a few days. I'll need some furniture."

"Can I see it?"

"Have you ever been inside?"

"No, Papa didn't like them."

"Don't tell me; it's because they grow inferior grapes."

She threw her head back and laughed. They pulled to a stop and got out. It wasn't a large house, but it was a similar style to her family's. He pulled out a key, and they went inside.

CHAPTER 23

A few weeks later, Patrick waited outside of Ben's hotel in his car. It was dark, early morning, and they needed to get to the set early. The dawn light was key to some of the scenes being filmed that day. He tapped the wheel impatiently, looking at the hotel door. He didn't have to wait long. The familiar figure came out and down the stairs.

The car door opened, and Ben got in. "Good morning," he said.

Patrick returned the greeting and moved the car onto the road.

"Going to tell me what the film is about this morning?"

"Rustling."

"What's that?"

"A man hiding out as a sheep rancher goes after people stealing his stock."

"And who does Jean play?"

"The postmistress; she'll save the rancher from an angry lynch mob. There'll be lots of horse stunts."

Ben laughed. "Jean's favorite."

"That and airplanes," Patrick agreed. "How are things going with your new business? Lottie mentioned the contracts are done."

"We have things on track. The vineyards have been secured, and we've found the best way to sell wine legally."

"Lottie mentioned the bricks and the loophole. Are you sure it's legal?"

"Right now, it is. But I'm sure it'll be tested in the courts once Prohibition starts. Will Harry be on set today?"

"Yes, he will be there, if you need to discuss the projects with him."

The conversation settled into a comfortable silence.

"Any word from Annabeth?" Ben asked. Patrick pounded his fist on the wheel. "I'm sorry, I shouldn't have brought it up."

"No, it's all right," Patrick assured him. "It's been so long. We'd like her to just come home."

"You think Frank's dead?"

"So many people died, and we've had no indication that he survived."

"And no body has been found?"

"No. So many won't be returned home. They've been buried in graves around Europe."

They went silent, lost in their thoughts about Frank again. "We're headed far away from the studios," Ben pointed out.

"Yeah, we're going to need a lot of room for the filming today."

When he didn't continue, Ben asked, "Aren't the camera cranks operated on the right? How do you do it?"

"Jean and I brainstormed that, and what we came up with was a tripod. That way, I can stand and support my hand as I crank."

"What if you need to move it around?"

"I use different mechanisms to help sling it around me."

"I can't wait to see you in action."

"Well, you're about to," Patrick said as they pulled into an open field. Horses were already lined up. Ben could see Jean talking to several men, walking horse to horse.

"We'll need to set up the camera," Patrick said.

"Tell me what to do."

"Grab the boxes from the back, and I'll get the camera."

"Got it."

Ben grabbed the boxes and carried them, following Patrick. They went to the area that had been built for the camera. Boards had been laid for support and the director's chair sat nearby. Ben assisted Patrick in setting up the camera and tripod. While Patrick loaded the film, Ben turned to him. "Who's yelling so much?"

"Ah, that's the director, William Stone. It's very normal; he wants to get the movie shot and that'll be his only goal today."

"And who watches out for the stunt people?"

"Jean's in charge of this one; she'll also be riding."

Ben nodded, and the people around the set got organized.

The director, Stone, began yelling orders. "We need the light!" He shook his fingers at Jean and the other stunt people. "You get up on the horses. You're chasing these two men, they've stolen sheep, and you want them back!"

Patrick looked at Ben. "We'll be moving to at least three or four locations. Be ready."

Ben spent the next few hours hauling equipment from place to place. He had little time to concentrate on the movie.

Ben wiped his head and said, when they were finally on a break, "This is work."

"Yeah," Patrick agreed. "It's all fun and games on screen, but to get it there takes a lot of effort."

"What next?"

"We're done. Everyone will start getting ready to head back."

"Is Harry around?" Ben asked, looking around.

"Over there." Patrick called out, "Harry!" A tall blond man in the distance waved to them and walked over.

"Hey, Patrick, sorry I didn't come over sooner. Stone keeps changing the plans for the type of building in the background."

"No problem. Ben wanted to talk with you."

"Have you had a chance to quote those projects we talked about?" he asked.

"How about tomorrow morning?" Harry asked.

"That's perfect."

"Meet me at my boarding house?"

"I can give him your address," Patrick told Harry. He'd stayed at the same boarding house as Harry when he arrived from New York.

"Tomorrow, eight am. I'll be there." Harry sauntered off.

"See you then," Ben said. He looked at Patrick. "What now?"

"Now, we get these film canisters into the car and go to the editing room. We'll take the film and run it through, making the scenes line up."

"Is that why we did so many different takes of the same thing?"

"It is. It'll look like multiple cameras are being used. It'll give the scenes more depth."

"Can I watch you put that together?"

"Sure. Are you going to be able to spend the next few hours with me?"

"My day's all yours," Ben assured him.

Jean walked over, pulling her hat off her head and hitting it on her leg, dislodging the dust. "That was a fun morning. Did you get it?"

"I did," Patrick assured her.

Stone yelled, "Patrick! I'll be over to the editing room around three pm."

"We'll be ready," he assured the director.

As they moved the equipment to Patrick's car, they saw some trucks pulling up.

"That's my cue," Jean told them. "I'll see you at the studio." She gave Patrick a quick kiss and ran off to see to the loading of the horses.

CHAPTER 24

Patrick and Ben ate sandwiches in the editing room. After they cleaned up, Patrick moved to the equipment to begin editing the movie. He started the film, Ben watching with interest. There were scenes of Jean throwing a rope, pulling one of the bad guys off of his horse. "Wow!" Ben exclaimed.

"It gets better from another angle," Patrick said.

"How do you get that portion in that spot?"

"That's easy. I cut the scene out, then attach it to the film in the new place for it." He held up the film and found the scene he was looking for.

"How can you find the different scenes?"

"You saw the small man running around before each scene?"

"Yes."

"That was the director's assistant; he has a slate and uses chalk, and he erases it between scenes. It allows me to manage each scene in order."

"Do you have to watch the whole film first?"

"No, I have a pretty good memory for the scenes I shot." He stopped the film at the scene he needed and used the film splicer to cut it. It was put back together using a special glue that partially melted the film together. Patrick waited a few minutes for the glue to dry, then played it back. There was a better view of the rope being tossed and close-ups of Jean and the man being taken down.

"That part was slower," Ben observed.

"Yeah. It's called over-cranking. I move the crank faster, and it looks like slow-motion. If I slow it down, it's called under-cranking, and it makes the action go faster."

"How do you know which speed is right?"

"Practice, practice. The studio let me take a camera home and film the kids running back and forth. It helped me get the hang of it."

"And he hums," Jean said, entering the small room.

Ben grinned at his friend. "What do you hum?" Patrick mumbled something. "What was that?" he prompted.

"Opera," Patrick said a little louder.

"Opera?"

"'The Anvil Chorus' by Verdi has the right beat for me to be consistent."

"And the slower scenes?"

"I just slowed the song down."

"And from then on, you were able to operate the camera?"

"No," Patrick laughed, "my first film had to have several retakes, but I had a good director who was willing to give me a chance."

"Some stunts I've seen on film look far too dangerous."

"Some aren't real stunts," Jean pointed out.

"How's that?" Ben asked her.

"Glass shots, it's a matte technique. We use a piece of transparent glass in front of the camera. The artist will paint on the background. If we don't have a budget for a castle, we paint one in place," said Patrick.

"You said it was used for stunts?" asked Ben.

"Yes, especially edge ones, where the actor will want closeups and not see the stunt person; that's when we'll use that technique," said Patrick.

"Did you see 'Modern Times'?" asked Jean.

"Chaplin? Sure, it was amazing," said Ben.

"Remember the skating scene when he was close to that drop off?" asked Patrick.

"Yes," said Ben, "it was nerve racking."

"Glass shot," said Patrick.

"Just don't use it too often or you will put me out of business," said Jean.

"No chance of that," said Patrick.

PART III

New York, December 1919

The club was coming together and would be ready for its opening. The band could be heard rehearsing in the background.

"Lauren," called Jemma from the bar area, "get those girls trained. They're hostesses, not hookers. No heavy makeup and remind them why they're here."

"I will," Lauren called back. She turned to the line of girls and saw several rolling their eyes. "Listen up, if you want to stay here, you'll follow the rules."

"And if we don't?" asked a girl, smacking her gum.

"You'll be out, and there's no second chances. Terri, get rid of the gum." She watched the girl take the gum out and put it in a small piece of paper.

"Satisfied?" Terri asked.

Lauren nodded and looked at each girl. "Any more questions?" The girls shook their heads quickly; they needed the jobs.

Charlie leaned over the bar and asked Jemma, "Why not let the girls have some fun? We'll make more money."

Here we go again, she said to herself. "We're not doing that. There'll be plenty of money in the booze sales. I want this place to be classy."

"I guess it's up to you," he grumbled.

"You'd be right about that. Are the food and alcohol in place?"

"Yeah, Darren's set up teams and has been transporting the inventory. I have bartenders hired. Opening night's only a few weeks away," he commented.

"We'll be ready," Jemma said confidently. She looked around at the fully decorated space. Two levels of tables and decorative lattices separated the areas. They framed the dance floor.

"What's all this about coat checks, girls? Can't the customers hold their own coats?" he groused.

"It isn't coming out of your pay."

"You're sure it's a good idea to have women drinking in here?"

"You want the men dancing together?" she asked drolly.

"Women can be trouble, that's all I'm saying."

"I'm thinking that we might cater to the men at night and maybe the ladies in the afternoon."

"Why the afternoon?"

"Because ladies have taken up sports, and they want to go somewhere afterward to relax before heading home."

"You may have to take up a sport." Charlie smirked.

"Hmm, that's a thought." She didn't mention that Lottie and Lissette had already started that communication for her. He already thought he ran her business. She left him and went over to Lauren, where the girls were practicing carrying trays.

"Hey, boss, the girls are doing well," Lauren said, watching them closely.

Jemma looked the girls over and murmured, "Anyone look like trouble?"

"Just one," Lauren muttered back.

"The one with the short skirt?"

"That's Terri." Lauren nodded at the girl. "She might not make it through the days."

"You have control. I trust your instincts."

Lauren blushed but said, "Thanks, boss."

"We have people calling for the opening of the club."

"Anyone good?"

"The honorable mayor Hylan and his staff."

Lauren gasped and turned to face Jemma. "Won't that be a problem?" At that moment, one of the girls dropped her tray. Lauren whirled around. "Hey!" she exploded, "That could've been full of glasses! Be careful!"

"Sorry, I won't do it again," the girl promised.

"Okay, start again. We have to do this smoothly. You'll be carrying glasses and food trays soon."

She turned back to Jemma. "The mayor? Are you sure that's safe?"

"Hey, *they* called me. I think if we take care of them, then they'll take care of us."

"Lottie called to remind you about tonight," Lauren said.

"I'd forgotten," Jemma admitted.

"That just means you need to get out more." Lauren smiled at her.

"Yes," Jemma said and thought about what Ben had said. She needed to start building relationships with people she trusted. "Lauren, would you like to join us?" Lauren didn't say anything. "Never mind, forget I asked," Jemma said and turned to go to her office.

"I'd love to go," Lauren said.

"Well, good. Be ready to go at seven. We'll be eating at their house."

Lauren nodded and tried not to squeal in glee. *Try to be calm,* she thought. *Try to be calm.*

 arren entered the apartment he shared with Lauren. He'd planned a quiet evening at home. A dress hit him in the face. He pulled it off his head and looked at his sister, "What're you doing?" He watched her hold up a dress or a skirt and reject each one. The pile of clothes on the floor left her with only a few garments hanging.

"I just don't have the right clothes," Lauren fretted.

"Where're you going?"

She went over to him and grabbed him by his jacket. "I got asked to go to dinner with important people!"

"Who?" he asked, trying to pry her fingers off his jacket.

"Jemma."

He stilled. "Are you and her friends now?"

"I want to be."

"Oh, okay. Just be careful. She's our boss."

She let him go and went back to her closet. "I got it." She pulled out a green dress with blue flowers. "What do you think?"

"Yeah, sure," he said and moved to the icebox to take out a beer. He sat at the small table and put his face in his hands.

"Is something wrong?" she asked as she came out of the bathroom with the dress on. She hesitated at the mirror and touched up her makeup.

He lifted his head and said, "No, no. I met someone."

"You did?" she asked as she finished her makeup and picked up her bag. "Is she nice?"

"She's pretty," he said dreamily.

"Not what I asked," she muttered. Her brother had lousy taste in women. He was also unreasonable when it came to them. "I'm on my way now," she said, pulling on her coat and adjusting her hat.

"I'll be going out later."

"Okay, bye."

He watched the door close, and he dropped his head on the table and pounded it with his fist. He was getting in too deep.

CHAPTER 27

*L*auren ran up the metal stairs to Jemma's apartment. She'd never been inside, but she'd taken items to her before this. *Deep breaths*, she thought, and lifted her hand to knock. The door opened quickly, and Jemma stood there in a robe.

"Oh, I must be late. Come in, I got distracted," she said.

Lauren followed her into the large space. There were bookshelves on the back walls, and art covered every spare white wall. The couches were a dark red. "Colorful place," she said.

"I like color," Jemma said simply. "I need to get dressed, so make yourself comfortable."

"I will, thanks!" Lauren walked around the room and found a table with pictures. She recognized Jemma but not anyone else. *Wait, isn't that…* She leaned toward it. *I know that face.*

"Ready?" Jemma asked, coming out of the bedroom.

"Yes," Lauren replied. She was still trying to think of who the man in the picture was.

"Anything wrong?" Jemma asked, adjusting her earrings.

"No, I was just looking at the pictures. You have a nice family."

Jemma smiled. "Yeah, they are."

"Which one is Ben?"

Jemma walked over and pointed to the tall man hugging her. "Right there."

"He's nice looking."

"Yeah, he is, and he's a good guy."

"No chance of him moving to New York?"

"He's settled in California, unfortunately."

"Miss him?"

"I do. We're close."

"Who is that?" asked Lauren, pointing to the older man with Lauren and Ben.

"My grandfather," Jemma said, her voice distracted. "I forgot my purse, just a second."

Lauren stared at the pictures, and it came to her. That man hugging Jemma and Ben was John Harden! Jemma was the granddaughter of an infamous gangster!

Jemma returned, clicking her purse closed. She looked at her watch with a sigh. "Late again. Grab that bag. Let's go."

Lauren picked up the bag and heard bottles inside clang together. "Are we going with your driver?"

"No, I thought something else might be more fun."

Lauren followed Jemma down the noisy stairs and looked around. "I don't see a car."

"No, there won't be a car."

They continued down the steps to the back of the building, stopping at a door. Jemma pulled out a key and unlocked it.

"I didn't know there was a room here," Lauren said.

"No one but me and Jojo have a key." Jemma walked into the dark space and returned with a motorbike.

"What kind of bike is this?"

"It's a converted military motorbike."

"Is there room for both of us?" Lauren asked doubtfully.

"We'll make it work. Hand me the bottles." Lauren handed

the bag over; Jemma inserted them in the side saddle. Jemma got on and started the engine and directed, "Climb on the back." Lauren shrugged, hiked up her dress, and climbed on. "Want to go fast or slow?" she asked over the hum of the engine.

"Fast!"

"Okay then." Jemma revved the engine and called, "Hang on!"

Lauren gripped Jemma's waist, and they sped off. A few blocks later, they slowed. They got off the motorbike, and Jemma moved it into a small garage under a tall brownstone.

"Glad I had my hat," Lauren remarked.

"It does help."

"You're finally here!" called a voice from above them.

They looked up and saw Lottie leaning out of the window. "My fault," Jemma told her.

"As usual."

"Yeah, yeah, let us in."

"Hey, Lauren."

"Hey, Lottie."

They went up the stoop and waited. Moments later, Lissette answered. "Hello, Lissette. This is my friend Lauren." Jemma introduced the two women.

She said I'm her friend, Lauren thought giddily. "Nice to meet you," she said to Lissette.

"You too. Come in, we have the food ready upstairs."

The home entryway was grand with polished wood paneling and a beautiful rug. They headed up an ornate staircase. At the top of the stairs, they found Lottie sitting in a large living area with comfortable couches, deep chairs, and large rugs. There was also a lot of art covering the walls.

"This looks like Jemma's place," Lauren said, looking around.

"Lissette helped me decorate when I moved here," Jemma told her.

"I enjoyed it." Lissette smiled. "Let's sit. We can eat around the low table in the living room and talk."

"I have something to help with that," said Jemma. She pulled out two bottles of wine.

"Perfect, I'll get them open," Lottie said. She retrieved a corkscrew from the kitchen and opened each bottle. The drinks were poured and the food eaten.

"Do we have the ladies lined up for the afternoon teas?" asked Jemma.

"I've been to my clubs. They're excited for it," Lissette responded.

"That's good," Jemma told her.

"Call me and let me know when the first ones will be scheduled."

Lissette looked at Lauren. "I hear you applied for your job in an unusual manner."

"I needed a job, and that seemed the only way."

"She's a fine employee," Jemma said. "I expect good things from her."

Lauren smiled. She was glad to hear her hard work had been noticed.

Lottie looked at her. "Are you dating anyone?"

"That's a little personal, don't you think?" Jemma protested.

"We're all friends, right? Nothing wrong with friends gossiping," she said, picking up her wine glass.

"If she wants to answer, she can," Jemma huffed.

"No one serious. I'm having fun right now."

Jemma and Lottie knew Jojo would love to go out with her, but kept their mouths shut.

"I may be hiring some new bartenders for the afternoon teas soon," Jemma said.

"Oh, can I interview them?" Lauren asked, rubbing her hands together.

"I don't know. Charlie normally hires the bartenders."

She scrunched her nose. "I know who he'll pick, and it won't be any good-looking men. Jemma, we need good-looking men for the teas," she said earnestly.

"You're right. I'll run interference," Jemma said.

"Yay!" Lauren looked at Lissette. "Can I ask you a question?"

"Of course."

"Well, I read in the society papers…"

"Oh, my. You read those?"

"Just sometimes," Lauren answered. She felt silly admitting that.

"I apologize." Lissette could tell she'd hurt the girl's feelings. "I stopped caring about the society papers a long time ago after Lottie and I got together. They only ever said nasty things about us."

"Oh, I'm sorry," Lauren said. "Anyway, I read a couple of years ago you were going by Elise, and now you're going by Lissette?"

"Elise is my middle name," she explained. "I'd decided to go by that for a while. It sounded so cosmopolitan, but after a while I got bored with it and started going by Lissette again." She smiled. "Who knows, I may decide to go by Elise again sometime in the future."

They talked into the night, each sharing stories and laughs. By the time the evening ended, each felt they had a new friend.

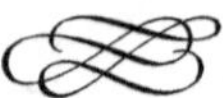

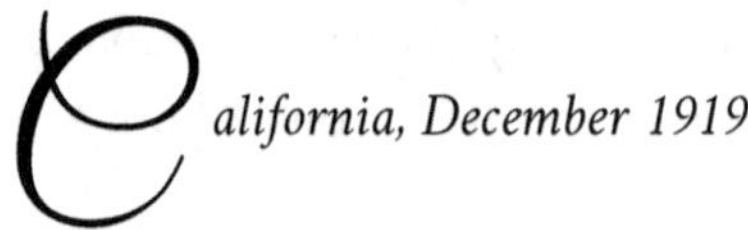

alifornia, December 1919

The first bricks were rolling off the line. The packaging was being hand-wrapped around them. Marisol handed the first packaged bricks out to Angelo, Bella, Patrick, Jean, and Ben. Each one was marked with their brand: *Grape, Vin de Table.*

"This is it," Marisol told them. "The orders have been coming in from all over the country."

"This is only the first shipment," Ben cautioned. "We still have orders that'll take all of our current inventory. It'll all be gone in several days."

Angelo shook his head. "I thought we'd lose everything. Instead," he said, looking at the busy factory floor, "our family has grown and we're going to thrive."

"We'll need these boxed up for the train. Chicago, Pittsburgh, Philadelphia, and New York will be receiving our products."

"And if the government comes after us?" Angelo asked him.

"That's why we have Lottie," Ben replied.

CHAPTER 29

*N*ew York

Lottie laid down the phone. "The first rail cars are on the way," she told Chris.

"It'll be an interesting first test of Volstead. Do you think the feds will stop the distribution?" he asked.

"The law says no."

The phone rang, and Chris picked it up. "Hello? Yes, she's here." He held out the phone to her.

"Who is it?" she asked cautiously.

"The Prohibition director."

"General Woodcock?" He shrugged. She held out her hand for the phone and put it to her ear. "Yes, this is Lottie Flannaghan."

"Do you represent Grape, Vin de Table by the Valdez family in California?"

"Yes, sir, I do."

"Is there intent to violate the law with the sale of grape bricks?"

"No, sir. The intent is to save the vineyards of honest, hard-working families."

"I understand the instructions have a warning statement on the packaging?"

"They do. The instructions are very clear about what isn't to be done with the concentrate." The line went very quiet, and she could've sworn she heard laughter. "Sir, are you still there?"

She heard him clear his throat. "Yes, yes, I am."

"Will you be pursuing a case against the manufacturers of Grape, Vin de Table?" she asked.

"Intent is very hard to prove," the man replied.

"That it is, sir, that it is."

She slowly hung up the phone and turned to Chris. "Ben and that little whirlwind of his may have found a way to beat Prohibition."

"You still look worried," he observed.

"Yeah. How will the bootleggers respond to the competition?"

hicago

"The bars are set up, Al," Frank Capone said to his brother.

"Are the prior owners being civil?" Al Capone asked.

"Most," Frank said cautiously.

"We'll have to do something about Harden. Approach him again." Capone rubbed his hands together. "We'll be making a lot of money. People will be desperate for drinks."

"Well, maybe not so desperate," Frank said.

"What're you talking about?"

"This." Franke turned the newspaper toward his brother.

"Grape juice?" Capone scoffed. "Why do I care about that? It's a kiddie's drink."

"Al, it's the wording on the label."

"Well, what does it say? Read it to me," Capone demanded.

Frank picked up the paper and read from it. "It says right here, 'Do not store the grape juice in a jug. Do not put away in a dark area for twenty one days, because this could accidentally turn into wine. To prevent fermentation, add 1/10% Benzoate of Soda'."

Capone frowned. "Wine bricks? The Prohibition guys will shut it down."

"I don't think so. There seems to be a loophole."

Capone was furious. "They can't do that! They're interfering in my profits!"

CHAPTER 31

New York, December 1919

"How do we tell the Prohibition guys from the regular people?" Lauren asked Jemma.

Jemma tapped the table with her fingernails. "I've been thinking about that. We could initially handle it like a party, only bring in people that we know or who've been recommended," she said.

"Since we won't know what they look like, we'll have to be careful. Maybe we could have a password. Maybe our guests can whisper it to get in. "

Jemma pondered that. "Hmmm, I like that idea. Instead of a word, maybe a phrase? Not a long one, though; we need something easy that people can remember. "

Lauren snapped her fingers. "I got it, 'the sun is shining'."

"That works. I think we may need multiple, though. One for the night crowd and a different one for the afternoon crowd. Maybe 'tea for two'?"

Lauren laughed. "I like it."

Jemma nodded and went to the bandstand; the band was setting up to practice. She called out, "Attention, everyone. I have an announcement."

"Here, use this," the band leader said, handing her a microphone.

She took it and waited while people filed in from all areas of the club. She noticed Charlie didn't move from his position at the bar. "Is everyone here?" They looked around and nodded. "We'll be opening soon. Prohibition has started, and we'll be selling alcohol here. Do we all understand that?" The employees nodded. They'd been asked when they were hired if they could be loyal to her and the job. "We need customers, but federal agents might attempt to mix in. We've worked out a way to vet all who enter and have determined that a phrase will work. The phrase is 'the sun is shining'. When someone in the line says that, Casper—the bouncer at the door—will know they have been thoroughly vetted and will be allowed in. Anyone not knowing the phrase won't be allowed in."

"Obviously, we can't have someone shouting out the phrase so everyone else in line can hear it, so the phrase will need to be whispered in the bouncer's ear."

"We may also need to change the phrase every so often, but we'll communicate with everyone before that happens. Any questions?"

Jemma could see Charlie out of the corner of her eye; he was shaking his head. She focused on the group in front of her.

"Now, what I want you to do is to share the phrase with people you know we can trust."

"What is it?" Casper called from the entranceway. He had just walked into the meeting and had caught the ending.

"Sorry, Casper. The phrase is 'The sun is shining.' The person will, hopefully, whisper it in your ear so that others in the line without the password can't get in. We are hoping that our crowds will grow, and we'll be able to build a regular list of customers."

The crowd started to talk. "What about raids?" one worker asked. "What do we do if we get raided?"

"Yeah, how do we get out?" one of the male waiters asked.

"You and the customers must get out safely. We'll be using the back door to 86th Street."

"Won't the agents know about that?" Charlie asked.

"No, the door isn't visible from the outside," Jemma replied shortly.

"Could we be arrested?" asked one of the bartenders.

"It's too soon to tell. We have a lawyer on retainer, and she will represent anyone who might get arrested."

There was more grumbling, and Jemma fought the urge to sigh. "Just to be clear, we are in an illegal business; if you don't think you can handle that, then maybe you should find other employment."

The bartender who'd asked the question spluttered, "No, no, boss. I want my job; I just want to know what to expect." The other waiters and staff nodded.

Lauren called out, "Then back to work!" The employees broke away to their individual jobs. She walked up to stand with Jemma on the bandstand. "They're good kids; the whole thing's unsettling."

I need to let Ben and John know about the passwords, Jemma thought. "For all of us."

"You're worried, too?" Lauren asked, surprised.

"Yeah, this is new for all of us."

"Is there anything you can do to stop the raids?"

"I have something in mind," Jemma murmured. "I'll be going out to follow up." She stepped down from the bandstand and crossed to her office.

Lauren motioned to one of the waitresses. "I'll be right back."

She followed Jemma into her office and watched her pull on her coat and hat.

"Can you tell me what you're going to do?" Lauren asked.

"No, not yet."

She walked over and took Jemma's hand. "We're friends now, aren't we?"

"Of course we are."

"But you can't share this with me?"

"No, it might get complicated. And I don't want to drag you into it."

"But you'll let me know if you need anything?"

Jemma smiled easily. "Yeah, I will. I think you have something to do also?"

"Yes, boss." Lauren saluted and went back to her duties.

Jemma smiled and shook her head. Ben had told her to find someone she trusted; now, she had Lottie, Lauren, and Lissette. She had to find a way to provide additional protection for her club and her people.

John had the answer; there was a federal agent who might be willing to look the other way on certain matters. He'd sent Jemma the man's address. John's note was concise: "Make an agreement and pay on a schedule." He'd said that most agents were underpaid, and this man would agree because he needed the money.

Okay, Grandpa, I'll do it, she thought.

She looked at the address; it was in Brooklyn. Rocky, her driver was waiting. He stood quickly and went over to her. "Ready, boss?"

"This is the address," she said, handing him a small piece of paper.

Rocky looked at it and nodded. "Yeah, I know this place." He held the door open for her. Jemma got in the backseat and watched as he got behind the wheel. The scenery flew by, and soon they were across the bridge and into Brooklyn.

The area is similar to that of Greenwich, she observed as they pulled to a stop in front of an apartment. *I don't think the offer of money will be rejected.*

"Boss," Rocky said as he looked around the area, "you want I should come up with you?"

The area looked a bit seedy, but she straightened her shoulders and said, "No, I've got this." She went to the door of the apartment building and walked in. The man's apartment was on the third floor. She looked down at her heeled shoes and sighed. *My best shoes. They'll have to do.* She moved quickly up the first flight, and by the third, she was cursing the shoes. She sat down and took them off. They were so pretty but not built for climbing. She started to stand when a voice asked, "Can I give you a hand?"

She looked up slowly. A man leaned toward her. He had light brown hair and dark brown eyes. She nodded and put her hand in his, allowing him to pull her to her feet. She had to tilt her head to look him in the eye. "Thank you."

"Quite a walk up here," he commented.

"It was," she admitted with a laugh, holding up her shoes.

His laugh joined hers as he asked, "Seeing someone on this floor or one above?"

"No, I think if I had to go higher, I may have just gone home. Well, I'll need to go now," she said as she started to pull her hand from his.

He let it slide away and said, "I hope you find who you're looking for."

"Me too." She nodded and started down the hall, looking at the door numbers. When she got to the door, she needed, she stopped and glanced to the right. The stranger stood there. She frowned. "I don't need more help."

"You don't?" he teased.

"No," she said firmly and reached up to knock on the door.

Still, he remained next to her. "Look, I don't need you to be here."

"I beg to differ."

She put her hand on her hip. "And why's that?"

"'Cause this is my apartment," he commented.

"You're Dan Nolan?" she asked in disbelief.

"Yeah, I'm Danny."

She smiled and quirked an eyebrow at him.

"Don't." He pointed his finger at her.

"Don't what?"

"Ever since that stupid song came out, everyone sings it to me. They think it's so funny."

"I wasn't…" Jemma started to protest.

"Yeah, you were."

She looked abashed. "All right fine, I was going to sing it. But it's a good thing you stopped me since my singing isn't that good."

Danny smiled. "You're looking for me?" he prompted.

"We need to talk. In private."

"Sure." Danny reached past her and unlocked the door. Pushing it open, he said, "After you."

Jemma hesitated at the door. *Should I have brought Rocky with me?*

"You scared?" he taunted.

Jemma straightened her shoulders. "Not for a moment," she said and walked into the apartment.

Danny stood in the open door. "You can loosen the death grip on that bag. I'm not going to try to take it."

She relaxed her hand and asked, "Can we talk now?"

"I don't see why not." He closed the door and turned on the lights, illuminating the small space. "Make yourself comfortable in my large abode."

She glanced around the small room; it contained a kitchen

area on one side and a twin bed on the other. A small table sat in between. She moved to the table and sat down.

When she didn't say anything, he asked, "Who are you? Why are you here?"

"I'm Jemma Hardison," she said, using her pseudonym.

"Ok, I have the who, now the why?"

"I got your number from my grandfather." He waited. "He said that you might be able to help me with my business venture."

He stood and went over to get a beer from the ice box. "Can I get you one?"

"Yes, thank you."

Danny carried the bottles and two glasses to the table with him. She watched him pour the drinks. When he finished, they both drank. "You mentioned a business venture?"

She examined her glass and said, "Funny that you have beer."

He stilled suddenly and asked, "Just what's the venture you want to discuss?"

"I understand you're working for a federal agency that's looking to shut down anyone selling, manufacturing, or distributing alcohol."

Danny drained the glass and slammed it down. "Just who's your grandfather?" he demanded.

"John Harden," she answered truthfully.

He gripped the glass so tightly that Jemma thought it might crack. "And what did you expect to happen here today?"

"An agreement of sorts," she said idly.

"What kind?" he asked warily.

"I'll be opening a club shortly. It'll have entertainment and a restaurant."

"And alcohol?" he asked warily.

She nodded. "That's the plan."

"And what's my role in this?"

"I pay you not to raid my place," she said boldly.

He tossed back his head and laughed. "I think you overestimate my powers. I'm just a low-level employee."

"All I'm asking is that you let me know if we need to clean up before the agents come around."

He tilted his head. "And what's in this for me?"

"You'll be nicely compensated, of course."

"How much?" he asked, sitting back in his chair.

She looked around the apartment and met his eyes. "Enough to get you to a better place than this one."

He followed her gaze. "Um, no. I think I'll stay here. If I, all of a sudden, can afford a better place, my superiors might get suspicious and think I'm on the take."

"Hmmm, you're right," she acknowledged with a nod of her head. "Will you do it?"

He didn't respond right away. Instead, he asked, "How much?"

"Ten dollars a day?"

"That's higher than the going rate. You got a deal."

Jemma nodded. "How will I get it to you?" she asked.

"Oh, don't worry. I'll be around."

She stood and said, "If we have a deal, I think I'll be on my way."

"No, I think we have a thing or two to discuss."

"We do?"

He stood and reached out his hand, taking her arm and pulling her toward him. He lowered his head and, with his lips just touching hers, he said, "Yes, we do." He kissed her long and deep.

Jemma didn't know this man, but she felt the pull of him. She wrapped her arms around him and pulled him closer. The slow kisses seemed to drug them both. Finally, he pulled back.

"I'll see you in a week."

"What?" she asked, confused.

Danny grinned at her and adjusted her slightly askew hat. "I'll meet you in a week."

She shook her head to clear it. "Where?"

"Your place."

"You don't know where I live," she protested.

"Don't worry, I'm a federal agent; I think I can find it." Jemma walked toward the door. "I think you're forgetting something?" Danny said.

"No, I don't think so," she said, holding up her purse. Her brain was still fuzzy from the kiss. He brandished her shoes. She flushed. "Oh, yes, I'll need those."

"Want me to help you put them on?" Danny asked, dangling the shoes.

"No," she said hurriedly, "I'll put them on downstairs." She walked over to get them.

He wanted to pull her in close again; instead, he handed her the shoes.

She seemed to hesitate when she got them. "How does John know you?"

"I'm Mel O'Bannion's son."

Jemma was gobsmacked. "Son! I've known that man my entire life; he doesn't have children."

"Well. I'm here." She continued to study him. Looking for any trace of Mel in him.

"It's the eyes," he said.

She looked at him intently and said, "They're the same."

"Just the eyes," he assured her.

She hurried out.

"It was nice to meet you!" he called down.

She stopped and stared up at him. "Yes, it was."

CHAPTER 32

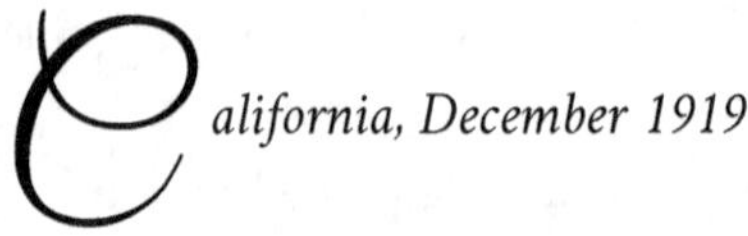

alifornia, December 1919

The roar of a car engine could be heard outside. Marisol put down her book and went to the large window overlooking the porch. "Who is it?" asked Angelo from his chair.

"Ben's expecting some deliveries today," she said absently.

Angelo came up behind her, and when the dust settled, he walked over to get his gun. "It's RL," he said, adding two shells and swinging it up to close it.

"No, no, not again. I thought he got the message last time he was here." She looked over her shoulder toward the kitchen, where Ben was talking to Mama. She approached Angelo and touched his arm. "Papa, let me reason with him."

He nodded. "He was a good employee. See what you can do. I'll be here watching."

Marisol walked out onto the porch. "RL, what're you doing here?" she asked.

"Marisol." RL smiled broadly and ran over to her. "For you! I'm here to be with you."

She stepped back from his approaching form. She tried again. "RL, you need to find another job and someone who returns your feelings."

"No! You see, I have so many plans for the two of us," he said and grabbed her by the arm.

She sighed. *This isn't going well.* "Papa!" she called.

Angelo walked out with his gun. Holding it to his shoulder, he pointed it at RL. "It's time you left."

"No! I'm taking Marsol with me!" RL ranted, dragging her across the porch.

"She doesn't want to go with you," Angelo said, leveling his gun at the man.

"And if I decide to report you and your illegal business?" RL threatened in a low voice.

Ben walked through the doorway and strode briskly over to RL and Marisol. Grabbing the man by the collar, he pulled him from Marisol and shook him.

"Hey, stop!" RL pleaded.

"You won't be reporting anything to anyone," Ben snarled in his face. "You have no business here anymore. Angelo fired you."

"That isn't up to you," RL whined as he tried to get loose from Ben's grip.

Angelo said, "I've told you this is a family business."

Ben dropped the man to the ground. RL scrambled to his feet and pointed at Ben. "He isn't family!"

"You would be wrong there; he's my partner. You need to gather your things and leave. I told you before that you're fired."

"Marisol," RL pleaded. He saw Bella step out onto the porch. "Mama! Please?" he pleaded.

"I'm not your mama. You must go," Bella insisted.

"Marisol," he tried again.

"RL, please go."

"But… but we…"

"There was never a 'we'," she told him quietly.

That statement from her changed him; his face hardened, and he looked at Ben, then Marisol. "Is that how it is?"

Ben said, "It's time to go."

RL slammed his hat on his head and stalked down the porch.

Angelo followed him to the stairs. "We need to make sure he leaves." He put the gun down and walked back into the house.

Ben watched the truck drive off. They knew that man was going to be trouble. Marisol and Bella stood with him.

"What are we going to do?" Bella asked. "Do you think he will turn us in?"

"For what?" Ben asked her. "We have records to prove it's a legal business."

Marisol took her mama's hand. "We'll be fine."

Ben nodded. A car came around the house and followed the truck out of the vineyard. "That's all that can be done now. Why don't we go inside?" Marisol took her mama by the arm and guided her inside.

A little while later, Angelo joined them, his hair sticking up and his face a deep red. "Papa, are you okay?" Marisol asked him worriedly as she walked over to him.

He didn't say anything; he crossed the room and sat in his deep leather chair. "Changes, so many changes. RL was with us for years."

"He should have been gone a long time ago," she told him. "He always overstepped."

"Marisol, he seems to think he was going to marry you. Did he have reason to believe that?"

"Not in any way, Papa." Ben, Bella, and Angelo watched her intently. "No," she said forcefully, looking at the three of them. "He made assumptions, but I never encouraged him."

That seemed to satisfy them.

Ben looked at her. "That could be worse. That means he's fixated on you. There's no telling what he might do to get you back."

A car engine could be heard near the front of the house. Ben walked to the window and saw two cars pulling up.

"Is he back?" asked Marisol, running over to him.

"No, it's Jesse with our cars. Angelo and Marisol, can you come out? I have someone I want you to meet."

Angelo stood. Bella went to him and smoothed down his hair. "Your color's better. Do you want some lemonade to take with you?" she asked, watching him closely.

"No, I'm all right." He looked at Marisol and Ben. "Let's go greet our guests."

Ben and Marisol followed him out of the house and down the stairs to the two cars.

"Hi, Jesse. It's good to see you," Ben greeted. "Jesse Harrison, this is Angelo and Marisol Valdez. You'll meet Mrs. Valdez soon."

"It's nice to meet you," Jesse said, shaking their hands. He pointed to the other car. "That's my other driver, Shorty."

"We should probably move the cars to the back," suggested Angelo.

"Good idea," Ben agreed.

"We can do that. Ben, you want to show us where?" Jesse asked him.

"Sure, I'll ride with you," he said and walked to the passenger side of the car.

Before they got in, Marisol called, "Mr. Harrison, did you pass anyone on the way in?"

"I did. The truck blasted by me like a bat outta hell and almost ran me off the road."

The group was silent, looking at the road that led out of the vineyard.

"We'll meet you in the back," Marisol said. She and Angelo walked back into the house.

As they got in the car, Jesse looked at Ben. "Is that truck someone we're gonna have to keep an eye on?"

"Yeah, he is."

"Give me the details later; we can do something about that."

Ben nodded.

Jesse drove the car around to the back and stopped. He waved to Shorty to get out, then used a handkerchief to wipe his head.

Bella walked onto the porch and called out to Shorty, "It's too hot. Come into the house."

Jesse nodded, and Shorty jogged up to the house. "Thank you, ma'am," he said when he got inside.

"Come with me. I might even have some cookies."

"That'd be nice, thank you."

"Come down and take a look at the car," called Jesse. Angelo and Marisol headed to the first car. It was flashy and looked sleek and fast.

"Not that one," Jesse told them.

Angelo frowned. "Not this car?"

"You thought it'd be the one that looks the fastest?" Jesse asked.

"Yes." Marisol stood by with a frown.

"That's the point," Ben told them, standing at the other car. "Our drivers will be going past checkpoints, and this car won't stand out."

"It definitely doesn't stand out," Angelo said doubtfully.

They walked over to look into the car. The backseat had been removed, leaving the rear space open. "Are all the modifications in place?" Ben asked Jesse.

"Yes. It's stock on the outside, but on the inside, it's outfitted with high-powered engines that'll leave the coppers in the dust. We also installed heavy-duty shocks and springs."

"And plenty of room for alcohol." Marisol grinned.

"That's the main reason for the modifications," Jesse assured her.

"Show me the engine," Angelo demanded. Jesse led the way and opened up the engine cover.

"That's not the engine that comes with the car," Angelo observed, bending down to examine it.

"No," Jesse admitted, "but this will outrun any cop cars."

"Can it handle the load of bottles?"

"That's the reason for taking out the backseat and the added shocks and springs. Though I'll expect you also want to pack the bottles to withstand the trip."

"And if we get stopped?" Marisol asked.

"They'll be carrying letters stating that it's sacramental wine," Ben said.

"Will that be true?" Angelo asked him.

"Sometimes. Some of it'll be meant for sacramental wine, but others will be shipped to bars in Chicago and New York."

"What if the bottles are found in raids in those areas? Will they track them back to us?"

"They'll be told that the bottles were bought before Prohibition."

"Will that be enough?"

"We won't be selling the good wine to everyone; we'll keep it for a specific clientele."

"We might want to change the labels for those locations," suggested Marisol.

"That will make it harder to track back to us," Angelo replied, mulling over the idea.

"Yes."

"How many cars will we need?" Angelo asked.

"I've ordered two," Ben told him.

"If needed, I can provide more," Jesse assured them.

"January's coming quickly," said Ben. "We'll need to test

routes to Chicago and New York starting this week. The drivers need to know the routes and not draw attention to themselves."

"Who do we get for that?" Angelo asked. "I only have regular drivers; I don't want them involved in anything dangerous."

"That won't be a problem," Ben assured him. "I have two people coming down from Chicago to take the route. They're already familiar with the areas." His sister and John knew both men, which would make it easier to take the deliveries. Trust was going to be an issue until this thing was over. He'd heard that Prohibition agents were going to be paying for information on alcohol related activities.

Angelo sighed. "Why must we be involved in this?"

"Because, Papa, we need to make sure our winery survives Prohibition," Marisol told him.

"How long?"

"There's no set limit right now," admitted Ben. "It could go on for years."

"Or forever," Jesse observed.

"It seems we have no choice then," Angelo lamented.

"Sure, we do, Papa," teased Marisol. "There are always orchids."

"Bah, orchids! Ben, get it organized. Marisol, get measurements so we know the size of the boxes."

"Yes, Papa," she said and watched as he went inside. As soon as the back door closed, she rounded on Jesse. "Can I drive the car?" asked Marisol.

Ben hid his grin.

Jesse was used to strong ladies and said, "We'd have to drive at a normal pace until we get out of sight of the vineyards," he suggested.

"I can do that," she said confidently.

Jesse looked at Ben, "There's only two seats."

"You go with her; I'll take my turn after."

Marisol grinned and went to the driver's door and got in.

Jesse's eyes widened. "She can drive, can't she?"

Ben kept a straight face and said, "I don't know."

"Oh, no, why didn't you stop me! That car's too powerful for a non-driver. I need to get her out." He started toward her.

Ben grabbed his friend's arm. "Hey, I was kidding. She drives the trucks all over the vineyard."

"Oh, okay. Then we'll get going." He turned back to him. "You're sure?"

"I am. Go!"

Jesse climbed into the passenger seat.

"Ready?" Marisol asked, revving the engine.

"Remember, we don't want people to know what the car can do," he cautioned.

"You're right," she said, gripping the wheel. "I'll behave," she assured him.

Marisol drove slowly to the outer edge of the vineyards. "We can go a little further, and then we'll be out of sight."

Jesse nodded, and they continued down the road for a few more minutes. He looked around to make sure the coast was clear, then said, "All right, you can start increasing speed here."

Marisol pushed on the gas pedal a bit hard, and they took off, throwing their heads back.

"Careful!" Jesse warned.

"Sorry," she said, pushing the pedal harder. "Whoo! The car has speed!"

"Yeah, it does," he said, gripping the dash, "Okay, I think that's far enough."

She listened to him this time and reduced the speed to turn around. "It handles well," she commented.

"We'll do the maintenance on them between each trip to make sure they perform as they should."

"Jesse, why should we trust you?" Marisol asked him.

"Ben trusts me," he pointed out.

"He does," she acknowledged. "Why is that?"

"We're family."

She frowned. "You're related?"

"Yes." He didn't explain how they were related.

CHAPTER 33

$\mathcal{B}$en's bars were all located on the same road. They were all smallish locations, nothing like Jemma's club in New York. He'd parked his car and was walking for a few minutes when he noticed someone following him. He deliberately passed his bar entrance, in case it was a Prohibition agent trying to get the jump on him.

He stopped abruptly, and the man ran into him. He turned and got a good look at the man. He was on the shorter side, about thirty-five, with thinning light brown hair, and looked like he had missed a few meals. "Is there something I can do for you?" Ben asked.

"No... Yes," the man stuttered.

"Well, which is it?"

The man crushed his hat in his hands. "I need a job," he said in a rush, his hair falling over his eyes.

"People are looking for jobs in odd ways," Ben muttered. Jemma had told him about Lauren, who had climbed in through a high window and asked for a job. Now, he was being stalked. "What kind of job?"

The man looked around and said in a low voice, "I know you own some bars."

Ben frowned. "How did you hear about that?"

"Harry Brown at the studio; he told me there might be jobs."

Ben shrugged and said, "Let's go inside."

"Where?" the man asked, looking at the solid brick walls.

"Around the corner."

The man followed and watched as Ben tapped on the door. A small window opened, and a person inside said, "Hey, boss." The door opened quickly.

Ben walked in and waved to the man behind him. "Well, come on in."

The man looked around the space as he entered. Ben's four bars were all similar: low lighting, rich interiors, intimate booths, and long bars that ran the length of the rooms. Other locations would be opened as they were needed; until then, they would be used as storage.

"You... you look ready to open," the man acknowledged.

Ben nodded and moved to sit in a booth. "Sit. Tell me your name and what kind of job you're looking for."

He joined him in the booth. "Johnny Bellavar."

"Ben." The two men shook hands.

Johnny said in a rush, "I'd like to be your manager for all of your locations."

"I have four," Ben commented. "For now."

"I can handle that," Johnny replied, his voice steady.

"What's your experience?"

"I've run multiple restaurants here in the city."

"Were they successful?"

"For a time," Johnny admitted.

"Then why work for me?"

"Prohibition. If we can't sell alcohol, we can't stay open. We made more money on the drinks than we did on the food. I've had to close all my places and have paid off the vendors and employees." He looked down. "There's nothing left."

Should I take the chance with him? Ben thought as he studied the man sitting in front of him. He looked in Johnny's eyes, and Johnny's met his unflinchingly. "Okay," Ben decided, "I'll give you a chance."

"Thank you."

Ben chuckled. "Don't thank me. With four locations, it'll be a lot of work."

"I can handle it." Johnny was adamant.

Ben noticed the man's hand shaking. He saw Ben's interest and tried to move his hands under the table.

"When did you last eat, Johnny?" Ben asked, concerned.

"Honestly?" Johnny said, rubbing his shaky hand on his forehead. "I don't remember."

"Do you have a place to stay?"

"I'll find something."

"I'll front you the money to get an apartment. But first, we get you some food," he said firmly. Ben stood, and Johnny followed quickly behind.

CHAPTER 34

"Where are you going?" Marisol asked. She saw Ben putting papers into his briefcase. They were at his house in the other vineyards.

"I want to make sure Johnny has things under control in town. Opening night's coming."

"Can I go with you?"

"Sure, you can leave?" Since she'd taken over as foreman at the new vineyard, she'd been working long days.

"The brick order has been packaged and shipped off, and the vines are being monitored. I'll notify my supervisors that I'll be out today."

"Is Angelo going to be okay with you being with me?" They'd made strides as partners, but there was still tension when he and Marisol went off the vineyard alone.

"Papa's changing his attitude. He's allowing me more freedom."

"Just not with me," he muttered under his breath.

"What was that?" she asked sweetly.

"Me? I didn't say anything." Ben looked at his watch. "Meet me back here in twenty minutes?"

She nodded and left out the back door and headed to the supervisor's office.

He stood at his car twenty minutes later and waited. She walked up, her hair pulled into a bun, and she'd changed into a dress.

"Nice," he commented.

"Thank you," she said, giving him a slow smile. He returned it and went around the car to open her door. She got in, and he closed the door and moved to the driver's seat. The car they took was one of the models outfitted to move alcohol. They stopped at the edge of the street and parked.

"How many bars do you own?" she asked in a low voice.

"Four. Most are on this street, small ones. I have others that can be converted later."

"How big is your sister's bar in New York?"

"It's big," he said. "It's a full club. There's a band with a huge dance floor."

"Does Jemma also have smaller locations?"

"Yes, but most of them are being used for storage to support the main club. She has plans to expand at a later date."

"We will be meeting Johnny at the first bar?"

"Yes."

"And how's he working out?"

"He seems to be doing okay. I put him in charge of the booze deliveries. We're here to find out what progress has been made."

He offered her his elbow, she took it, and they strolled down the street. He sidestepped and walked quickly with her down the long alley. He stopped suddenly and tapped on a dark door. A small opening appeared, then shut quickly. The door swung open. "Hey, boss. Johnny's in the back."

"We'll head that way."

"Johnny!" called Ben.

Johnny stepped out. He was wearing the same suit as the day

Ben had hired him. Ben asked, "Have you had a chance to get a place to live?"

"I padded down in the back here. I didn't think you'd mind."

"Johnny, take some time and get a place to live."

"I… I will," Johnny promised.

"Introduce me," nudged Marisol.

"Marisol Valdez, this is Johnny Bellavar, my new manager."

"Nice… nice to meet you," Johnny stuttered.

Ben took pity on the man and asked, "Do you have an update on the inventory?"

Johnny seemed to turn into another man; he straightened and said, "Follow me." They entered the room, there were barrels of beer, bottles of gin, and whisky. "I have champagne still coming," he assured Ben.

"We'll provide the wine," Marisol told him.

"I tasted the bottle Ben dropped off; it'll sell well."

"Johnny, I'm amazed you got organized this quickly," Ben praised. "Is this the only one stocked?"

"No. All of the locations have had their deliveries."

"How did you manage that?"

"You know the trolley system?"

"No, can't say I do," Ben confessed.

Marisol interrupted. "The Pacific Electric passenger trolleys."

"Yes," said Johnny.

"How does that work with our alcohol?" asked Ben.

"It's an underground network that supplies transportation of heavy boxes and barrels. The tunnels branch off into basements in the area. It keeps us out of the eyes of agents looking for cars and trucks. I've found ways to use the system, with the driver's involvement."

"Bribes?"

"Yes, and well worth the money."

"Great," said Ben absently. "We're further along than

expected. Good job." Johnny flushed. "The next time I see you, Johnny, I want to see you in a new suit." He took out a hundred dollars and handed it to him.

"But that's too much," he protested.

"Then get two. We're headed out."

"Wait a sec. Ben, I have an idea I'd like to run by you."

Ben and Marisol stopped and waited.

Johnny began with, "I have my eye on a little larger space."

Ben rubbed his neck; he had a lot on his plate now. "Tell me about it."

"The property I found has a soda shop in front and a large back area that would work as a bar."

"I hadn't thought of that type of location. Can you show it to us?"

"Really? Thanks." Johnny grabbed his hat and coat to follow them to their car. The drive was a few streets over. "Over there." He pointed. They pulled over and got out.

Ben peered in the window. "We wouldn't have to hide if this were part of the cover. I'll have to call Terry to get access."

"I have keys," Johnny said.

"You do?" He studied the man. "Is this one of the places you used to work at?"

"Yeah," he admitted. "It was a little restaurant, which I believe will make a great soda shop."

"Show us around." Johny opened the door, and a bright open space greeted them. There was a bar with soda dispensers. Tables and chairs were already in place.

"It wouldn't take much to make the changes out here," Marisol observed.

"Hmm. Johnny, show me the back," Ben told him.

They went to the back, and Johnny pushed the door open. Ben saw there was enough room for a sliding door. They entered the extensive space.

"This is a perfect cover," Ben told Johnny. "Get with Terry

and Lottie. We'll need this taken care of immediately. Can you handle the soda shop and the back bar?"

"I can," Johnny said confidently.

"Get your plans drawn up and meet with our carpenter."

"I will, thanks for your support."

As they dropped him off, Ben called to his departing back, "Remember to get a suit!"

Johnny didn't turn but raised an arm to wave at them.

"That was nice of you," Marisol said.

"Not so nice, the man has an eye for business."

CHAPTER 35

hicago

Mel walked into John's office. "We've closed down the gambling operations."

"Are we ready with the bars?" John asked.

"We are. All of the buildings have been finished and furnished. We moved everyone from the gambling establishments to those."

"Have you talked to Ben and Jemma?"

"Both operations are ready to go; our men are supporting them. The first wine deliveries will be driven here. We'll move the wine bottles through the basement tunnels."

"The larger alcohol deliveries are on schedule?"

"The ships will be easily accessible. Once the barrels have arrived, they'll be distributed."

"Jemma recommends a password at each location for the customers to keep the Prohibition agents out."

"It's a good idea; we'll put it into place. Though I don't think it'll be a concern since we have agents on the payroll." Mel sat in front of John's desk. "You had Jemma contact Danny?"

"Yes, I knew he could be trusted, and she needs family supporting her."

"I don't want him to get into trouble."

"He is with Jemma; they'll work it out."

Mel nodded. John always took care of the family. "Capone's sending men around again to the bars not under his control," Mel said. "So far, he's taking over bars in nonviolent ways."

"You think they wanted to sell?" John scoffed.

"No, I'm sure it was coerced. I hear he's building his own breweries."

"There's money for everyone during Prohibition. One man doesn't need to have it all," John stated.

"I got word. Mouse is with Jemma now," Mel told him. John was helping Jemma build a group of people she could trust.

"He's a good man to have in times of stress."

CHAPTER 36

*N*ew York

"How's our stock?" Jemma asked Charlie.

"We're good. All areas are full. The high-speed boats will be able to outrun the Coast Guard ships."

"How's Darren doing?"

"He's fine. The drums made it in, and the shipments were confirmed."

"Good."

The private deliveries of wine had arrived from California and were in the special room along with French champagne. She'd already been approached about private tastings. Charlie wouldn't know anything about that.

CHAPTER 37

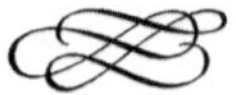

New York, January 1920
Prohibition has started

The night of the club's opening, Mayor John Francis Hylan was the first customer. He swept in and waited for his overcoat to be taken. Several men and women were with him.

Jemma went to greet him. "Sir, welcome."

"Thanks for sending over the password. I've been looking forward to it," he replied,

"Sir, just to be sure, can we count on you to not be involved in a raid?" she asked him.

He and his entourage laughed loudly, and he said, "That's a federal law; let those boys take care of their own business."

"Well, if that's the case, welcome." She waved to Lauren. "Please escort these people to their tables."

Lauren smiled brightly. "If you'll follow me, Mister Mayor?"

Jemma waved to the band, and music flooded the building.

She went to check the door. "How's it going?" she asked Casper.

"We have a line out there."

She looked through the peephole. "That's good and bad; drawing a crowd will be hard in this kind of business. Make sure everyone uses a password."

"No problem, boss. You think we'll be okay to open tonight?"

"I have it on good authority that we'll be just fine."

"The mayor?" he asked.

"Yes," Jemma replied. *The mayor and my source,* she thought.

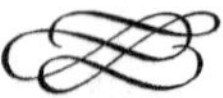

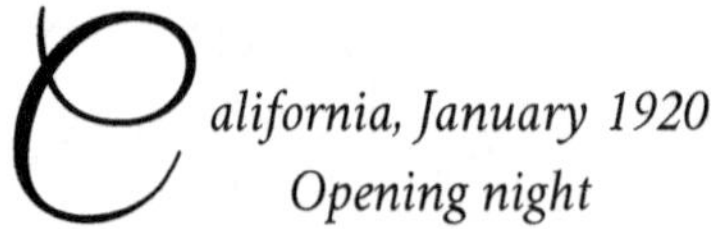

alifornia, January 1920
Opening night

Ben had been to check on each bar. They were set up, and each employee had been briefed on the passwords at the door. Word of mouth would bring in the customers.

Patrick and Jean had put the word out at the studios that would bring in the initial crowds.

"We have customers," Barry, a large man who managed the door, said.

"Make sure they know the password," Ben reminded him.

"Will do, boss."

The first group entered; it was Marisol, Jean, and Patrick. "I don't know, Barry. This group looks disreputable."

Barry started walking toward the group aggressively, ready to throw them out.

"Ben!" Marisol yelled.

He grinned. "Never mind, Barry, they're with me."

He waved them inside. The interior of the establishment was

dark and lit with lamps. The room was surrounded by soft, burgundy-covered banquets. The bar itself stretched the length of the room.

"This is nice," commented Jean, rubbing her hand on the soft seat.

"Can we get a drink?" Patrick asked.

"I have a surprise for you." He waved at Johnny.

"Group, this is Johnny Bellavar; he's my manager."

"Nice to meet you," came from around the table.

"Five of the specials, Johnny."

"On their way," he said, waving at the bartender.

"Oooo, what's the special?" Jean asked.

"That's a surprise," Ben told her.

"Marisol, I requested more bottles of the 'good' wine from your vineyard," said Johnny.

"You think it will be popular?"

"I know it will be."

She smiled. "I'll tell Papa that you said that."

"It tastes better than the brick wine, that's for sure," Patrick said drolly.

Jean hit him. He grinned and took her hand in his.

The drinks arrived. "Mmmm, fruity," Jean said as she took a drink.

Patrick took a drink, grimaced, and called over to the bartender, "Bring me a beer."

"Not your thing?" Ben asked.

"No." The beer came, and he took a long drink.

"Better?"

"Much."

"I like it," said Jean, taking another drink.

"You'll have to be careful in some speakeasies where you don't know where the alcohol's coming from," Ben told them. "These cocktails can be used to hide the flavor of bad booze."

"Is it dangerous?" Jean asked.

"It can be. Just don't take alcohol from anyone you don't know."

"We won't," said Jean.

"What are speakeasies?" asked Marisol.

"Speakeasies, because when you're at the door, you speak quietly or easily when discussing the location and avoiding law enforcement," said Ben. "There're other names for them, too. Blind pigs or blind tigers."

As the evening went on, more and more people filed in.

"Want to try the other locations?" Ben asked them. Everyone nodded. "Johnny, we're going to the next one."

"I'll be along to check on each of their progress," Johnny said.

They spent the night going from bar to bar.

CHAPTER 39

 ew York

A few weeks after the club opened, Jemma walked by the lines of staff, each dressed and ready for that night's customers. She noticed one or two were smoothing their skirts and their hair. "There's nothing to be nervous about. You work in a club; we have music, food, and a few other vices." She nodded to Lauren.

Lauren called, "Everyone at their stations." They moved and stood waiting for the first customers. Jemma nodded at Casper to start letting people through the door.

The small window was opened; individuals and couples who gave the right phrase entered. Jemma watched each one closely. A lady entered with a young gentleman. As their coats were taken, Jemma smiled slightly and whispered to a waiter passing by.

"Yes, boss." She spoke to him in a low voice. "Right away, boss." He walked over to the duo and guided them to a table held for VIP guests.

Lauren came over to her. "Who is that?"

"Lottie contacted Lois Long for me."

She tilted her head and said, "I don't think I know that name. Is she famous?"

"She's a writer for *The New Yorker*."

Laurens' eyes widened. "Shouldn't we get rid of her? Won't they find out that we're serving alcohol?"

"We want someone like her. Don't worry, this is a good thing."

Charlie charged across the room toward the door. Jemma stepped into his path. "Going somewhere, Charlie?"

"Yeah. They just let in—"

She didn't let him finish. "Customers, Charlie. They're customers."

He tried to get around her, but she stayed in his path.

"What, you're going to allow colored people in here?"

"Prohibition's changed the rules. Everyone's welcome."

"First it was women, and now this. I say no to it all," he groused.

"It's my club, Charlie," Jemma reminded him.

"Not for long," he muttered.

"What was that?" she asked, her face hardening.

"Nothin'. I didn't say nothin'." He stomped off toward the bar. "Blacks and tans shouldn't be allowed, is what I'm sayin'."

Jemma waved at Darren. "Keep an eye on Charlie, will you? Make sure he doesn't offend anyone."

"Who would he offend?" She nodded at the group Lauren was escorting to a table near the dance floor. His eyes widened. "I'll keep an eye on him, boss."

She walked to the door and told Casper. "We're full up. Shut down the door for the night."

"Boss, there're a lot of people out there," he said.

"Tell them to come back tomorrow night or to find other locations."

"Okay, boss." He opened the window, and word went down through the crowd. They broke up and went on their way, grumbling. There were more than twenty speakeasies on the road, but Jemma's place had become the place to be seen.

The band played, the people ate meals, as well as drank. The night went on, and Jojo tapped her shoulder. She'd been going table to table checking on customers.

"Hey, Jojo."

"They're here. I brought them in the secret entrance," he mumbled into her ear.

"All right." She fluffed her hair. "I'll be on my way." She looked around and waved Lauren over.

"Yes, boss?"

"Lauren, I need to step out for a bit."

"We've got it."

She spoke to Jojo. "I'll let them in." She waved at Casper and said, "I'll be back." She looked around. The crowd had broken up, and she turned the corner, down the alley to 86th Street. She pushed on the door, and it popped open. Mayor Hylan and his entourage were in the room. There was a small wooden table, and several bottles of wine and champagne had been set up.

"Jemma, it's so good to see you." Hylan walked over and took her hands in his.

"It's good to see you also, Mr. Mayor."

"What do you have for us today?"

"A California award-winning wine. And some imported champagne."

"Pour them up."

She popped the cork on both and poured a taste into each of their glasses. Everyone took a small sip and then swallowed. "That's excellent," Hylan said. His group agreed and they drained down the two bottles.

"Gentlemen, will you be joining us in the main club?" Jemma asked.

"Good crowd tonight?"

"A very good crowd. I've saved you a table," Jemma said. "And the kitchen is still open. Jojo will get you around." She knocked on the door and waited. A knock sounded back, and she nodded at the men.

"Jemma," Hylan said, taking her hand, "this was a lovely experience."

She patted his hand and said, "I hope you can bring your wife next time."

He blustered and his words came out quickly. "Yes, yes of course."

The group exited, and after a few moments, Jemma went around and back into the club. She saw Lois Long on the dance floor with two men and carrying a glass of champagne.

Lauren nodded at her.

She returned it and started toward her office.

CHAPTER 40

alifornia

"Don't I have a say in this business?" Angelo asked.

"You do," Ben assured him, "but you need to listen to reason. We're growing, and we need to add rails to our brick vineyards."

"This is going too fast; we're spending too much," Angelo vacillated.

"We're making a huge profit; we need to add it back into the business."

"No, we should be putting money back for the future."

"This is a family business, and we should put it to a vote," Ben said.

Angelo crossed his arms over his chest. "Fine, I'll accept that."

"Even if the answer isn't one you want?"

Angelo nodded slowly.

"Marisol, Bella," Ben called. "We have something to run by

you." They both entered. "Sit down, we have something that we need to vote on."

"What about your family?" asked Marisol.

"My vote is theirs." Ben presented his case. "We're being swamped with orders for grapes for San Francisco."

"Not the bricks?" asked Marisol.

"No, they want the grapes, and it's possible to ship them via rail as we harvest them."

"That's a lot of extra manual labor and transportation cost," said Marisol.

"That's why I'm suggesting we add rails to the vineyards that would allow us to harvest the grapes directly to the cars."

"Who would move them?" Bella asked.

"The railroad would be contacted to pick them up and deliver them back." Ben moved to the desk. "I've mapped out where I'd like the rails."

Marisol walked over to look at the drawing. Bella reached out to Angelo. He shook his head. Her mouth compressed, and she stood and moved over to look at the plans.

"This looks expensive," said Bella.

"We're making money, and I want to put it back into the business," Ben stressed. "I believe we'll get it back within one season."

"Papa, what do you think?" Marisol asked her father.

"You make your decision," Angelo said.

She looked at Bella, who discreetly nodded.

Ben asked, "Do you have enough information to vote?"

Both Marisol and Bella said, "Yes."

"All for the rail addition?"

Marisol's hand went up; Bella avoided Angelo's eyes, and her hand went up as well. Angelo sat like a stone.

"With my vote, we're three to one in favor of adding the rail lines," Ben said.

Angelo stood up and walked out. Marisol frowned.

"I'll talk to him," Bella told her.

Marisol moved back to the drawings. "I'd like to help with the project."

"I was hoping you'd say that."

Elsewhere, Bella caught up with Angelo.

"You voted with Ben," he responded wearily.

"I voted for the expansion," she corrected. "Why don't you want it?"

"It's getting too big. What happens if all of this ends? We have acres of substandard wine that no one will want."

"We plan for it."

"We?"

"You've chosen to stay away from that part of the business."

"Marisol wants something of her own."

Bella softened. "She does, but she wants her papa's input."

"I'll try to do better," he said gruffly.

CHAPTER 41

New York

A few days later, Lauren sent out one of the waiters for a few copies of *The New Yorker*. "I don't see her name listed," said Lauren, flipping through the pages of the magazine.

"Hmm, I found it," Jemma said. She read for a few moments, then laughed out loud. She folded it back and tossed it to Lauren. "Read that."

"*On January 17th, 1920, when Prohibition became the law of the land, a new kind of woman was born: a woman who drank, smoked, and (gasps) with members of the opposite sex in illegal watering holes known forever as "speakeasies." No one, man or woman, described these dens in such delicious detail as The New Yorker magazine's cabaret-reviewer and resident dancer til dawn, "Lipstick". Written by Lois Long in The New Yorker. (Lois Long, The New Yorker, 1920)*"

Lauren read quickly. "Wow, people are going to want to read this. It's so exciting. People will want to experience what she has."

"The club didn't get mentioned by name," Jemma frowned, "but it's good press anyway."

"I watched her; she drank, danced, and partied along with everyone else," Lauren told her.

"These are good things. Make sure Casper and his boys know Lois gets in, whatever the crowd."

Lauren noted it down. "Got it."

"Are you off tonight?" Jemma asked her friend.

"I am," Lauren said. "But I can cancel if you need me here."

"No, you deserve it. Go out and have fun."

"Thanks!" Lauren started to head out of the office.

"Is anyone going with you?"

"Yes, Darren." Lauren hesitated. "Jemma, may I borrow a dress?"

"Sure." Jemma tossed her the keys. "Drop those off with Casper on your way out."

"I will! Thanks!"

Jemma nodded goodbye. "See you tomorrow."

CHAPTER 42

*B*ang! Bang! Bang!

Jemma looked at her clock; it was four am, and she'd only been asleep for an hour. "Yeah, yeah, just a minute!" she yelled. The banging continued. She pulled on her robe and yanked open the door. "You'd better have a good reason to be here."

She stopped abruptly when she took in the scene in front of her. It was Darren and Jojo, and Jojo was carrying Lauren. "What happened?" she asked.

"We'll tell you," Jojo said, "but can we lay her down first?"

"Of course." She stepped back and let them into the large room. Jojo started to take Lauren to a couch. "No, not there. You can put her in my spare room." Jojo moved Lauren to the offered room. Jemma pulled back the bed covers, and he set her down.

"Why didn't you take her to Bellevue?" she asked, moving the hair off of Lauren's face.

"We tried, but they said that they were full of people with the same problem," Darren said,

"I heard someone say forty-one people have died so far," said Jojo.

"From what?" Jemma asked, bewildered.

Jojo hung his head. "Alcohol poisoning."

"Alcohol poisoning?" Jemma exclaimed. "From where?"

"I took her," Darren said.

"No, we did," Jojo corrected.

"Will somebody tell me what happened?" she demanded, getting a wet cloth to press to the restless girl's head.

"We went to Punchy's speakeasy."

"Why?"

"We heard they had some cheap hooch," Darren explained. "She was drinking aviations and bees knees like they were going out of style."

She shook her head. "They do that to cover the taste of the woodgrain alcohol."

"Yeah, so, isn't all alcohol the same?" asked Darren.

She continued to stare at Lauren. "I've heard rumors that the government's adding poison to liquor."

"No! That can't be true. Why would they do that?" Darren asked, astonished.

"They figure people won't drink alcohol if it has poison."

"But bootleggers don't care," said Jojo.

"No, they don't."

"What do we do?" Darren asked.

"We get her to purge as much as she can. Get her to the bathroom. It's going to get messy."

Jojo picked Lauren up and carried her to the bathroom. He started to put her by the toilet.

"No, sit her in the bathtub," Jemma directed.

He moved her and asked, "What now?"

She grabbed the swaying girl by the chin. "This won't be comfortable, sweetie, but it has to be done."

"Help me, please," Lauren moaned.

"I'll take care of it. You both go make some coffee," she told Darren and Jojo. They quickly left the bathroom.

Jemma opened Lauren's mouth and stuck two fingers down the girl's throat as far as she could. Lauren gagged and struggled weakly, trying to get the offending digits out of her mouth.

"Don't struggle!" Jemma ordered.

"Oh, god!" Lauren moaned again.

Jemma pulled out her fingers, leaned Lauren forward, and the sick girl proceeded to throw up. It seemed to go on forever. She finally stopped and wiped her arm on her sleeve. "Oooh, I puked on your dress! It's ruined!"

Jemma laughed; Lauren sounded more like herself.

"Am I going to be okay?" Lauren asked blearily.

"I don't think you got much in you. You're doing better than I expected."

"I only drank one drink," she mumbled.

"They said you had multiple."

"I poured them out. They taste different than at our place."

"Our place? Then why were you there at all?"

Lauren shook her head, ignoring the question, and asked, "Can I get washed up? I smell."

"Yes, you do. Let's get you up and out of your clothes."

Jemma helped Lauren take off her clothes, then dropped them in the tub. She brought wet rags from the sink and helped wash Lauren off. After patting her down with a towel, Jemma got her a nightshirt out of a drawer. "Put this on and wash your face. I have an extra toothbrush in the cabinet."

She watched to make sure Lauren was steady on her feet. When she finished, Jemma said, "Sit there." Lauren sat on a small chair and watched Jemma clean out the bathtub into a trash can. Next, she rinsed the bathtub.

Lauren slumped in the chair and started to cry. "I'm so sorry. I don't know why they brought me here. I didn't want you to see me like this."

Jemma pulled herself up from the floor by the tub and walked over to Lauren. "I'm glad they brought you here."

She sniffed. "Really?"

"Yes, I've come to rely on you."

"Me and not Charlie?"

"Definitely not Charlie," Jemma replied and didn't say anything more. She walked over to Lauren. "Let's get you to a bed."

"I can stay here?"

"For tonight." Jemma put Lauren's arm around her neck and waist. They moved slowly tow the door. Jemma reached over and pushed it open with her free hand. Jojo and Darren were sitting on the couch, talking in low voices. They sprang up when Jemma and Lauren appeared. They both rushed over.

"Is she okay?" Darren asked.

"I'm fine," Lauren answered her brother. "Jus' tired."

"She's staying with me tonight," Jemma told them. Both men stopped in surprise. "Move her back to the spare room." They followed her direction and settled Lauren in the bed. She went right to sleep, and the three moved to the living room.

Jojo looked at Jemma. "Is the alcohol really being poisoned?"

"Yes, illegal alcohol can be dangerous."

Darren asked, "Then why's Lauren doing better? So many other people died tonight."

"She told me she didn't drink much," Jemma responded. "She said it tasted funny and was pouring it out."

"She's a little thing; it probably affected her faster," Jojo observed.

Darren stood. "This can't be legal," he seethed.

"Darren, nothing about this business is legal. You know that. We're selling illegal alcohol in the club," she said, sitting back and lighting up a cigarette. "Still, something should be done."

The two men looked at each other and shrugged. Jojo

cleared his throat and said, "What about meeting the other bar owners and suggesting that the alcohol might be poisoned?"

"Yeah, that's not going to happen," Jemma retorted.

"Why not?" Darren asked. "Surely the government doesn't want to kill people."

"I agree. Owners killing customers isn't an ideal business plan," Jemma said.

"Is it the bootleggers and not the owners?" suggested Jojo.

"Exactly, they're so eager to sell product—any product—to meet the demand. Even if it kills people."

CHAPTER 43

The next night, Danny held his wine glass up to the light; the color sparkled. "This is better than the juice brick wine," he commented

"Desperate people will drink anything," Jemma agreed, taking a sip of her wine. She was thinking about how easily Lauren could have died.

He took a drink and said, "Tomorrow afternoon."

"What's going on?"

"A raid."

She sat up. "At my place?"

"Yes. It's definite."

"When?"

"Tomorrow, teatime. One of the lady's husbands reported that his wife came home drunk from attending a tea at your establishment."

She stood and paced up and down. "Do you know which one?"

"Someone named Blake."

"Yes, she was rather sloshed, and she seemed depressed."

"What'll you do?"

"Oh, we'll still be there, and we'll be serving tea."

Danny looked at her with raised eyebrows.

The next day, Jemma was ready.

"Boss! Here they come," Casper called out.

"Okay, ladies, here we go," she said and strolled over to the seated women. Their teacups were filled, and the ladies were eating cakes and snacks. Banging coming from the front door was soon heard throughout the club. Jemma nodded to Casper to open the door.

Rows of men with guns and axes charged in and surrounded the ladies sitting at the tables. The women sat quietly and watched Jemma.

The lead agent stormed in. "I'm Agent Bonner, and this is a raid!"

At that moment, an older woman walked out of the back, leaning on her cane. She looked at the agents with guns drawn and axes brandished. "Oh, my," she said nervously, "may I sit down before you start?"

"Ethyl, come sit over here," Jemma coaxed her.

The agents waited while Ethyl slowly made her way to her seat. Once she sat down, she smiled. "Thank you, you may begin."

Bonner frowned at her, and Jemma hid a grin. He turned to her.

"Jemma Hardison, we're here because you're violating the Volstead Act by selling alcohol!" Bonner shouted. He was a rather slim man in a suit with a hat that looked too big for his head.

Jemma strolled over to him and asked, "Would you like to taste the tea?"

"Bring it to me," he said to the man standing next to him. "Now we have them."

Another man walked up to him and said, "There's nothing funny behind the bar."

The bartender held up his hands. "That's what I told you."

Jemma called over to him, "Tommy, bring me a cup."

Tommy lowered his hands and took a cup over to Jemma. She filled the cup from the teapot sitting on the table and handed it to the agent.

Bonner smiled at her as he took the cup. He had her dead to rights. "Get ready, boys," he told his men. They moved around him, ready to pounce as he took a drink. He swallowed. "Gak!" he choked out. An agent next to him pounded on his back.

"Sir, was it too strong?" one of the agents asked.

Bonner wheezed and pointed at Jemma. "That was tea!" he coughed.

"Was it?" she asked. "How peculiar serving tea at an afternoon tea." The women sitting giggled. "What else did you boys expect?" she asked innocently.

"Boys," he wheezed again, "check the back rooms."

They spread out, following orders. One of the agents found bottles. "Hey, what about these?" he asked.

"That's near beer," Jemma said. "There's no law against that."

The agents returned from the back and reported, "Lots of food, no alcohol."

Bonner angrily pointed his finger at her. "I don't know how you did it," he snarled, "but you haven't seen the last of us. We'll be back."

"Come back anytime, gentlemen." Jemma waved at them.

As the agents filed out, the door was shut and locked behind them. Casper called, "All clear boss."

"Oh, Jemma, I'm so sorry," Rachelle Blake apologized. "It was David. He doesn't like me leaving the household in the afternoons."

"You're allowed a life," Jemma told her.

"He doesn't think so." Rachelle wiped her eyes with her handkerchief. "Though, I guess I could've drunk less before going home."

"Why not come for a few weeks but cut back on the alcohol?" suggested Jemma. "We have some cocktails that have the flavor without the alcohol."

"We'll help you remember," Lauren told her.

"Thank you," she said and hugged Jemma and Lauren.

Jemma looked at Rachelle. "My dear, if you need help for any reason, let me know. I have contacts who can help."

"No, David isn't like that," Rachelle protested. "He just likes things to be a certain way."

Jemma wrote down her number and placed it in the woman's hand. "Keep this just in case."

"Yes," Rachelle said, staring at it, "I will."

"So, I guess it's just tea today?" called one of the other ladies from another table.

"Well, we don't have any alcohol on site just now, but if *you* have any on you, it's legal for you to drink and share." Jemma smiled.

"Well, now that you mention it," said Ethyl. She picked up her cane and popped off the end. "Gin, anyone?" The ladies whooped and held out their cups. She moved spryly between the tables.

Lauren clapped her hands. "What a great actress."

"Well, I did tread the boards during my youth," Ethyl said modestly.

"Will you be open tonight?" asked one of the ladies.

"We plan to be. Just don't bring David," Jemma teased Rachelle.

"No, no, he wouldn't go to a club, even if he were home."

"Ladies," Jemma got their attention, "stay and enjoy the food and tea on the house." The ladies cheered and went back to their conversations. "Lauren," Jemma called. Lauren waved at the bartender she'd been talking to and went over to Jemma. "My office."

She nodded and followed her in.

"Where are we with inventory?" asked Jemma.

"Jemma, thank you for last night," Lauren rushed to say.

"I told you there's no need to thank me; we're friends."

"Okay." Lauren grinned. She was still giddy that Jemma considered her a friend.

"How are you feeling?" Jemma asked, concerned.

"A little wobbly," she admitted. "I guess I'll never be loaned a dress again?" she asked with a small smile.

"I'll have to think about it." Jemma smiled wryly. "Inventory?" she prompted.

"Charlie's moving barrels back here now, and the cars will be here soon with more," Lauren reported.

"Good, we'll have time to decant the hard liquor and beer."

Lauren leaned forward and said, "Jemma, maybe we should wait. What if the agents come back?"

"I think that they were embarrassed enough to give us a break."

"Okay…" Lauren didn't sound like she agreed.

"I'm not worried; you shouldn't be either," Jemma assured her. Lauren turned to leave. "Oh, by the way, did you finally go on a date with Jojo?"

"No, we were just friends out drinking."

"Maybe *you* were," Jemma muttered under her breath.

"What was that?"

"Hmmm? Oh, nothing. I'll talk to you later." Lauren nodded and left the office.

Jemma picked up the phone and dialed a number. When Danny answered, she said, "It's over."

"Any problems?"

"No, we were ready."

"Glad I could help."

"Do you know anything about David Blake?"

"How do you know his full name?"

"His wife is a regular at my teas. She said he was making a lot of threats about shutting them down."

"Hmm, I heard he was out of sorts when he made the report."

"Is he considered dangerous?"

"Not to us."

"To his wife?"

"I'm not sure."

"I'll keep an eye on him."

"How will you do that?"

"I have my ways."

"Learning all kinds of new skills?" he asked.

"I'm a business owner, and I have to think on my feet. We want to open tonight. Will there be any issues?"

Danny laughed. "I don't think so. You hit them where it hurt, and you embarrassed them. Do be extra careful, though, and watch for any questionable people trying to get in."

"I'll warn Casper to be extra careful."

"That'd be a good idea."

"Are you stopping by tonight?" she asked idly.

"Are you asking?"

"I might be," she admitted.

"I'll be there. We have another event scheduled tonight. I'll come by after."

"If you get anything good, bring it." The raiders took plenty of pictures to show the public they were serious about Prohibition. They destroyed a lot of the alcohol, but a larger part was taken by the men and either sold or drunk by them.

"I'll see what I can get my hands on," he promised.

"See you then," Jemma said wryly and hung up the phone. She walked back into the main club. The ladies had started home, and she could see Lauren holding on to Rachelle, guiding her outside.

Lauren walked back after they exited and asked, "Will she be okay?"

"I have some ideas about that," Jemma said, opening her cigarette case.

Lauren didn't say anything. She knew Jemma liked to keep things to herself.

Jemma walked away, lighting her cigarette. She called, "Mouse!" John had sent Mouse to her. She thought the name was due to his diminutive size. When she asked why, John only said that Mouse was a man you needed when nothing else would work. She didn't understand what he meant, so when Mouse arrived, she'd assigned him a job as the chef's assistant.

"Yeah, boss," he said, coming out of the kitchen and wiping his hand on his apron.

"Mouse!" yelled the chef.

"With the boss!" he called back.

"Whattaya mean? I'm your boss!" the chef yelled back.

"I'm with the boss boss, boss!" Mouse yelled. Clanging of pots could be heard as a response.

Jemma waved him over to the corner of the bar, away from everyone. "Can you follow someone for me?" she asked.

"The nervous tea lady?"

"Yes, how did you know?"

"I've found her crying in the hallway a few times."

She tilted her head and looked at him thoughtfully for a minute, then continued. "I'd like you to keep an eye on her and her house."

"Mouse!" yelled the chef again.

"I'm assuming after we close?"

"I think tomorrow would be fine. I just want to make sure she's okay."

"Got it," he replied. They heard something dropped in the kitchen. "For now, I'll be in the kitchen," he said, turning back.

"Good idea," she said.

CHAPTER 44

A few days later, early in the afternoon, Jemma's office door swung open. She looked up and saw Mouse, and he had a woman wrapped in a blanket.

"Who is that?" she asked, going over to them. She pulled back the blanket. It was Rachelle! "Mouse! I told you to just keep an eye on her, not kidnap her."

"I had to." He moved the blanket away from the woman's face. The right side was blackened.

Jemma gasped at the sight. "Rachelle, are you okay?" When she didn't answer, she directed, "Mouse, go get some ice and a wet towel."

He raced out to follow her directions.

The poor woman was shaking so hard she could scarcely move. "Wait here," Jemma told her. She pulled a heavy chair over to Rachelle and pushed her down into it.

"Can you talk to me?" Jemma asked her.

"He hit me." Rachelle's voice was barely above a whisper.

Jemma kneeled in front of her and took her shaking hands in hers. "Has he done this before?"

Rachelle looked down. "Never this bad," she acknowledged, "and he always promises it won't happen again."

"But it did."

"It always does."

Mouse came back in and brought the wet cloth to her face. Rachelle clutched it, her eyes staying focused on him.

"What happened, Mouse?" Jemma asked him.

"I was doing what you asked," he explained. "I was checking on her because she hadn't been out for a couple of days. I saw her lying on the floor through the window."

"He broke the window and got me out." Rachelle's voice was muffled by the towel.

"Rachelle, what do you want to do?" Jemma asked. "Do you want help?"

"What are you talking about? Of course she does," Mouse said.

She looked at him sharply. "Mouse, we have to let her make that decision."

"Yes, I do," Rachelle answered.

Jemma stood and went over to her desk. She pulled out her small notebook and flipped through it. "I know of a safehouse where you can stay, but you won't be able to go back home."

"But my things," she protested.

"For now, you won't be able to get to them. It's too dangerous." She sent a warning look to Mouse, and he nodded. "Let's get you settled and then I'll get you with our lawyer."

Rachelle reached out her hand to Mouse, and he started to take it. Jemma grabbed him by the collar and moved him to the door. "We don't need any more complications, especially of a romantic kind," she whispered fiercely.

He hung his head. "You're right, I'm sorry. We need to get her somewhere safe."

She released him. "Get her to Baker house."

"I know that one."

"It's the best place for her. Get her there, and keep her covered up."

"I will, boss."

"Go now! Out the back. Rocky's out there. He'll drive you." Mouse covered Rachelle with the blanket again and guided her out of the office and the club.

The chef ran over. "Where's Mouse? I need him for prep."

"He'll be back soon," Jemma told him

"What do I do in the meantime? We have customers coming in."

"I'll help," she said.

"You?"

"Yes, me," she said and went to the kitchen. He followed her.

"But you don't cook."

"Don't I?" she asked. She took the apron from the hook on the wall and put it on. "Where do I start?"

He waved vaguely at the cutting board and carrots

She went over and took up the knife. "Rounds, diced, or julienne?"

He stopped, and his mouth hung open. He found his voice and said, "Diced, please." He watched as the knife moved swiftly and somewhat professionally through the carrots. "Do celery and potatoes next."

"All diced?"

"Please."

The chef moved back to his pot, adding spices and checking the oven for the meat. They worked together efficiently. About an hour later, Mouse ran in and stopped abruptly.

"Good, you're back," Jemma said. "You can take over now."

"You did all of this?" he questioned, staring at the piles of vegetables.

"Ha! She could teach you a few things," the chef gloated.

"High praise indeed." She took off her apron and handed it to Mouse. "I trust that errand has been taken care of?"

"It has."

"Good."

CHAPTER 45

That night, Lissette, Lottie, Lauren, and Jemma were sitting in Jemma's living room for what had become their weekly dinner. It was Jemma's turn to host. They had an enjoyable evening. They waved goodbye to Lauren and watched as she made her way down the stairs. Lottie and Lissette started to leave, and Jemma called, "I do have someone who needs to talk to you."

"Who would that be? Another bar owner in need of advice?"

"No, I sent one of the tea ladies over to Baker house."

"Has she been abused?"

"Yes, she wants to get a divorce."

"I can talk to her. But even if she's serious, divorce is hard on women. Even with all of our freedoms now, voting and employment."

"What's the main issue?" Jemma asked.

"We'd have to prove the abuse. Which is almost impossible."

"There are also the financial concerns."

"Yeah, she won't be awarded any money; the husband will keep it all. Does he know she's gone yet?"

"Not yet; she said he works late. And he doesn't check in on her until late in the day."

"He thinks she's a pushover then. I'd recommend you get someone over there to get her things. Otherwise, she'll have nothing," Lottie told her.

"I'll do that," Jemma promised.

"I'll come over tomorrow, early afternoon, and we can go to the safehouse together to talk to her."

Jemma watched the two of them leave and gathered up her coat. She went to the kitchen. "Mouse, I need you." He nodded and walked toward her. "And bring the truck keys." He headed back to get them off the hook on the wall.

"Chef, we'll be back to clean up in a little while," Jemma told him. He nodded and watched them leave.

Mouse started the truck. "Where are we going, boss?"

"Rachelle's house." He nodded and turned toward the wheel. He whipped back around when he realized what she said.

"We are?" he exclaimed.

"Yes, she'll need her things. Lottie said her husband might not give her anything."

"Then we go."

They arrived at the large home, which was at least six floors high. She looked up at it. "Are there servants?"

"He dismissed them before he beat her and left her on the floor." Mouse's voice dripped with anger.

"All right. For now, let's concentrate on getting those things. How do we get in?"

"Why do you think John sent me to you?"

She frowned and watched as he pulled out a lockpick set. "Perfect, we'll be quick about it."

He moved to the door and opened it swiftly. They entered and moved quickly, up the stairs to the second floor. "Which room?" she asked.

"Second from the left, that's where I found her."

She didn't ask why he'd be looking into a second-floor window; she just followed him. They entered the large room, and she headed across to the closets. "Find the suitcases."

He looked around and under the bed. "Here they are." He pulled them out, opened them, and placed them on the bed.

She started putting in dresses and assorted items sitting out on the dressing table. With all three bags full, they looked around. "Where's her jewelry?"

"They usually keep it near the bedside," Mouse offered. She quirked an eyebrow at him. "What?" he asked. "It's just what I heard."

"Uh-huh, right," she huffed. "Try that large box on the bedside."

He ran over and picked the lock. "Jewelry," he said triumphantly.

"Grab it, we need to get out of here." They heard a door slam. "Now!" they said at the same time.

They exited the room and started to the stairs. "Not down," Jemma said. They ran up the stairs. "Attic," she said and pushed him toward a smaller staircase. The door was unlocked, and they went quickly into the large dark room. "Barricade the door," she directed.

While he did as she asked, she ran to the window. Mouse joined her, and they managed to open it. "Come on." She climbed out onto a ledge. Mouse handed her the bag and then climbed out.

"Where to?" he asked.

"I see a light in a window next door." They carefully shuffled down the ledge with the suitcases until they reached the window. Jemma looked in and tapped on the glass.

A boy of about twelve stared at her. She mouthed, "Open the window."

He opened it and watched as they climbed into his room

with the suitcases piled around them. "What're you doing?" he asked with a yawn.

"Getting Miss Blake's things," Jemma replied.

"The nice lady next door," the boy said, acknowledging the name. "The man there hits her."

"Yeah, we got her out the other day, and we came back for her stuff."

Mouse looked at the boy. "Will you tell anyone we were here?"

"No, he's not a nice man. Need some help getting those down?" Mouse handed him a bag.

"Is anyone else here?" Jemma asked as they made their way downstairs.

"Everyone's asleep. You should be fine."

"Thanks for your help," said Mouse.

"Anytime." The boy walked them out of the house. They piled the bags into the back of the truck, then drove away. "We'll take these over tomorrow when I join Lottie to meet Rachelle," Jemma said.

"He won't be happy that we got her things," Mouse said.

"He'll never know."

PART IV

CHAPTER 46

*N*ew York, 1921

Lottie slowly put the phone down. "It passed," she swore, slamming her hand down on her desk.

"What?" Chris asked, looking up from his law books.

"The Mullan-Gage Law."

"Adding more layers to an already convoluted law."

"Their dragging the local cops into this mess."

"The courts are already inundated. How can adding to that help?"

"It won't," she said shortly.

"We have a steady business with Volstead," he pointed out.

"Yes," she murmured. "We need to let our clients know what's going on."

"We can split the clients up. Will you talk to Jemma?"

"Yeah, she's family. I'll talk to her."

CHAPTER 47

*N*ew York
The club that night

Things were swinging, the band was going, and several dancers were demonstrating the latest moves. Everyone was joining in. Alcohol and food were being served. The alcohol was the main draw, but the food and music kept them there.

Someone grabbed Jemma by the elbow. "We have to talk," the voice growled.

She yanked her arm away from Charlie. "About what? And don't grab me."

"Then move to the back. We need to talk," he shot back and stalked off.

She frowned. He kept forgetting she was the boss. She followed him and saw that he was standing in the hallway with his hands gripping the edges of his coat.

"Okay, what is it?" she asked as she reached him.

"The missing inventory you found on the audit, we believe it's being taken."

"From which locations? Lauren's records aren't showing any deficiencies."

"I think they were just never delivered."

"From the contact boats?"

"Yes."

"That would involve Darren."

"It would. We need to question him."

She sighed. "Fine. Keep it quiet for now."

He nodded.

She went back to the main floor and saw Lauren laughing with customers. They'd gotten close, and she hated to jeopardize that, but the family relied on this business. She would do what she had to keep it going.

CHAPTER 48

The next morning, Jemma stretched and stood up. Danny looked on, admiring her from his place on the bed. When she pulled on her silk robe, he said, "You don't need to get dressed."

"I do, actually. I need to go to the club. I have a meeting with the staff about some delivery irregularities."

"Wouldn't you rather stay here with me?" he said and patted the bed next to him.

She pulled the robe closed and sent him a side look. "Don't you have somewhere to be?"

"Yeah, I guess I do," he said, not moving out of his current position.

She shrugged, then turned to him. "Your money's on the dresser." With that, she sauntered off toward the bathroom.

"Like always," he muttered and shoved the covers off. He pulled on his pants and went to the dresser. The money sat just where it normally did. He scooped it up and silently counted it. When he finished, he slid the bills into his pocket. He wandered over to the bathroom door and tapped on it.

"Come in."

He pushed the door open. Jemma was in the tub. He walked over and scooped up some water, pouring it over her shoulders.

"Are you leaving?" she asked, moving her rag up her arm.

"Things are changing," he said.

"What things?" she asked.

"The local police are getting involved in our operations."

"Oh, the Mullan thing. Lottie mentioned it as a possibility."

"Mullan-Gage. It's been approved, and it doesn't just involve federal agents anymore. Local police will be involved now."

"Oh, they don't want anything to do with us, and most of the officers are my customers," she scoffed.

"You may have to pay more," he warned her.

"Is that all?" she asked and stood up. He held out her towel. She took it and slowly wrapped it around her. "I still have you on the payroll. Can't you just give us a warning like you have in the past?"

"They'll be cutting the phone lines when raids are announced at the office." He put his hand on her arm.

She pushed it off. "What're you saying? What am I paying you for?"

He stared at her, and she stared back. "I wonder about that all of the time."

CHAPTER 49

Jemma pondered Danny's words as she made her way carefully down the steep stairs from her apartment to the ground. "Need to replace those," she muttered as her heels clanked down each stair on the metal staircase. At the bottom, she walked around the wide brick building, which ran the length of the block, following the dark and light bricks that formed a line around the corner and down the street. The solid walls ran the length of the building with a break for a solid door. The cool breeze lifted her skirts; she pulled her fur-lined coat closer and hurried toward the door.

A man ran past her, jostling her. "Jojo!" she called after him.

Jojo skidded to a halt and turned slowly toward her. "Oh, hey, Jemma. Sorry about that."

"I'm okay. Running a little late?" she asked, idly walking over to him.

"Just a little." He grinned, pushing the cap back on his head, and hurried to the door. She watched him knock and then hesitate before the door opened, giving him access.

She took another moment to review the old building. In its

prior life, it'd housed a small bar surrounded by larger office areas. Since 1919, they'd made significant changes to get ready for Volstead.

She'd had an idea that liquor would be more in demand when it was limited, and she wanted to see it through. She'd been right; the club was a success. The new law that had just passed was worrisome. They'd been raided before, but she'd always been forewarned. Small stashes of liquor had been taken, and a couple of employees had been arrested, but Lottie had been able to take care of things.

She knocked on the door, and the small window opened. The large, heavy door opened immediately. "Morning," she said to Casper.

"Morning, boss."

"Charlie around?" she asked, starting to remove her coat.

"You might want to leave it on," he suggested.

Jemma paused. "Is the employee being questioned…"

"…on the roof," he completed her sentence.

She nodded and headed through the club. "Morning, Maeve." Jemma waved at the new female bartender. She'd learned that men seemed to buy more alcohol served by a good-looking woman. Maeve returned the greeting. Jemma didn't stop and headed to the back and up the stairs. She could hear faint screams coming from outside.

The higher she climbed, the louder the screams became. She exited onto the roof and found the man in question. There were two other men there, too: Charlie and Bob. Charlie held one leg and Bob held the other, dangling a man upside down over the side of the building. They were shouting down questions to the man.

"Where are they, Darren?" Charlie asked again. "What did you do with them?"

"I didn't do it!" Darren screamed.

"Yeah, you did. Admit it!" yelled Charlie. He shook the leg he held.

"No!" Darren saw Jemma leaning over the edge of the building. "Boss, I didn't do it, I promise!"

"Well, Darren," she drawled slowly, "we're missing a lot of barrels. And you were in charge of them."

"It was the cops, boss. They chased us in the boat, and I had to drop it over the side."

"You know, Darren," Jemma said, lighting up a cigarette, "we've heard this story before. Haven't we, Charlie?"

"We sure have," he confirmed. "Maybe we drop him a little further." He nodded at Bob, and they lowered him even more.

Darren screamed again. "It isn't a story, I promise!" The desperation was apparent in his voice.

"Darren, we had you followed," Jemma said simply.

He went limp.

"Charlie, Bob, pull him up," she directed. The two men pulled him back over the ledge. "Ready to tell us the truth?"

He hung his head.

"Darren," Charlie prodded. "Tell her how you did it."

"I got the barrels to shore," he began, "and the men would meet me. They paid cash. But, boss, it wasn't that many, and it was just a couple at a time."

She tapped her cigarette and let the ashes fall to the ground. "Darren, we have losses of just over a hundred barrels. The losses began almost as soon as you started working for us." He looked at her, nonplussed. "Where's the money?" she asked.

"Money?" he croaked.

"Money." Bob nudged him to answer.

"There ain't any money."

She looked at him with a raised eyebrow. "Should I ask Lauren where it is?"

Darren's eyes went wide. "No, no, please don't talk to her," he pleaded.

"Does she know what you were doing?" Jemma asked. She needed that question answered. Lauren was part of her inner circle; she trusted her with her business and personal life. If Lauren was a liability, she needed to know.

"No!" he shrieked. "She's not involved. She thinks I got an extra job."

Jemma made a decision. She glanced at Charlie and then to Darren. "You have two weeks to get the money."

"Two weeks?" he gasped.

"Yes."

"And if I can't?" his voice grew hoarse, and suddenly he couldn't swallow at all.

"You don't want the answer to that, Darren," Charlie advised.

"I'll get it, I will," he promised.

"Let him go," Jemma said.

Charlie and Bob looked at her and then released him.

"Darren? I'm giving you a chance to make this right." He turned to run off. "Darren! I mean it—one chance."

He turned back to her. "I get that, boss. Really, I do."

"Go," she said. He ran as fast as he could to get away from them.

"Why did you do that? He stole our money," Charlie griped.

"*Our* money?" she asked with raised eyebrows.

"Oh, uh, your money, of course," the big man stuttered.

"That's what I thought," she said and dropped her cigarette onto the ground. She smashed it with her heel and said, "He seemed pretty sure he hadn't stolen as many barrels as we accused him of stealing."

"Yeah, well, what do you expect? He's a thief and a liar," Charlie said.

She looked at him for a long moment and then turned to exit the roof. "We have work to do."

Charlie and Bob followed her to the bottom of the stairs. He sent Bob on his way and followed her down to the office.

"We have talent coming in this morning," she said at her office door.

"I'll set up the band to be ready to back them up. What time do you want to start?"

"9:00am."

"I'll meet you in the main area." She entered her office and sat at her desk. There was an undercurrent that Charlie believed the club belonged to him. He'd progressively been getting involved in things he shouldn't. She'd so far managed to keep the tasting room for the high society and political crowd away from him. He could be a bull in a china shop, and she didn't trust him.

Maeve stuck her head in the door. "Boss, you have a guest."

"Who is it?"

"Lottie."

"Show her in."

Lottie swept in; she wore a dark velvet dress and a matching hat.

"Nice outfit," commented Jemma.

"Thanks, I have several appointments with clients today."

"Did we have one scheduled?"

"No, but we need to talk." They both moved to the table and sat down. "Mullan-Gage has been put into place."

"Oh, that."

Lottie slammed her hat down on the table and stood up. "You have to listen; this new act is going to cause more problems."

Jemma sat back and said, "I have men on the payroll; they're keeping us informed."

"You aren't listening. This'll be local cops; the mandates are for them to now come after the speakeasies. And it'll be a felony if you get caught!"

Jemma laughed. "That's supposed to scare me?"

"This place has gotten big and popular."

"And that's a bad thing?"

"In this environment? Yes." Lottie sat back in her chair and crossed her arms over her chest.

"We've had arrests before," Jemma reminded her, sitting back in her chair and putting her legs up on the table. "And you've been able to get them off or have the charges reduced."

"I have, but those were just a slap on the hand."

"My people know we'll get them out." Lottie walked over and pushed Jemma's legs off the table. Her feet hit the floor, and she jumped up. "What? Do you want to fight?"

"I would…" Jemma started toward her, but Lottie stopped her with a hand. "But it wouldn't solve anything." She sighed and continued. "I think they'll be targeting the owners next."

Jemma frowned. "I heard from my source today that the agent's phones will be cut off before the raids are announced."

"Then it's starting."

"Okay, I'm taking it seriously. What do we do? Shut down?"

"It won't help unless it's a permanent move."

"Not likely. We like it here." She looked over at Lottie. "So, what do we do?"

"Just do business as normal. You have your security measures in place?"

"We do. Lauren has some ideas."

"What are they?"

"Currently, we use passwords."

"Yes, the phrase that changes periodically."

"Another idea is an ID card. It would be personalized with our club's name."

"I like that."

"The innate trouble is that, like the passwords, they can be passed on to the wrong people."

"If you get raided…"

"I'll make sure you're notified."

"That's all we can do now. I'm on my way to my next client."

"Thanks for letting me know."

Lottie nodded and pulled on her velvet hat and headed out to meet her other clients.

CHAPTER 50

*J*emma approached the bar. "Is Lauren in yet?" she asked Maeve.

"Yes, boss, she just got here. She's in the back, managing the food deliveries." Maeve poured a drink and placed it in front of her.

"What's this?" she asked, looking at the drink.

"A new drink that our rum guy recommended."

She took a sip and said, "Tasty, what's it called?"

"It is from Cuba; It's called the Hankypanky cocktail."

"What's in it?"

"Gin, sweet vermouth, and Fernet Branca."

"I like it. That'll work out well for our afternoon teas. Add it to our list," she directed.

Maeve smiled and said, "I will, boss."

Jemma went to the back to find Lauren. She found her there, hip deep in boxes. "Everything in order?" asked Jemma.

Lauren turned to her. "Yes. All foodstuffs are here. The alcohol has to be stored away."

"Get Maeve to help with the booze and get Mouse to help you unload the foodstuffs." Lauren nodded. "Double the Fernet

Branca liquor order. We'll probably need more after the after-noon tea crowd gets a taste of the new cocktail."

"Maeve poured that one up for you?" Lauren grinned.

"She did, and I liked it."

"Me too."

"Make sure that the back door stays accessible at all times. If we have to 86 customers, we won't want them hurt trying to leave."

"I'll clear it before any customers arrive," Lauren assured her. "Are we expecting trouble?"

"Maybe. Can you come to my office?"

"Sure, as soon as I'm done here."

Jemma nodded and walked to her office. She went in, settled at her desk, and reached to the right to access her books. They were open and her pen poised when there was a knock on the door.

"Come in."

Lauren stuck her head in. "Got time now, boss?"

"I do." Lauren walked in quickly and sat. "I have something to share with you." Lauren waited. "I was talking with my source this morning." Lauren was aware of the source, but she hadn't met the man. "Changes are coming that might affect our operations."

"What are they?"

"The local police are going to be doing searches starting soon."

"The new laws passed?"

"Yeah, I hate to admit when Lottie is right."

"Will the raids be arranged in a coordinated effort by the federal agents and the police?"

"I expect they will."

"Then we'll be fine," Lauren said, relieved. "Your source will still be able to help then."

"Except that now the phone lines will be cut during times when the raids are being announced and organized."

"Then what're we paying for?" Lauren asked, exasperated.

Jemma laughed. "That's exactly what I said."

"What was the answer?" she demanded.

"There wasn't one. There may be more arrests in the next few months."

"The arrests aren't that big a deal. It's their careless disregard for our products."

"Yeah, they do like the photo op. Big, strong men using axes on barrels and crashing bottles. The recovery will be harder."

"Should we move our storage around?" Lauren asked, thinking about the current inventory they were carrying.

"Tell me what you think."

"We keep a lower inventory here on site."

"The trouble with that is we have to move the alcohol around more often. It could get caught in transit."

"I have some ideas for that," said Lauren.

"What're you thinking?"

"Well, it won't help with the barrels, but we could move the bottles."

"How?" Jemma demanded.

"Let me bring in someone to demonstrate for you."

Jemma sat back and tapped her pencil on the paper. "I'll be very interested in what you have to show me. You have good ideas."

Lauren grinned. "Good enough to move to assistant manager?"

"Working on that," Jemma said. Lauren stood and walked to the door. "And, Lauren, we need to move forward with the ID cards. Get a couple hundred in each color."

"Yes, boss!"

A knock sounded on the door; it was Maeve. "Lauren, the new hostess interviewee is here."

"Thanks, I'll be right out." Maeve closed the door.

"If she passes your inspection, give me a few minutes, and then send her in," Jemma told her.

Lauren went out into the main club. She looked around and spotted the woman who was to be interviewed. She was attractive but cheaply dressed, and her makeup was applied with a heavy hand.

Lauren walked over to her. "Hello, I'm Lauren O'Brian."

"Dolly Smith," the girl introduced herself. "Look, am I going to be a hostess or what?" she said with her hand on her hip and gum smacking in her mouth.

"It depends, and get rid of the gum," Lauren said, looking the woman over. While Dolly ditched the gum on a piece of paper, Lauren thought, *she could be cleaned up*. "The boss will see you in a few minutes. I have a few questions first, where did you work before this?"

"Several bars downtown."

"As what?"

"A hostess."

"Not the kind we need here." Lauren rolled her eyes.

"What is that? Speak up," Dolly demanded.

Lauren stared at her. "Gimme a minute." She walked over to Jemma's door, knocked, and stuck her head in. "Not a great first impression, boss."

"Send her in. I'll see if we can handle her."

"Right, boss." Lauren closed the door and went back to Dolly. "She'll see you." She pointed to the office.

"*She*? A woman? Why are you calling her boss?" she asked, fluffing her hair and putting on more lipstick.

"Miss Hardison is the boss, and if you want to work here, you'll show her respect." When the girl didn't respond, Lauren said, "This way." Dolly followed her, hips swinging. "Through that door; hand her your papers," she directed. Dolly walked to the door and looked back at Lauren. She waved her in.

"Come in and sit down," Jemma directed. Dolly sauntered to the chair in front of the desk and handed Jemma her papers. Jemma looked down at it. "Dolly, where was your last job?"

She named a small hole in the wall speakeasy in Brooklyn.

Jemma stopped a sigh. She knew that location and their reputation. She decided to be blunt. "We don't operate like that establishment, and prostitution will get you fired here."

"But how do we keep the customers happy and drinking?" Dolly asked, frowning.

"We do it with quality entertainment and alcohol. We charge them plenty for the privilege of being here."

"But what about extra money?"

"We pay well; there won't be a reason for a side hustle."

Dolly thought about that for a minute. "Okay, I'll give it a go."

Jemma frowned at her and said, "Stand up." Dolly stood. "Turn, please. Your clothes and makeup…" she started.

"What's wrong with them?" Dolly said defensively, quickly opening her purse to find her compact. When she stared into it, she saw that nothing was out of place.

"They're cheap. Meet with Lauren, and she'll get you set up and show you how your makeup should be done."

The girl snapped her compact closed. "And if I don't want to?"

And there's the attitude Lauren alluded to, thought Jemma. She sat back and said, "It makes no difference to me if you want to or not. There're plenty of people who *DO* want to be here." She moved files around on her desk and looked up at Dolly abruptly. "Are you still here?"

Dolly squirmed. "I want the job."

"You understand the requirements?"

"I do," she said in a rush.

"Follow Lauren's instructions. To the letter. You'll be on

probation for a while." Dolly stayed where she was, unsure what she should do next. "You can go now."

Dolly turned and almost ran to the door. "Tell Lauren to come see me," Jemma told her. "And, Dolly, remember, one foot out of line and you're out."

"Yes, boss," Dolly called on her way out the door.

It was a few moments later that a knock was heard on the door. "Come in," Jemma called out.

"You wanted to see me, boss?" asked Lauren.

"Sit." She sat. "Your impression of Dolly?"

"Cheap, pretty, but might be trouble."

"You have good instincts. I saw the same thing." Jemma sighed and sat back. "We are short on waitresses currently."

"We'll give her a chance. Just one, though."

Jemma smiled. "That's what I told her. Get her cleaned up and watch her closely. You might get Maeve and Casper to help with that."

"I'll get her to the makeup room and give her the uniform for tonight."

"Good." When Lauren didn't move, Jemma asked, "Is there something else?"

"The new bartenders are here for their interviews."

"Have you seen them?"

Lauren's lips curved into a slow smile. "Mmm, yeessss," she purred.

"I take it you approve?" Jemma's smile was genuine for the first time since entering the club that day.

"If we want more women customers, that's the way to do it," she said.

"Nice looking?"

"You could say that."

"That's good. I want to start them on the afternoon shift with the tea ladies."

"You promised I could interview them," she reminded her

cheekily.

"I thought about doing it myself, but I have so much paperwork to do here…" Jemma trailed off.

"I'll take care of it," Lauren rushed to answer.

"I don't know, you're so busy."

"I can work it in," Lauren assured her. She stood and walked toward the door.

"Lauren, have you seen Darren today?"

She turned back and said, "No, he was gone before I got up this morning." She hesitated. "Do you need him for something?"

"No, I think he knows what I want from him," Jemma said, her voice even.

She frowned. "Boss, is there something I need to know?"

"Not now. I need you to concentrate on the tasks you were given this morning. And don't let Charlie influence your decision on which bartender to hire."

"Oh, he won't," Jemma assured her and headed back out to the bar.

Jemma shook her head. Back to business; even illegal businesses had paperwork and accountants.

Lauren walked out and looked around.

"They're over there," a low voice came from under the bar.

She leaned to the side and saw Jojo there. "And who is it I'm looking for?"

"The new bartenders," he said, working industriously on the hinges for the hidden cabinets. "Don't know why we need new ones."

"Ladies are drinking more now; they want something pretty to look at."

"You too?" he asked.

"Me?" She looked over at the men. "I like to look."

"Hmph," he said, and his screwdriver slipped. "Ouch!"

"Are you okay?" she asked, her concern genuine.

He shook his hand. "I'm fine." He looked past her. "Charlie's with the guys."

"Oops, the boss doesn't want him involved. Gotta go."

"Sure, sure," he muttered, flexing his hand. "I guess I'm not pretty enough." He went back to work, testing the hinges.

She hurried over and tapped the big man on his shoulder. "I've got this."

Charlie waved her off. "Get outta here. I got it taken care of."

She tapped his shoulder again. "No, the boss says I'm to take care of it."

He continued to speak in a low voice to the men, disregarding her presence.

Lauren started to raise her voice, but Jemma's voice rang out from her office door. "Charlie, can I speak with you?"

Lauren was so close, she could see the man's neck muscles tense up and his hand make a fist. When he turned toward Jemma, he seemed to be a different man. He was even smiling. "Yes, Jemma."

"Let Lauren handle that. I have a delivery to review with you."

Charlie hesitated but followed her direction and headed to her office.

Lauren mouthed, "Thanks."

Jemma waited for him to enter, then closed the door to her office.

Lauren turned to the group of nice-looking men. She said, "Boys, it's time to talk. Follow me." She led them to a set of tables and had them sit.

Dolly walked over to the bar. "What's she doin'?" she asked Jojo.

Jojo ignored the question and leaned on the bar to watch Lauren interact with the men.

"She's supposed to be helping me," she whined.

"Sit down. She'll be back," he ordered.

"You can't tell me what to do," she huffed, but sat on a barstool anyway. "You like her?" she asked, looking from him to Lauren.

"Never said that," he commented.

She sent him a side glance and hmphed.

Lauren stood and nodded at the men, pointing toward the door. One stayed behind.

"Looks like someone make the cut," Jojo muttered, picking up his tool chest and striding away.

Lauren called after him as she neared the bar. He didn't stop; he raised his hand and continued on his way.

Dolly said, "You finally remembered me, huh?"

Lauren turned slowly to her. "Listen here, girlie, your first day could be your last."

"You're not in charge; you can't fire me."

"No? I can provide reports to the boss, and she can fire you." That shut her up. "Ready to follow my direction now?" Lauren inquired.

Dolly's eyes flickered behind Lauren and then back to her. "Yes," she said begrudgingly

"Follow me. You'll need makeup lessons and new clothes."

"Hey!" she screeched. "What's wrong with my makeup and clothes?"

"They're cheap," Lauren said, turning to walk away.

Dolly grabbed Lauren's arm. "You can't call me cheap."

Lauren looked at the hand on her arm and waited. Dolly slowly dropped it.

"I didn't call you cheap. I called your makeup and clothes cheap."

Dolly frowned and touched her face. "I have to change?"

Lauren's mouth twisted. "Do you want the job or not?" The girl continued to frown, seemingly unsure. "The door is that way," Lauren told her, crossing her arms over her chest.

Dolly turned toward the door, looking like she'd storm out.

Good riddance, thought Lauren and moved away from her.

"No, no, I want to stay," Dolly faltered, abruptly running over to her.

"Why the change? I thought you were leaving."

"Well, I was wrong." She seemed to be looking at something over Lauren's shoulder. Lauren turned in that direction and saw the new bartender, Nate, Charlie, and Maeve.

Lauren shook her head and said, "All right, let's go."

They walked behind the stage to a long hallway that housed dressing rooms and makeup rooms. They went into the makeup room, and a tall woman with gray curls stood at the mirror, moving the tubes of makeup in front of her.

"I have someone for you, Shirley," Lauren said.

Shirley walked over to the duo. "Turn around, girlie," she told Dolly. The girl started to argue, but instead she did as she was told. "Good bones," Shirley commented. "Go wash your face. You have a lot to learn."

Dolly drew her mouth into a tight line, but she asked, "Where?"

"There's a sink over there." Shirley pointed to the far side of the room. "That one is going to be a challenge," she muttered to Lauren.

"Her attitude's bad, and I'm not holding out a lot of hope," Lauren replied in the same tone. Dolly returned fresh-faced and surprisingly pretty. "I'll leave you to it," she told Shirley. She pointed at Dolly. "Mind your attitude!"

She went back out to the club floor, looking around at the workers getting the area ready for the afternoon tea. At that moment, she saw Charlie out of the corner of her eye. *Now, what's he up to?* she wondered. He looked around before entering Jemma's office. She strode over to the bar. "Where's Jemma?"

"She stepped outside to get some air," Maeve said.

"Hmm," she said and glared at Jemma's office door. "I need to talk to her." She charged toward the front door. One of the bouncers saw her coming and opened it quickly.

She went out and looked around. Jemma stood with a tall man. They were facing each other, and it looked like an argument. Lauren started to run over to her, but Jemma held out a hand to stop her. The man nodded at Lauren and turned to walk in the other direction. Jemma turned toward her. "You have something for me?" Lauren looked to where the man had gone. "Don't ask questions," Jemma cautioned her.

"I won't."

"You were out here for a reason?"

"What? Oh yeah, Charlie's in your office."

"Is he? I wonder what he's looking for." Jemma shook her head. "I guess it's time to remind him who's the boss here." She went back into the club determinedly and headed toward her office. Lauren followed close behind.

Jemma stopped at the door and glanced at her. "I've got this. Why don't you go see how Dolly's doing?"

She nodded and backed away slowly.

Jemma entered the office and quietly closed the door, waiting for it to click shut before turning to face Charlie. He was sitting in her chair with his feet on the desk. "Comfortable, Charlie?" she asked, leaning back against the door.

He leaned back in the chair. It squeaked out loudly. "I'd say it fits just right."

"We've talked about this before," she reminded him. "This is my place."

"Yeah, *the boss lady*," he sneered.

"That's what they call me."

"Well, I don't."

"No," she agreed and pushed herself off the door. "You don't. I think it might be time we separated this relationship."

His smiling face changed; his brows lowered, and his mouth

turned down. "I'm just having a bad day; it's Pop's birthday today."

"Charlie, Charlie," she chided, "that was, what, back in June? Or was it August? You've told this story before."

He reached into his pocket, and she tensed. He laughed suddenly and pulled out his hands and held them up. "Look, I don't mean anything. I just got carried away."

She continued to study him. "Consider yourself on a short list. If I see you trying to undermine my authority, you're out. "

"Is that a threat?" he asked idly.

"No. It's a promise."

They continued to stare at each other. He broke contact first and stood. "I guess I'm in your chair." He hesitated and said, "*Boss.*"

Jemma moved past him to the chair and said, "Get back to work, Charlie." He didn't say anything, just left the office. She shook her head. A final confrontation was coming, and she had to be prepared for it.

She walked out to the bar. She saw Maeve and Lauren staring at Nate, the new bartender. "Still staring at the new bartender?" she asked.

"Yeah," Lauren sighed. "He's dreamy."

"I think he might not be your type," she said, studying him.

"Tall, dark, and gorgeous isn't my type?"

"No, I believe he's more of Chris' type."

"Lottie's Chris?" Her eyes widened. "No," she whined. "Aw, he's so pretty. Why do the pretty ones have to be a Nance?"

"He is dreamy," Jemma acknowledged. "Did you order the cards?" she asked.

She continued to stare at him and said, "Yes, I'll pick them up in a few days."

"I'm going home for a few hours to rest."

"I have things here."

When Jemma returned that evening, the club was already loud and boisterous. "Evening, boss," Casper said as she entered.

"Any problems?"

"Jojo came in; he seems depressed."

"Where is he?"

"At the bar."

She went to check on Jojo. People greeted her as she moved through the tables to the back of the club. She smiled and shook hands, trying to make her way to Jojo. When she finally got to him, he sat with his head lying on the bar. She shook his shoulder. "Jojo, what's wrong? You're off tonight. Shouldn't you be having a good time?"

"I just got this letter from Ma." He pulled the letter out of his pocket and handed it to her.

She unfolded it and sighed as she read. "Oh, Jojo, I'm sorry."

"Ma didn't find him," he said morosely.

"I'm so sorry," she said again, hugging his shoulder.

"Yeah, me too."

"Do you want to go home?"

"No, I need the distraction," he said, staring down at his drink; it was still full.

"We have plenty of that." She mouthed to Maeve, *Water this down*, and pointed at Jojo's drink. She nodded.

Jemma turned Jojo toward her and said, "There must be something we can do." Maeve moved quickly, poured out half of the drink, and refilled it with water.

Lauren came walking up quickly. "Boss, there was a commotion at the door." She noticed Jojo. "Is he okay?"

"He will be, eventually." She sighed. "You mentioned the door," Jemma reminded her.

The commotion got louder. *Mullan-Gage,* she thought. *Lottie was right.* She straightened her shoulders and headed to the door. The music stopped, and everyone looked at her. "Keep the music going. I'll see what's happening." The music started again, but the people watched her go to the entryway.

"What's going on here?" She stopped abruptly and grinned at the people standing in the doorway.

"Boss, they don't know the password!" Casper complained.

"No, they wouldn't. It's okay, they're my private guests."

"They could've said that," he muttered and moved out of their way to allow them to enter.

"Follow me. I have someone who'll want to see you." She took the man's elbow and pulled the couple into the main club area.

"Jojo!" she tried to call over the noisy crowd. The band leader heard her and stopped the music. "Jojo!" he called from the bandstand.

Jojo pulled himself up and looked around. He blinked, unable to believe who he was seeing. It was his mom AND Frank! "You found him!" He ran over to them. They grabbed him in a bear hug.

People were watching. Jemma waved to them to go back to what they were doing. "It's a family thing." She looked around and saw the man she was looking for at the kitchen entrance. "Mouse," she called, "bring some food for five." He sent her a thumbs-up. She called to the band leader, "Start the music back up; this is a night for celebration!"

The crowd cheered, and the music played loudly.

Lauren walked up. "Is that who I think it is?"

"Yes, go call Lottie and tell her I need her here as soon as possible."

"What if she asks why?"

"Just tell her to hurry."

"I will," Lauren said. She went over to Jojo and hugged him tightly. "I'm happy for you." She turned to leave.

"Can we talk later?" he asked her.

She looked at him searchingly. "Sure, after we close. I have to go now." She turned and hurried off to call Lottie.

Jemma turned back to the group and said, "We can use my office for this reunion."

Once the office door closed, Jojo looked at his mother. "Your letter, you didn't say you found him."

"There was just too much to explain," said Annabeth.

"We wanted to do it in person," Frank told him.

"How did you find him?" asked Jojo.

"She didn't stop looking, thank god," Frank replied.

"How could I? I knew you were there," Annabeth said, her eyes shining.

"What happened? Where were you all this time?" Jojo asked.

"Got hit on the head," Frank said.

"And shot," Annabeth reminded him.

"They kept moving me from hospital to hospital. My dog tags were taken at some point, and I was a little out of it. They just called me John Doe."

"Where did you finally find him?"

"In Belgium," she said.

"There were four divisions of us. I was injured in the last days of the war."

Jemma let them talk. When they slowed down, she went to the phone and called Patrick. "Hello, Patrick, it's Jemma. I have someone here who'd like to speak with you." She held out the phone to Frank.

He walked slowly over and said, "Hello, Patrick."

Silence on the other end, then a shout. "Frank, is that you? She found you!"

"She did. I'm finally home. Thank you for supporting her efforts."

"I did what I could. Brother, you have to come see me soon."

"Let me settle here first, then I'll see about coming out there."

There were tears flowing from every eye in the room. A

knock sounded on the door. Jemma wiped her eyes and opened it. She was surprised to see not only Mouse, but also the chef. "I thought I might offer a hand," he said.

"Thank you."

The food was set on the table and the plates filled for all the guests. Frank put down the phone, wiping his eyes. The chef walked over to him. "Thank you for all you did. I lost my son over there."

"I'm sorry for your loss."

Jemma said, "Chef, I didn't know. I'm so sorry."

He nodded and left the room.

"Can we eat?" Jojo asked. Everyone laughed.

"Of course," Jemma said. "Let's all sit."

The door swung open, and Lottie and Lissette ran in. Lottie stopped short and shouted, "Frank!" She ran over to him, and Annabeth hugged them both. "I'm so glad you're back," she wept.

They sat and ate, telling them the story of his return.

"Somebody's gotta call Patrick!" Lottie exclaimed.

"Jemma's already called him so we could talk," Frank told her.

"Thank you, Jemma," Lottie said to her. Jemma nodded. "What'll you do now, Frank?" asked Lottie.

"Rest first, spend time at home, with my family."

"*YOU* can stay at home as long as you like," Annabeth said. "I'll need some help getting my business going again."

"I know you sacrificed a lot for me. Thank you," he murmured, laying his forehead on hers.

"It wasn't a sacrifice."

Frank lifted his head and said, "Then I'll be helping out there first and probably eventually rejoin the police department." He looked over at Jojo. "What're you doing now? Have you finished your architecture degree?"

"I did," he confirmed.

"And are you designing buildings?"

"Among other things," Jojo admitted.

Jemma said, "He works for me."

"Jojo works here with you?" Frank asked.

"He does; he has amazing building skills."

"I take other jobs in design, but this one's the most consistent," Jojo told him.

Frank started to ask more questions, but Annabeth interrupted. "Why don't we continue the conversations at home?"

"Home, yes, that would be wonderful."

"Jojo, why don't you take my car and get them home? You don't need to come back; you can bring me the car in the morning," Jemma told him.

"I can do that."

She went to her desk and tossed the keys to him.

"Are you sure about this?" Frank asked her, looking at Jojo dubiously.

"He's a good driver," she assured him.

"Hmm, things have changed," he mused. The group laughed, and the three exited.

Lottie and Lissette stayed behind. "Thanks for including us," she told Jemma.

"You're welcome."

"I heard the raids have started."

"I kind of thought that the commotion at the door was a raid. You're right about what's coming."

"It could be bad."

"Now that I know there could be more trouble, what can I do about it?"

"What does your informant say?"

"He said things are getting out of his control, and the first raids might be bad."

"Can you tell me who your informant is?"

"I'd rather not."

"You don't trust me?"

"No, it isn't that," Jemma assured her. "I'll keep that to myself for now."

Lottie nodded. "It looks like money well spent in the past year."

"It was." *In more ways than one*, she thought.

"You have police officers and the mayor in here all the time. Have you thought of approaching one of them?" Lissette asked.

"I haven't yet," Jemma admitted.

"If you do it, be careful." Lottie looked at her watch. "We have to be going. Thanks for the food and the company."

"Anytime. You two should come by more often," Jemma told them.

"I don't know," Lottie vacillated. "Other clubs are freer for us. I don't think we ought to be dancing together here."

"There're lots of rules being broken nightly," Jemma said. "One day, that might be one you break."

Lottie laughed. "I don't think that'll happen in my lifetime."

CHAPTER 51

$\mathcal{L}$auren stepped out into the cool air. The club had closed for the night, and the evening guards were in place.

"Lauren," she heard a voice say. She turned toward Jojo.

"I thought maybe you wouldn't make it tonight."

"I told you I would," he said softly.

"Walk with me?" she asked.

He nodded. "When I saw Frank tonight, I knew I couldn't wait any longer." They stopped, and he reached for her hands. "Lauren, I really like you."

"I like you, too, Jojo."

He shook his head. "No, I don't think you get my meaning."

She put her hand up to his face. "I've been waiting for you to say something. Why do you think I drank that bad liquor? I was trying to get up the nerve to find out if you liked me as much as I like you."

"Would you mind if I kiss you?" he asked nervously.

"Not at all."

He gently kissed her, and she responded.

"I thought you liked that bartender, Nate."
"I hear Nate's more of Chris' type."
He grinned. "Good."
"When did you first notice me?" she asked him.
"When you fell right into my arms."

CHAPTER 52

$\mathcal{L}$auren walked into her apartment humming softly. She started to put her key into the lock and saw a crack of light coming from under the doorway. She frowned, unlocked the door, and entered quickly. Clothes were all over the floor, and broken dishes were strewn about. Her brother sat on the couch holding a picture frame. She ran over to him. "Darren, what's going on? Did someone break in?"

"It's all my fault," he mumbled over and over. "It's all my fault."

She held him. He was her little brother, and even at the age of twenty-five, he needed her. He finally stopped mumbling and pulled away from her. She reached over and took the picture frame from him. The glass had been shattered, and his hands were bleeding.

She looked at the familiar picture. It was an image of their family in happier times. He reached out toward the picture and said, "They didn't have to do that." His blood dripped onto the floor.

"Darren! Your hands!" She jumped up and looked around at the destruction. She grabbed a shirt off the floor and tore it in half. Then brought it back to where he was sitting and wrapped it carefully around his hands. "Tell me why you think this is your fault. Did you make this mess?"

"No, it was like this when I got home."

"You think you know who did it."

"It's because of me."

Her eyes narrowed. "A couple of weeks ago, Charlie and Bob had someone on the roof. Did you have anything to do with that?"

His head dropped down; he couldn't face her.

"WHAT. DID. YOU. DO?" she seethed.

Darren stood and pushed his feet through the debris, walking to the window. The night was dark, and the moon wasn't shining. "I got caught. But, Lauren, I didn't do everything they said I did."

"And what did they accuse you of?"

"Taking liquor barrels and selling them."

She shook her head and put her head in her hands. "I can't believe this. Jemma trusted us; she gave us a job when no one else would."

"She trusted you, not me."

"No, Darren, she trusted *us*."

"She had them watch me."

"Who?"

"Charlie and Bob."

"Was that who caught you?"

"Yeah, they caught me with a few barrels."

"What did you do with the money?"

He mumbled, "I gave it to Betty."

"I knew it! She put you up to this, didn't she?" she pounced.

"You never liked her," he accused her.

"How'd you feel about her when you were dangling over the roof?" she prodded him.

He rubbed a hand through his hair and grinned, shame-faced. "Well, I did question my life choices at that time."

"Finally, some actual thought. At least it's over." She looked up, her mouth pulled tight. "It's over, right?"

"Well…" he hesitated.

"Well, what?" she asked, stomping her foot. "There's no well here. It's either over or it's not."

"I need to talk to Betty; tell her the money's dried up."

Good luck with that. The bitch won't stick around much longer once she hears that, thought Lauren. *Good riddance.* "Do you still have a job?"

"Sort of. Jemma said I have to pay the money back."

"I have some money saved up. I can ask Jemma for a payment plan."

He hung his head again. "I don't think that'll be enough money."

"Why? You said it was just a few barrels."

"Maybe a little more," he guiltily admitted. "But Charlie's blaming me for a lot more losses."

"Oh, god," she moaned. "This keeps getting worse and worse. How many more barrels?"

"A hundred or more. Charlie wasn't clear."

She paled. "We could never save enough for that."

"Now you know why I was held off the roof."

She looked around. "Why did they search the apartment? The barrels wouldn't be here."

"I'm not sure who did that; somehow, I can't see Charlie or Bob doing this."

CHAPTER 53

The next night, Darren waited outside the library for Betty. Since he'd met her, she'd told him not to come inside. She stepped out and immediately took his arm. "Where're we going tonight? To dinner or a club?"

He pulled her over to the side of the building. "We need to talk."

"Of course, sweetie," she said and patted his cheek with her gloved hand.

He grabbed her hand. "Do you love me?"

"Of course I do," she said, but her eyes narrowed. "Did you get the barrels yesterday?"

"I got 'em."

Her face relaxed. "Then what's the problem?"

"I just can't do it anymore."

She laughed. "Oh, you're just nervous. Hasn't it gone well each time?"

"I thought so," he muttered.

"You know," she said, putting her hand on his chest, "my rent's due soon. Do you have the money with you?"

"Betty, I got caught. There's no money."

"No money?" she asked blankly.

"None."

"Hmmm. How'd you like to come to my apartment tonight?" She smiled lustily at him.

"You… you aren't mad?"

"Let's head to my place, baby, and I'll let you know how I feel when we get there."

Darren felt his mood lift. *Lauren was wrong,* he thought. *Betty cares more about me than the money.* They walked a few blocks and went into a new apartment building. This was the first time he'd been invited to her place.

"Fourth floor," she said with a smile. He returned it and followed her up the stairs. She pulled out her key and opened the door.

They entered, and Darren looked around the large apartment. "This is nice," he said. "Better than ours…" His voice trailed off when he saw a large man in the doorway across from him.

"Why've you brought him here?" the man asked Betty.

"He ain't got the money, Jacky. He says there won't be anymore."

Darren's head whipped around to her; her accent had changed entirely.

"What do you mean, no money?" Jacky demanded as he advanced on Darren.

Backed into the corner, Darren croaked, "Who are you? Her brother?"

Jacky paused in his pursuit. "I'm her husband."

"Her husband? But she… we… love each other," Darren said lamely.

"Listen, lover boy," Jacky growled, "your part of this relationship is to give the money to Betty, who then gives it to me."

"Money? She gave it to you?" Darren said dumbly. Betty

pulled out a cigarette and lit it, not saying anything. "Don't you work at the library?" Darren asked her.

"He's a little slow, ain't he?" Jacky asked her.

She exhaled a puff of smoke. "Oh, all right, might as well admit it now. I'm married, and I've never worked at the library."

"What do you do for money?" Darren asked her.

"Suckers like you give me money. And now I'll have to get another man for your slot." She sighed.

"Slot?" Darren asked slowly. He couldn't wrap his head around what Betty was saying. She'd never loved him; she was married, and she was just using him for the money. *Oh god*, he thought, *Lauren was right!*

"You never questioned that I could only see you on Wednesday and Thursday evenings," she jeered. "So trusting, and so stupid."

"You… You said your mom needed the money to help her," he protested.

"My mom died years ago, the old bat. She couldn't support me neither."

"If all of this was a lie, why did you bring me here?" Darren asked.

Jacky sneered at him. "To *encourage* you to go back to stealing the barrels for money."

"I can't, they caught me."

Betty looked disgusted. "He's useless now. What're we going to do with him?" she asked her husband.

"That sister of his, would she pay to get him back?" he asked Betty.

"She doesn't have any money, either," said Darren.

"Yeah, I could tell," Jacky mocked.

"It was you! It was you at my apartment!" Darren accused him.

"Yeah, it was me. We wanted to make sure you weren't keeping any money for yourself."

"I want to leave," Darren said miserably.

"I think it's time to let him go," Betty told her husband.

"Well, let me give him something to think about on his way home." Jacky folded his hand into a fist and slammed it into Darren's stomach.

Darren thought he was going to throw up because the pain was so bad. "I'm sorry," Jacky said. "Let me help you up."

The man extended his hand, and Darren took it. Jacky helped him up and then punched him in the stomach again. Darren fell to his knees, retching.

"Don't you puke on my floor!" Jacky warned. "Get 'em up and get 'em outta here," he told Betty.

Betty kicked at Darren until he struggled to his feet and stumbled out the door. She called out after him, "Tell your sister you still owe us."

CHAPTER 54

alifornia

"The Flame Tokay and Emperor grapes were a good investment for areas that don't want the bricks," Angelo admitted.

"We've sent out two thousand train carloads, and all are being returned empty. We're fully sold out of the product, again," said Ben.

"They're hearty, but that doesn't make them taste good," Angelo muttered.

"I don't think people care, Papa. They just want booze," Marisol said. "And it's profitable."

Angelo shook his head. "We are losing the ability to differentiate between a fine wine and a common table wine," he bitterly complained. He turned and walked away from them, his head hanging.

"It's going to take time to build the fine wine business back after Prohibition ends," Ben said.

"And if it doesn't end?" she asked.

"Then we continue as we are, making sacramental and medicinal wines with the fine wine and bricks with the substandard grapes." Ben checked his watch. "I need to make a call, Marisol. It's about the railcar delivery."

"Oh, now?" she asked wide-eyed.

"Yes, now."

"I'll come with you." They started walking to the house.

Angelo continued to walk down the barrel inventories in the large building. Loud engines could be heard outside. "I'm not expecting deliveries," Angelo said to himself as he walked to the door.

Before he got there, several men pushed past him into the building. "Over there!" one yelled and pointed. A couple of men with axes ran to where the first man pointed and drove the axes into the first barrel. Wine gushed everywhere.

"Wait! Wait! Stop!" Angelo yelled at the men.

Ben ran in. "What's going on? Who are you?"

"Federal agents. Angelo Valdez, I'm Special Agent Mullins," the man said, flashing a badge at Angelo and Ben. "Distributing alcohol's illegal."

"We're not distributing alcohol," Ben protested. "This is sacramental wine. We have paperwork that proves it."

"What's that?" Mullins said.

"Papa, bring the papers from your office," Marisol directed. Angelo strode away quickly.

"Wait. Henderson," Mullins pointed to one of his agents, "go with him and make sure there's no funny business."

Henderson started after Angelo. They entered the office and then exited quickly, Angelo holding the papers.

"Bring them to me," Mullins said. He read through the papers. Henderson directed the other agents to pull down another barrel.

"No, please!" Angelo pleaded.

"Hold up there," Mullins said. "This looks to be in order."

"They can legally make the wine?" Henderson asked.

"Yeah, seems they found a loophole." Mullins turned on Angelo. "We'll be keeping an eye on you," he threatened as he handed back the paperwork. "Come on, men, we have other places to be."

Marisol, Ben, and Angelo stood with their feet covered in red wine.

"What a mess, and a loss of years' worth of work." Angelo crinkled his nose and put his finger into the smashed barrel, tasting it. "This isn't my wine!"

"Look at the side," directed Ben.

He did and saw there was an "X" marked on the side. "What does that mean?" Angelo asked.

"It means that I set that barrel up to be damaged," Ben admitted.

"You! You were aware of the raid!" Angelo thundered.

"I was."

"I had the wine brought over, Papa," Marisol told him. "We wanted to protect the fine wine."

"Why wasn't I told?"

"You told me you didn't want to be involved in anything illegal," Ben replied.

Angelo's eyes widened. "Did you bribe them?"

"Agent Mullins is on the payroll. He gives me a heads up. We were able to limit the damage and loss of inventory."

"Is this the way we are to do business?" Angelo asked him.

"If we want to survive, yes," said Ben.

"In the future, you will include me in information like this," Angelo ordered Ben and Marisol.

"If you're sure," said Ben.

"I am."

ew York

Jojo rounded the corner of the building and felt someone tap him in the shoulder.

"Aren't you a bit late this morning?" Jemma asked.

He snatched the hat off his head and said, "Frank and I were up late talking."

"I get that. I was teasing. Any idea which side of the alcohol debate he'll be on?"

"I hope he doesn't work with the dry's," he responded. "And considering the amount of beer he drank last night, I don't think he supports them."

"Well, let me know if that changes," she said in a wry voice. "Did you return my car?"

"It's parked in its usual spot in the back."

Jemma followed him into the bar with a wave at Casper. She walked over to the bar to where Lauren was standing. "Oh, hey, boss," Lauren greeted her.

"Good morning."

Lauren had promised Darren, she'd give him some time before she mentioned anything to Jemma. "You're sure about him?" she asked Jemma, their attention surreptitiously on Nate.

"I asked Chris to stop by this evening to meet him."

Lauren nodded. "That's okay. I like someone else. Always did."

"And did this someone else finally say something to you?" Jemma inquired.

"Who?" Lauren asked innocently.

"Don't give me that. Has Jojo finally made a move?"

"Shh, keep your voice down, and yes, finally." Lauren grinned at her boss.

"Sooo, is he a good kisser?"

"Mmmmm, yeah."

"Watch that, girl. We need your mind on business," Jemma teased her friend.

"Of course, boss," Lauren said with mock gravity.

They took another look at Nate. "Well, the ladies sure will like him at the tea," Jemma commented.

"They will. That was a good idea to cater to them."

"Did you test him to be sure he can make drinks?"

"Oh, was I supposed to do that?" Lauren laughed. "Yes, he had a lot of experience around town. He came highly recommended."

"Where's Charlie?" Jemma asked.

"Haven't seen him since he stormed out of here the other day."

"It's better that he's not here for the teas. He can be disruptive." Jemma looked around and saw that everything appeared to be ready. "Time to talk to the troops." Jemma clapped her hands. "All right, everyone, the ladies will be in soon. Manners, please. Remember, women are part of our future."

The waiters and bartenders nodded.

Lauren tapped on Jemma's shoulder. "My answer to your question on moving bottles will be here soon," she said in a low voice.

"Let me know when arrive," Jemma said.

"The ladies are here," Casper called from the doorway.

The tea ladies started coming in from shopping, golfing and other idle pursuits. "Jemma!" called Ethyl. "I like the decorations." She waved the cane at the walls and other décor. "Does it look different at nighttime?"

"Thank you. Yes, during the day, the rose colored walls and Italianate décor really stand out when the lights are bright, and then, in the evening, with the lights low, it's just accents."

Maeve called, "Ladies, we have a new cocktail we'd like you to taste." The ladies cheered, and Lauren waved to the waiters to move the cups over for them to try the new drink.

"What's this called?" Ethyl asked.

"It's called the Hanky Panky," Maeve told her.

"Well, bless me. That sure puts the hanky in my panky." Ethyl waved at Maeve. "Bring me another one, please. Jemma, can the cute new bartender bring the next set of drinks over?"

"Yes, he can. I'll leave Lauren to take care of it."

The ladies cheered again. "Young man," Ethyl called to Nate, "why don't you come sit by me."

Nate grinned at her and took her the first drink. She tapped him with her cane. "Sit."

He looked at Lauren; she nodded and helped carry the other drinks over to them.

A little while later, Lauren knocked quickly and walked into Jemma's office. "The tea ended," she said, "and the ladies are headed home."

"How did it go?"

"There were lots of compliments about Nate." Lauren smiled as she sat down at Jemma's desk. "He was a good choice."

Casper stuck his head in. "Your friend's here, Lauren."

"Thanks, I'll go get her," she said. Lauren walked out of the office and quickly went to the door. She saw her friend Amy, who wore a long coat and a hat pulled down over her dark brown curls. "Right on time," Lauren told her.

"I strive to be efficient."

Lauren looped arms with her and escorted her to Jemma's office. She knocked and was called in. "Come on, it's time for your interview." They entered.

Jemma stood and walked over to her. "Jemma Hardison," she introduced herself and held out her hand.

"Amy Greene," she held out her hand, and they shook.

Jemma looked her over and asked, "What're your ideas for smuggling for us?"

Amy looked at Lauren. She nodded and said, "Show her."

Amy opened her coat and pulled up her skirt, revealing holders for bottles. "Spin," Lauren said. She turned and dropped the coat; she wore a shirt with compartments that held bottles on her back. There was also a large flask on her hip, about a foot long, and attached with a belt. Jemma started to laugh. "That's perfect. What if you're stopped?"

"I cry and say my boyfriend abandoned me for the drink."

"Does that work?"

"They usually let me go."

"All right, you're hired. We'll be sending bottles back and forth each day. We have to limit the inventories we keep onsite."

"I'm your girl."

"Lauren, get her some money to get her started. She can help in the kitchen until we need to send her to our other locations."

Amy nodded with excitement and said, "Thanks!"

"And, Lauren? Be sure to unload her out of sight of Charlie."

"I'll take care of it."

During the lull between the tea and the club opening, after things were cleaned up and the staff turned over, the band came in to rehearse and warm up for that evening. As the later hours advanced, the club sounds started to penetrate the peace of her office. Lauren stuck her head in. "Got a minute, boss?"

"I do." Jemma closed her books and sat back.

"You need to come out on the floor now."

"Is it a raid?" she asked, ready to stash her books in the floorboards.

"No, it's Dolly. She's starting trouble with the customers."

"Damn, already? She just started."

They walked down the long hallway that opened to the main floor of the club. The band was playing, and the sultry notes of the singer floated through the crowded space. Tables were filled with happy customers enjoying food and drinks.

As they wound their way through the tables, there were a few shouts to Jemma, and they were stopped numerous times by happy customers. Jemma kissed cheeks, shook hands, and smiled in response to their comments. She waved and continued on her way. A loud conversation could be heard as they passed. "I didn't know you drank so much," complained a young man to his companion.

"I drink a normal amount," the young woman argued.

"No. The women at home don't drink like that."

"This is New York City; a bachelor woman can do anything a bachelor man can do."

"Yes, hon, they can," Jemma said with a throaty laugh as she passed them.

"See," the girl said, "I told you."

They passed more tables, and Lauren nodded toward a dark corner off the stage. "Over there," she said. As they approached the couple in the corner, Jemma motioned Casper to meet her. It was apparent that the duo was in an intimate embrace.

"Break them up," Jemma ordered Casper. After they were pulled apart, both started to complain. "Take him to get some coffee," she told Casper.

"All right, buddy, let's go." Casper grabbed the man's arm and hauled him off to the bar.

When Casper started to haul the man off, Jemma stopped him. "Hang on a second," she said, and turned to Dolly, holding out her hand, palm up.

"What?" Dolly asked, wrapping her arms around her and sticking her chin out. Jemma didn't move; she just stared at the girl, her hand still outstretched. "Fine." Dolly pulled out a large man's wallet and threw it at Jemma. She caught it deftly and handed it to Casper. He took it and pulled the inebriated man away from them.

Jemma looked at Lauren. "Get her out and make sure she doesn't come back."

"Hey, what do you mean?" Dolly demanded, sticking out her chest. Her breasts were clearly visible even in the low light. Jemma ignored the question and made her way back through the crowd. "What does she mean?" she asked Lauren.

"Put those things away," Lauren told her. Dolly grabbed the shirt edges and started to button them up. When she was finished, Lauren grabbed her arm. "Let's go; this way." Lauren started pulling Dolly toward the back door.

"Waitaminnit! Hold it, hold it," Dolly begged, dragging her feet. "I want to talk to Jemma. I want to talk to Jemma."

"Girlie, she's talked to you as much as she's ever going to. You are so not worth her time. Come on." Lauren grabbed the woman's arm again, pulled her out the back door to the alley, and pushed her out.

"You'll be sorry!" Dolly screamed, shaking her fist at Lauren.

"No, girlie, I don't think so." Lauren slammed the door in the girl's face.

"I know people!" Dolly's faint voice could be heard through the door as she pounded on it. "You'll regret this!"

"What people does she know?" asked Mouse. He stood nearby, wiping his wet hands on his long apron.

"Don't know, don't care," Lauren replied. "I do wonder who recommended her in the first place?" Lauren had an idea. "Hey, Amy," she called to her friend.

"What's up?" Amy asked, wiping her hands. Chef had put her to work washing dishes.

"We have a sudden opening for a hostess. How'd you like to make some extra money?"

"I'd like that a lot."

"Then let's get you a uniform," Lauren told her, and they walked behind the bandstand.

alifornia

The sun could be seen on the horizon. Marisol sighed and got up on the side of the bed.

Ben reached over and stroked her naked back. "You know it doesn't have to be this way."

She turned her head toward him, her hair fanning across her back. "You want to tell Papa about us?"

"It's your mother I'm worried about."

"No teasing," she warned.

"Who's teasing? She'd come after me with the shotgun."

What he said was true. Marisol shook her head and asked, "Any plans for the day?"

"Patrick called; he needs some help with his equipment on set today. Would you like to come see a movie being made?"

"Yes, I would. Will Jean be there?"

"I think so. And they want us to come over after for dinner and swimming."

"I'll bring a suit."

Later that evening, after watching the movie being made, Ben and Marisol were at dinner at Jean and Patrick's home. The pool seemed to shimmer in the moonlight. Patrick and Ben were in the pool with the kids, throwing a ball back and forth.

"That was a beautiful horse on set today," commented Marisol, sitting with her legs in the water.

"Black Beauty, and that's also the name of the movie," Jean said from the pool, her arm resting on the edge.

"The fox hunt scene was so interesting with the dogs, horse, and real foxes. Did it hurt when you fell off the horse?" Marisol asked.

"I try to land with less impact, but I'll be feeling the bruises tomorrow. Swimming helps loosen the muscles. The next big stunt will be the race. Will you come back for that?"

"Just tell me the date and we'll be there."

"Have you told your family about Ben yet?"

"No."

"Are you sure you've thought this through?"

"At the time, it seemed to be the right thing to do."

"And now?"

Marisol rubbed the slight curve of her belly and said, "The decision will be out of my hands soon."

CHAPTER 57

ew York

"You didn't make it one week," the man groused.

"You said to get her closed down, and the best way to do that's what I did," Dolly angrily retorted.

"I didn't think you'd get fired the first week," he muttered. "Now I'll have to think of something else."

"What about me?"

"I'm sure you can go back to your previous job," he said carelessly. "It makes no difference to me."

"Well, that's just peachy."

"Get out. I have things to think about."

CHAPTER 58

*L*auren had worked the late shift, and she was walking away. Jojo ran after her. "Can I walk you home?" he asked.

She turned to him and smiled. "Sure. Late night?"

"Nah, I wanted to give Ma and Frank some time alone."

"That's sweet. I'm sure they need it."

He held out his hand to her, she took it, and they walked slowly. "Yeah."

"Are you working on any other jobs?" she asked.

"A new building's going up downtown, and I'm designing the office spaces."

They walked along, enjoying each other's company, until she spotted a man lying in the street in front of her apartment building. "Drunk," she said in disgust.

"Everyone's drinking more with Prohibition in effect," he pointed out. When they got closer to the man, Jojo asked, "Isn't that Darren?"

"No! He went to see Betty again…" Her voice trailed off.

Jojo bent down by the man. "Lauren, it's Darren," he said, looking up at her.

"Oh God." She rushed over to look. His face was covered with bruises. He'd obviously been beaten.

"Mon... Money..." he muttered. "They just wanted my money."

"Help me get him inside," Jojo said. They picked him up and Darren cried out. "His arm's broken." Jojo wrapped Darren's good arm around his shoulder and Lauren wrapped her arm around her brother's waist. He was dead weight. Once in the building, Jojo asked, "What floor?"

"Third. Sorry," she said.

"Don't be sorry, you didn't do anything. Come on, old boy," Jojo said to Darren. "We need some help to get you upstairs."

Darren forced his legs to move, and the three finally managed to get him into the apartment.

"Where?" asked Jojo, his breath coming short.

"In his bedroom."

They carried Darren to the bed and laid him down. Lauren walked out to the hallway to the shared telephone.

CHAPTER 59

$\mathcal{J}$emma picked up her ringing telephone. "Hello?"

"Jemma, could you come to our apartment?"

"Lauren? Has something happened?"

"Yes, and please hurry!"

Jemma lay down the phone in its cradle and walked to the door. "Is Casper still here?" she called to the maintenance crew cleaning the floors.

"He's in the kitchen."

"Get him up here, please." She walked to her closet and started pulling out clothes. A light knock let her know Casper had arrived. "Come in," she called out.

The large man had to duck down in the doorway to enter. "You wanted to see me, boss?"

"I do. We have trouble," Jemma said from inside the closet.

"Here? At the club?"

"No, at Lauren's place. I think I might need your help."

"Okay, boss, want me to get Rocky?"

"Yeah, we need to go over now."

Once they were in the car, on their way to Lauren's apartment building, Casper turned to her. "What kind of trouble can I expect?" he asked.

"I'm not sure," Jemma admitted, "but I thought you might be helpful." Casper was another one of John's employees from Chicago. He'd relocated after the club was ready to open.

He nodded. "I'm ready for anything. "

Rocky pulled up to the curb. "Wait here," Jemma told him.

They went up to Lauren and Darren's apartment. Jemma knocked, and they waited. The door swung open, and they saw it was Lauren, and she'd been crying. Jojo stood beside her.

"What is it? What's wrong?" Jemma asked frantically.

"Come in, they're in the bedroom." Jemma and Casper walked to the bedroom. They saw the club's doctor, Dr. Kelly, leaning over Darren, checking him out; Darren's face was a mass of bruises, and his arm was broken, which Dr. Kelly had already set.

"Can I talk to him, Doc?" she asked the doctor.

"You can try," the doctor said. "I've given him some morphine for the pain. He might not be able to answer."

"Darren? It's Jemma. Who did this? Was it Charlie?"

Darren shook his head and moaned.

Lauren answered for him. "It was his girlfriend's husband."

"Her husband?" echoed Jemma.

"Yeah, they'd conned him into believing that she needed the money. Evidently, she has several men on the hook," Jojo told her.

Lauren spoke up. "He'd gone to talk to Betty the other day about the money, and her husband roughed him up a little. He went back tonight to talk to them again. Jojo and I found him outside when we walked home and brought him upstairs. I called Doc Kelly and then you."

Jemma took in this information and then turned to Casper. "I think we need to pay a social visit to this Betty person, don't you, Casper?"

"Yeah, boss, I think we do."

"Give me her address," Jemma said briskly and held out her hand.

Darren struggled to get up, and Jojo held him back. "He said the man's dangerous," Jojo told her.

"You think I'm not?" she asked. "They didn't just hurt him; they interfered with my family's business. Nobody does that to my family and gets away with it." Lauren handed Jemma a piece of paper with Betty's address on it. "Doc, send the bill to me, if you please. We'll show ourselves out." She turned and left, with Casper following behind.

Lauren sat on the bed with Jojo and Darren. "Wow, she's scary," Jojo said. Lauren and Doc Kelly nodded.

CHAPTER 60

ocky got out and opened the door for them. "Back to the club?" he asked.

"No, we have another stop to make." Her voice was grim. She told hm the location.

"Yes, boss."

They soon arrived at the address.

"You sure you want to come in with me, boss? I can take care of it," said Casper. Jemma just glared at him. "Yes, boss." He nodded, and they got out and headed upstairs.

"Rocky, go to the back and make sure no one tries to get away," she told the driver.

"Got it, boss." He exited the car and walked around to the back of the building.

Jemma and Casper entered the building and headed up to Betty's apartment. "We don't knock," she said.

"Got it."

Casper pulled a pistol from his pocket and kicked the door in. It splintered. Jacky and Betty were sitting on the couch with their mouths open in amazement. Jemma walked in and stared at the duo. She nodded to Casper, and he stepped back. She turned back to the couple.

"Who the hell are you?" Jacky demanded.

"Jemma Harden."

"Oh, shit," he choked out.

"Jacky, who's that?" Betty demanded.

"Just shut up," Jacky snarled. "What do you want?" he asked.

"I understand you've been embezzling money from me," Jemma said.

Jacky started shaking. He was scared, but he tried to talk his way out of this situation. "It wasn't me. It was that kid Darren."

"Because of her." She looked at Betty. "Betty, isn't it?"

"Yes," she answered tentatively.

Jemma looked around the rather big apartment and saw a chair. "May I sit?" When Betty nodded dumbly, she pulled the chair over in front of the couple and sat.

"Now, not only have the two of you been embezzling money from me, but you attacked one of my employees. You beat him and broke his arm." Jacky gulped and nodded. "Tell me why I shouldn't do the same thing to the two of you."

"We… we didn't mean to do it," Jacky stammered. "We were just messing around. Having some fun, you know? The kid got scared at something I said and tried to run away. He fell down the stairs and broke his arm."

"You hear that, Casper?" Jemma looked at him. "They didn't mean to do it. They were just messing around, having fun."

"Yeah, boss, that's a corker," Casper snorted.

"It is time you paid your debt to me," said Jemma.

"I–" started the man. Casper stepped toward him. "Fine, the money is over there in a box," he said, pointing to the mantel.

Betty whined. "But that is our money."

Jemma walked over and took her by the hair pulling her out of the chair. "No, that money is mine; you conned a nice young man." She released her with a shove onto the floor.

Jemma went and opened the box; she took all of the cash.

"This should take care of the money owed to me." Jemma turned back to the couple. "Here's my offer to you. You have five minutes to get out of here. You leave the city and never come back. You have nothing to do with my family. *EVER.*" She stared at Jacky. "And, Jacky, you know my family. If I hear anything about you ever again… Well, let's just say it won't be pretty."

"But… but…" Betty stammered.

"Just shut up," Jacky told her. "Look, Miss Harden…"

"Time's ticking, Jacky." Jemma looked at her watch. "Tick tock."

Jacky looked at Jemma, hoping for some sort of reprieve. Seeing none, he jumped off the couch, pulling Betty with him. He pulled her into the bedroom and started throwing clothes into a suitcase.

Jemma could hear Betty trying to get her husband to explain what was going on. With thirty seconds to spare, they rushed by her and clattered down the stairs.

"Well, that's that." Jemma stood and walked to the door. "Casper, let Rocky know we're ready to go."

"Got it, boss."

When they were in the car heading back to the club, she turned to Casper. "So, how'd I do?" she asked.

"The old man woulda been proud of you," Casper told her. "I had tears in my eyes."

"You old softie," Jemma told him. "Call Rocky, we are going home."

He went quickly around the building and returned with Rocky.

"What'd I miss?" Rocky asked, opening the car door for her.

CHAPTER 61

The next morning, Jemma was drinking tea at her home. A light knock sounded at the door. She went to find out who was visiting so early in the morning and saw it was Lauren and Darren. She opened the door. "Come in, sit down." They sat on her couch, their faces downcast. "Are you sure you should be up?" she asked Darren.

"Doc said it was okay for me to be out for a little while," he muttered. He was still in terrible pain, but he had convinced Lauren to take him to see Jemma so he could explain.

"Well, I've never seen a sorrier pair," she commented.

"Jemma, we're here to apologize," Lauren said.

"I don't see what you're apologizing for. I took care of things. Your debt is cleared."

They looked at each other. "But Betty… and her husband…" said Darren.

"They're no longer your concern."

"What does that mean?" Lauren asked. She lowered her voice. "Did you… did you kill them?"

Jemma threw her head back and laughed. "What, did I have them *rubbed out*? I didn't. However, Casper and Rocky…" She laughed again at their shocked faces. "No, they weren't killed, but I did put the fear of God into them. You'll never hear from them again. With any luck, they're on a boat somewhere getting as far away as possible."

"Thank you, Jemma," said Darren.

"Darren, you can work in the club until you get healed up."

"What? I thought..." he started.

Lauren poked him in the side. "Just say thank you," she mumbled.

"Thanks, boss."

"Can I count on you not to take any more of my barrels?"

"Yes, boss," he assured her.

She nodded. "And, Darren, you might want to be single for a while."

"Yes, boss," he said, trying to smile.

"Jemma," Lauren said, "Darren has something to discuss with you."

"About the shipments?"

He nodded.

"Go on, tell her," nudged Lauren.

"Jemma, I took barrels, but I never took a hundred or more."

"I had my suspicions."

"We think it's Charlie," Lauren said.

"That adds up, and I'll bet Bob's involved. Would you like to turn the tables on them, Darren?"

He smiled. "I'm in."

"Good." She outlined her plans with them.

"For how long?" he asked.

"Long enough to get evidence, both at pickup and delivery. I'm curious about their final plans."

CHAPTER 62

A few weeks later, Jemma was in the club reviewing the music for that evening when Lauren walked up.

"Jemma, can I talk to you?" she asked.

"Sure."

"In your office?"

Jemma raised her eyebrows and walked to the office. Once the door was closed, she moved to her desk and waited for Lauren to begin.

"What's going on?"

"I'm pregnant."

"Did you forget to wear your diaphragm?"

"I must have," she said faintly.

Jemma stood, took Lauren's hand, walked her to the couch, and sat down. "Did you do this on purpose?"

"Not consciously, I didn't. I think I want to keep her."

"Her?"

"Maybe more of a wish, though a boy would be nice also," Lauren said dreamily.

"Is Jojo the father?"

"Yes."

"Have you told him?"

"Not yet."

"Doc Kelly will be back from vacation soon. Do you want him to fix this for you?"

"I don't want it *FIXED*!" Lauren cried. "I want to keep it!"

Jemma took her hand. "I'm here no matter what. You have a job here as long as you want it."

"Thank you." The phone rang. "I'll get it," she said. Lauren walked to the desk and picked it up. "Boss, it's for you."

Jemma took the receiver and said, "Hello."

"Have they arrived?" Ben asked her.

"Has who arrived? Who are you talking about?" She heard him yell to someone in the distance.

"Tell them to go on. We'll get them some food," called Ben to people on his side of the phone.

Jemma waited until Ben came back to the phone.

"I just got about half of John's operating staff here," he told her. "They're arriving by train, and I hear some will be coming in alternate ways."

"Why would they be there?" she asked, bewildered.

"I have an idea about that."

"Jemma, you need to come over here," called Casper from the doorway.

"Ben, just a second. They need me at the door."

"I think you're about to have some personnel issues of your own." More yelling for Ben could be heard on the phone. "I'll talk to you soon." He hung up abruptly.

She stared at the phone before slowly laying it down. She walked to the door and joined Casper. "What is it?"

"Take a look." He held open the peephole and saw people she knew outside.

"Oh my. Open the door."

"Hey," Charlie called from inside the club. "Who're you letting in here?"

She ignored him. "Open the door," she said again.

Casper pulled it open, and people began flooding in. Men, women, and children crowded in. She knew these people. They were John's people. She hugged them as they walked by. Casper greeted his old friends. "Everyone, please move into the main room," she said when everyone had entered.

Charlie charged over. "Who are these people!" he raged.

She didn't bother to turn around. "They're family."

He glared at the motley crew. "Family, huh? They don't look much like you."

"Charlie, get the hell out of here," she snarled.

He grumbled and glared at her, but he decided to leave them to her.

She walked over to an older man, who'd been working for John for as long as she could remember. "Warren, talk to me. What's going on?"

"We were told it was time to leave Chicago. John wanted us out."

She'd had no idea that the situation with Torrio was so bad. She made a decision and said, "Hello and welcome." Kids were crying, and a majority of the adults were frowning. "How about some food while I work on getting you settled?"

The tired faces in front of her brightened. "Lauren," she called. "Let's get this crew fed."

"We can do that; I'll get with the chef. We may need some extra help."

A young man held up his hand. She recognized him; it was Warren's son, Davey. "I'm pretty good in the kitchen. Can I help?"

"Hello, Davey, it's so good to see you again," Jemma told him. "Thanks for volunteering. Follow Lauren over to the kitchen. The chef will tell you what's needed."

She watched him walk over to Lauren, wiping his hands on his pants nervously. He glanced back, and she waved him on.

She continued to survey the group in front of her and went over to an old friend she'd worked with in her younger days at John's establishments. She asked in a low voice, "May I have a word, Edna?"

She stood to follow Jemma to the office. Once the door was closed, Edna started to talk. "We were told to get what we could carry and that we'd be moving as soon as the trains arrived."

"So, what did you do?"

"We did as we were told and moved." She walked around the room. "Nice place."

"Thanks."

"We haven't heard much from you," she said idly.

"I've been rather busy," Jemma commented. Edna walked over to the desk and touched the flowers in a vase. "Where's Clay?" she asked.

"Still got a thing for him?" Edna asked, her lips tight.

Jemma glared and asked the question again. "WHERE IS CLAY?"

"All right, all right. He stayed behind."

"With John and Mel?"

"Yes, I tried to talk him out of it." Edna dropped her bag, and when she bent down to retrieve it, her hat fell forward on her head. She seemed undecided about whether to grab the hat or the purse. Jemma stepped over and put her hands on the woman's shoulders, gently pushing her hat back into place and retrieving her bag.

"Thank you," Edna mumbled.

"Edna, I'm happy that you and Clay got married."

"You didn't come to the wedding." She sniffed.

"No, I was rather hurt at the time."

"You still want Clay?"

She laughed. "No, I've moved on."

"Why did you ask about him?" she asked

"Because the two of you got together." That was something

that had helped Jemma make her decision to leave Chicago. "It's just odd he isn't with you."

Edna started to cry.

"No, don't do that, I'm sorry." Jemma put her arms around the woman and hugged her. "I'm sure he'll be with you soon." She waited for her to calm down and said, "What we need to talk about is how we're going to handle getting everyone here settled."

"How will this work? We can't just stay here."

"No," confirmed Jemma. "We have to open tonight. I have a thought, though." She picked up the phone. "Operator... please." She waited, and when they connected her, she said, "Maurice, take the sign down on the building. Yes, I know, I'm going to be sending over a large group of people. How many apartments?" She looked at Edna.

Edna quickly tallied up how many apartments they'd need. "Fifteen."

Jemma nodded and said, "Fifteen. That'll just about fill the place up. They'll be on their way after they eat. Thank you, Maurice. I'll let you know when they're on the way." She hung up the phone. Edna started to look hopeful. "I have a place for everyone."

"Will there be beds?" Edna asked. It had been such a long trip, and they had taken any seat available. Most were in second and third class.

"They are furnished," Jemma confirmed. "We'll need to keep the location within the family; no one here needs to know."

Edna nodded. She'd been in the family long enough to understand that Jemma operated like John, keeping her cards close to her vest. "Can I call in the leads from the families?"

"Of course. Let's do that now," Jemma directed and followed her out to the main club floor.

Jemma looked at the group as she called their names. She nodded at each one as they went by and down the hall to her office. She watched as Charlie milled near the group. No one seemed to want to talk to him. *Good*, she thought. They could already see him for what he was, untrustworthy.

"Can the family leads join me in my office, please?" she asked. Jemma walked back to her office, the leads following her. Once inside, the leads stood around, hats in their hands. Warren stepped forward.

"Jemma, you have something for us?"

"Yes, I do," she said. "We have apartments for you all."

"And they're furnished," supplied Edna. The men nodded to each other.

"Before we go any further," Jemma cautioned, "I want to let you know that operations here are not like back in Chicago. You are part of our family, but here we don't have the same trust in certain employees at the club. Please do not share any sensitive information outside of the family."

"What if they ask about why we came here?" Warren wondered.

"Yeah, that man, Charlie, he kept asking questions," another man, Jimmy, spoke up. "Nobody said anything," he assured her.

"Just say I invited you a while back and you decided this was the best time."

"And if they ask who we are?"

"Not that it's anyone's business, but you're my family," Jemma said simply. The leaders smiled for the first time. This was Jemma, whom most of them had known since she was a little girl.

A knock sounded on the door. Jemma held up her hand to quiet the room. Davy stuck his head in and said, "Lunch is ready."

"Thanks, Davey. Let's move out."

They'd set up a buffet, and they formed a line. "Everyone, eat your fill," she told them. They took her advice, and the men joined their wives. They each talked in low voices. The women nodded and moved the kids through the food lines.

Charlie continued to study the group as he walked over to Jemma. "Not a talkative group. Family, you say? From where?"

"Now, Charlie, we're not that close," she chided.

He sent a sideways glance at her. "Don't look much like you," he muttered.

"My father's side is dark," she commented and moved to get her plate. She filled it and sat with the group. They talked little and ate the food provided.

Davey joined her. "Did you get to assist Chef?" she asked.

"I did," he said eagerly.

His mother reached over to touch his hand. "He barely lets me cook anymore."

"I enjoy it, Mama." He grinned.

After she ate, she walked over to Casper. "I need to transfer these people to my apartment building."

He looked over at them. "I can get a couple of big cars."

"We need this to be kept quiet."

"How about the truck?"

"That might work."

"You thinking two trips?"

"That's my thought." She pulled out a cigarette and lit it. "Let's get organized."

He glanced at the door and said, "What about the door here?"

"We'll lock it down until you get back."

He nodded and grabbed his coat and hat. "I'll have the trucks on 86th street in a few minutes."

"I'll have everyone ready," she said.

Casper moved to the back door, and Jemma stayed in the alcove, going over the plans for the move. A few minutes later, she saw him waving from the back. She called Warren over to her. "We're going to be moving everyone to the new building.

We'll gather about fifteen at a time. Separate everyone into groups."

He nodded and spoke in a low voice to the groups. About half stood, and the other half stayed seated. He guided them toward the back, and once they were on their way, he returned to sit with the second group. *Good man,* she thought.

Charlie looked at Nate. "Where're they going now?" he asked in a loud voice.

"Not my business," Nate replied. "I need to get back to work. The tea ladies will be arriving in a little while."

Charlie frowned, continuing to watch the group.

It wasn't long before the back door opened again, and the final group was moved out. Jemma tapped her cigarette out in an ashtray and called, "Lauren, get this place organized. We have the tea coming up."

Lauren led the waitresses over. "All right, ladies, let's get this swept up and wiped down. Nate, come help with the flowers." He set down the glass he was polishing and followed her lead. The room became ready within a short period of time.

Lauren rushed over. "We're ready," she said.

Jemma checked her watch and looked toward the back door. Casper came in and walked quickly over to her. "Everything go okay?" she asked him.

"Yeah, everything went off without a hitch," he said and took off his hat and coat. "They're all settled."

"No one showed interest?"

"No, and I didn't advertise."

Jemma said in a low voice, "Make sure Charlie doesn't know where they're located."

"You think he'll do something?"

"I think he's quickly becoming a liability."

CHAPTER 63

"*D*arren's back, and that's all there is to it," Jemma said, glaring at Charlie.

"What about the money?"

"He's paid his debt to me."

"There's no way he had that kind of money."

"Charlie…" she started.

"Jemma, there's a call for you," Lauren called from Jemma's office.

"On my way," she called back. "We'll talk about this later." She left him and entered her office. Lauren sat at her desk, checking off inventory against the invoices.

Jemma picked up her phone. "Hello."

"Jemma."

"John," she said with a smile and leaned against the desk. She waved at Lauren to leave. She nodded, closed her books, and exited the room.

"John, how are things there?"

"You were right; the money's in alcohol. Even Ben's bricks are making a huge profit."

"Leave it to Ben to make our business legal." She laughed.

His tone changed abruptly. "Did everyone arrive safely?"

She moved to her seat behind the desk. "Yes, they're here with me in New York and with Ben in California. What's going on there, John? Do Ben and I need to come home?"

"No, we have things under control; we're just going to take back some of our properties."

"Who'll be there with you?"

"Mel, Clay, and a few others."

"John, I think we need to be there for you."

"No, the family must survive; you and Ben must stay and keep the business going. We'll work this out."

"Grandpa, I want you and Mel here with us. Why not just leave Chicago and come to New York or go pick grapes with Ben in California?"

"Chicago's my base, my home; these people have to be taught a lesson."

The line was disconnected. She stared at the phone for a long moment and then dialed Ben's number. The line connected, and a woman answered. "Hello, is this Marisol?" Jemma asked.

"Yes. Is this Jemma?"

"It is. Is Ben there?"

"He's out watching the last of the grapes being pressed. Is it important? I can have him call you?"

"I think it is. Yes, have him call me."

It was a few minutes later when the phone rang. "Jemma, Marisol said you called."

"I think John might be in trouble."

Ben sighed. "Yeah, it looks that way."

"Have you got everyone settled there?" she asked him.

"They're in housing all over town. Some are in the vineyard and scattered in apartments. What about you?"

"I have them housed in that apartment building I purchased. What do we do about John?"

"What're you thinking?"

"It sounds like John and Mel are alone and pushing back against Torrio and Capone."

Ben muttered an oath. "Yeah, that sounds like John. It looks like Capone's taken over several of his bars."

"Why didn't he tell me?"

"He didn't tell me either; it was one of my drivers who noticed something was wrong. I think John wants us out of it, for our own protection."

"Well, he can't get away with that."

"I agree. I'll be on my way tonight. I'll take one of the delivery cars."

"After the club closes tonight, I'll catch the train and meet you there."

"See you soon."

"You too."

Jemma went to her door and called, "Lauren, come see me."

"Yes, boss."

She was putting her logs into the secret compartment in the floor that Jojo had set up for her. It was invisible to anyone in the office, and given Charlie's proclivity for invading her privacy, it was best to hide them. Lauren came into the office.

Jemma stood and said, "After we close tonight, I need to go to Chicago. Can you get tickets for me?"

"Of course." She hesitated. "When you're gone, who's in charge?"

"You know who. Charlie," Jemma replied. Lauren sighed. "I don't have time right now to discuss this particular topic."

"Yes, boss. Don't forget the special guests tonight."

"Yes, I have that on my calendar. I'll be in the room with them at midnight."

Lauren checked her watch. "I'll go get the tickets now."

"Keep my trip quiet for now," Jemma cautioned her.

"Does Charlie have to know? I could tell him you're locked in your office and don't want to be disturbed."

"I wish I could. Get going."

The tickets were purchased, and Jemma added them to her purse. "Tell Rocky I'll be ready to go after we close tonight."

"Yes, boss."

Everything was going well, and the club was swinging that night. A few minutes before midnight, Lauren stuck her head in. "It's time."

"On my way now." Jemma walked around the club, greeting the guests, and made her way to the entrance. She nodded at Casper and headed to the secret room. She opened the door and set up the bottles for the small party. It was only a few moments before her guest arrived. She opened several bottles and mingled with the private guests.

A hard rap sounded on the inside of the door. "86! 86!" rang out from outside the room. She clapped her hands. "Gentlemen, ladies, it's time to leave and exit onto 86th street."

They got the hint and headed out onto the street through the secret exit. The door closed quickly behind them. She stood by and looked around to make sure the secret room was hidden. Jemma poured herself a glass of wine to wait out the raid. **Boom!** The room rattled around her. They were ramming the hidden inside door! Someone had told them where it was! **BOOM!** The room rattled again. She stayed where she was and waited.

The door splintered, and with a final hit, it fell into the room. She stayed put and watched the agents pile into the room. They held hatchets and a battering ram that'd been used on the door.

"Who the hell do you think you are busting in my place like Tom Mix or William S. Hart?" she demanded.

"We got you," Agent Bonner said triumphantly. He was the same agent who had raided the tea a few months ago.

She held up her glass to him, "Bully for you," and moved it to her lips to drink it down in one gulp. She set the glass down on the barrel. "Are you here for more tea?" she asked.

"Take her into custody."

"I'll do it," came a familiar voice from behind the agent. It was Danny!

Suddenly, someone yelled, "FIRE!" Gunfire started popping, and the bottle she was holding shattered in her hand. "STOP!" Danny roared.

Bullets were still flying. Jemma was looking at the now shattered glass in her hand when she felt something push her back. Guns were lowered, and Danny rushed over to her. She'd slid down the wall and was sitting on the floor. Her face was pale and her expression blank.

He knew that look, but ignored it and placed his handkerchief against her bleeding shoulder.

"Going to put cuffs on me, copper?" she asked. His mouth tightened. Jemma realized she had started feeling lightheaded.

Lauren pushed her way in and ran over to her. She saw the bloody handkerchief. "What the hell happened?" she demanded. "We need to get her to the hospital."

"She's under arrest," Danny said. Lauren recognized him; he had been with Jemma outside the club.

Jemma's eyes were closed. Lauren shook her and said, "Jemma! Jemma!" She looked around frantically. "She won't open her eyes! Do something!"

Danny picked her up, and Lauren guided them out of the room. The agents began destroying the room. Barrels were being split open, and bottles were crashing on the floor.

Sorry, Jemma, Lauren thought. The inventory in that room had taken time to build. Only the most discernible wines and champagnes were kept there. *Who ratted us out?* she thought. She, Jojo, and Jemma were the only ones who knew that the room existed. Jojo wouldn't have talked; she was sure about that.

Danny put Jemma in the back of his car, and Lauren got in next to her. He slid behind the wheel. Another officer leaned in and said, "I'll follow you." He nodded and started the car.

"She awake?" Danny asked Lauren.

"I don't think so," Lauren said, holding Jemma tightly. "I saw you," she told Danny. "I saw you and Jemma talking one night outside the club."

"I'm Danny Nolan. I was her confidential informant on the force. I gave her tips on when a raid was going to come so she could be prepared."

"So, what happened tonight? Did you call her and let her know?"

"No," he said, "the police cut the phones off at the office; there was no way to get to her."

"Did you shoot her?"

"No," he said and pounded his hand on the wheel. "I don't know who yelled to start firing. Did you see anyone?"

"I didn't, but I have some thoughts about that," said Lauren.

"Any you can share?"

"No, not yet. I need to talk to Jemma first." Maybe he was on their side. "How did you know about the room where Jemma was located?"

"An informant let us know," he said.

"It wasn't you?"

"No, I wasn't aware that room existed until we got into the club."

"Jemma kept that quiet. It was for special guests only, and they never left through the club. It'd have to be someone close."

"Could it have been one of the special guests?"

"I don't think so. They were the rich and powerful; they had no reason to expose her."

"Then you have a mole."

"Yeah, that's my guess." Lauren didn't say who she suspected. It was the same person she suspected of getting Jemma shot.

Danny stopped the car at the hospital, got out, and opened the back door to pick Jemma up. A nurse ran up to him and called for a doctor. He ran over and waved for a gurney.

"Will she be okay?" Lauren asked the nurse.

"We'll examine her and let you know," the nurse told her. Danny laid her down carefully on the gurney, and the nurse and orderly began to wheel her away.

"Can you call Dr. Peter Kelly? He's her personal physician," Lauren asked.

"We'll give him a call," the nurse confirmed.

Bonner walked up to Danny and said, "We got her, Nolan, the boss lady herself. She don't look so tough now."

Danny would've liked to slam his fist into the man's face. He forced his hand open and walked over to join Lauren in the seating area.

"I need to call her lawyer, Lottie," Lauren said in a low voice, "but I don't want to leave her."

"Go call Lottie," he said in a similar tone. "I'll wait here."

"Come get me if you hear anything." He nodded. Lauren hurried to the nurse's station. She grabbed the phone and sat down on the floor. Dialing quickly, Lauren waited. A woman answered the phone. "Lottie?" she asked.

"No, this is Lissette, just a second. Lottie wake up, it's for you," said Lissette.

"What? Who is it?" Lottie yawned.

"It sounds like Lauren," Lissette said, handing her the phone.

Lottie put the receiver to her ear. "Hello."

"Lottie, this is Lauren."

"What's wrong?"

"We were raided tonight."

"Which precinct?" Lottie asked briskly, sitting up and swinging her legs onto the floor. "

"No, Jemma's at the hospital. They SHOT her!"

"Dammit, which hospital?"

"Manhattan Metropolitan Hospital."

"I'm on my way."

"They want to have an officer here outside her room."

"I'll see what I can do. Wait for me." Lottie hung up the phone.

"What happened?" asked Lissette, watching Lottie pull on pants and a long-sleeved shirt.

"They shot Jemma in a raid. I'm going to the hospital."

Lissette grabbed her coat and hat. "I'm going with you."

Lottie picked up her notebook and scribbled down what Lauren had told her. She picked up the phone again and called Chris. "Chris, this is Lottie. I'm on the way to the hospital."

"Are you hurt?"

"No. Jemma was shot in a raid."

"Do you need me there?" he asked.

"No, I have this. Check with our other clients; we might have more arrests tonight. The feds are going to try to make a point with her arrest. They want the clubs gone; they never trusted the no alcohol talk."

"Until now, they've been considered legal entertainment venues."

"It's 1921, and I warned her about the new law, that they'd be looking at more than just the bartenders."

"Prohibition's been good for business. Next, they'll go after Jimmy Durante's club."

"Now that'd be someone I'd like to represent."

"Do they know of John's involvement?"

"No, and even if they did, Jemma's clean. She's kept her books separate from his businesses."

"You've seen them?"

"I have," she said, loading her purse for the journey to the hospital. "Emma and Jeremy asked me to review them to make sure she was safe."

"That sounds like her godparents all right." Lottie could hear the grin in her partner's voice.

"And also, my aunt and uncle," she confirmed. "I'm going to make a stop at Judge Mayer to see if we can get her released."

"Hey, call if you need reinforcements."

"I will. It's time the law was tested."

"Will Jemma want to be part of that?"

"She's a strong lady." She hung up the phone. "Ready?" she asked Lissette.

"I am."

They started out. "Hang on, I forgot something." She ran upstairs and came back with an additional bag. "Now I'm ready."

CHAPTER 64

*B*onner and Danny sat in the waiting room. Lauren rejoined them. She muttered, "She's been notified." He didn't respond; he stared forward.

The nurse came out and came over to them. "She's in surgery; we must get the bullet out. Dr. Kelly is assisting."

"We'll wait," Danny told her.

"The doctor will come out with an update when the surgery's completed." She walked back to the double doors and went through them.

Bonner tapped Dan's shoulder. "You don't need to stay. You've lost custody here; this is a police matter now."

Danny didn't comment; he crossed his arms on his chest and stared at the double doors.

"Well, aren't you going to leave?" Bonner asked.

"No, I think I'll see this through."

Lauren glared at the man.

At that moment, Lottie and Lissette rushed in. "How is she?" she asked Lauren.

"She's in surgery. Doc Kelly's in there with them."

"What happened?"

"Jemma was in a back room tasting some of the near beer we had in storage." Lauren pointed her finger at Bonner. "He burst in and rushed to the back. Next thing I know, I hear gunshots, and when I run back, Jemma's on the floor with a bullet in her."

Lottie whirled around and stalked over to where Bonner and Danny were standing. "Who are you?" she demanded.

"I'm Agent Bonner. I'm the person in charge. And who are you?"

"Lottie Flannigan, Miss Hardison's attorney. We'll see if you're still in charge when I get through with you." She stalked back to Lauren and Lissette.

"Who's the other guy?" she asked Lauren under her breath.

"He says his name is Danny Nolan and that he was Jemma's informant in the agency."

"I knew she had one," Lottie confirmed. "I didn't know his name. Why didn't he warn her?"

"He said the police had turned off the phone lines so he couldn't call out."

"You trust him?"

"I don't know. He did help carry Jemma out and bring her here."

Lottie turned and stared at Danny, thinking.

It was more than two hours before Doc Kelly came out. Lauren stood. Lottie, Lissette, and Danny went with her.

"How is she, doc?" Lauren asked him.

"She made it through the surgery. She was lucky; it could've been much worse."

"Can we take her in?" Bonner asked.

"Take her where?" Kelly asked, confused.

"Jail."

"The hell you are!" Lottie snapped.

"She isn't going anywhere but a hospital room," Kelly told him firmly.

"Then I'll put an officer outside her room."

"You'll have to take that up with the nurses and the hospital administration." Kelly turned on his heels and left.

"Well, I'm going in. She needs to be in cuffs," Bonner said and pushed his way into the ward.

Danny grabbed him by the arm and spun him around. "She's just been shot. You don't have to treat her that way."

"You'd best mind your business. I'm here to do my job," Bonner said and shoved Danny back into the wall.

"You're not going anywhere near my client," Lottie snarled.

"I most certainly am. She broke the law."

"Oh, she did, did she? Well, let me tell you something…"

Lissette turned to Lauren. "You should try to see Jemma."

Lauren hugged her. "I will, thank you."

Lauren snuck down the hallway to the nurse's station. She asked a nurse, "Where's my friend?"

"The gunshot patient?"

"Yes."

"Fourth door on the left."

She nodded and started to run down the hallway. She hesitated and turned back to the nurse. "Can you delay them?"

"Yeah, I can do that. Go!"

Lauren looked back. Lissette smiled and mouthed, "Good luck." Then she turned back to watch Lottie argue with the agent. She ran to the room and went in. Jemma was in bed; she looked so small. "Oh, Jemma…" she said and touched her cheek.

Jemma didn't open her eyes. She mumbled, "Get Lottie."

"She's here. She's arguing with the agent in charge."

Jemma laughed, then moaned in pain. "That sounds like Lottie." She was quiet for a minute, then asked, "Who shot me?"

"I think we both know who gave that order."

Jemma muttered, "Charlie." She drifted off to sleep.

CHAPTER 65

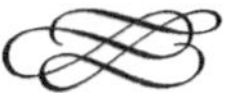

alifornia

Marisol watched Ben packing a bag. "The car's gassed up and waiting," she told him.

"Good, I need to be on my way soon."

"You think John's in trouble?"

He sat on the bed, bouncing the bag. "I do. And it's going to be messy."

"Is Jemma on her way?"

He nodded. "She'll be on the train late tonight." He stood again and started adding more clothes to his bag.

"Ben," Marisol hesitated. "I want to go with you."

"No, I don't know what I'm walking into."

"Then I should be there to back you up." He stayed silent. "I'm good with a gun."

"I'm aware of that, but do you think you should?" he asked, putting his hand on her belly.

"Yes, I do. We should be together. And," she continued, "we'll be able to go faster if I'm there to help drive."

He snapped his bag shut and headed toward the door. Marisol stayed where she was. He turned around and looked at her. "Well, what're you waiting for? Pack your bag."

She grinned. "I already did." She pulled her bag out of the closet. He shook his head and walked over to get it.

They walked downstairs together.

CHAPTER 66

hicago

"Everything's changing," John muttered, slamming his fists down on his desk.

"He wants to meet," Mel said in a low voice.

"Who?" John asked.

"Capone."

"Torrio's lackey?"

"Yes, he's taking over all of the bars now."

"Which ones?"

"North Side, West Side, and O'Donnell's, among others."

John scoffed. "Ah, none of those are as big as our operation."

"Boss, I think we should take the meeting." Mel had seen the burned-out establishments where meetings weren't taken.

"You think I'm scared of that two-bit punk?" John sneered. "Time was that they feared me and would've left town at just the thought of me. Ben and Jemma are right; things have changed."

"They've taken our gambling joints. That army of his just invaded."

John sat quietly, mulling over his options.

"Do we take the meeting?" Mel asked.

"We take the meeting."

"Who do you want in standby?"

"Clay's still here, along with a few others."

"Do we call Ben and Jemma?"

"I contacted them and told them not to come and to take care of our people. Did you put the signs up?"

"I did. The signs say that the businesses are closed due to illness."

"Good, that's good."

Mel hesitated and tried again. "Boss, wouldn't it have been better to compromise with Capone? Other owners have."

"What, and just hand over everything I've worked to build?" Mel stared back at him but didn't say anything. John sighed. "They'll take everything and turn it into something we don't recognize. I won't be part of their enterprise. Get Clay and the others to surround the location chosen for the meeting. We're not going down without a fight."

Mel knew better than to argue. If this was the final fight, he wanted to be there with John. *I'm sorry, Danny,* he thought. *I'd hoped we'd have more time.*

Mel contacted Clay and told him to stay outside. After that, he boarded up the windows as John wrote letters and put the final notes into his books. John carried them to the wall safe and locked them up. *At least that'll be there for the family. Jemma and Ben will take it over.*

Mel walked into the darkened space. "What now?"

John handed him a gun. "Now? We wait."

CHAPTER 67

Bullets from dozens of machine guns penetrated the wood covering the windows John and Mel huddled behind. "Well, I guess the meeting's started." John laughed, and he checked his gun. He sprang up, shot out the window, and dropped down. Bullets rained back in answer.

Mel stood, took aim, and fired. He dropped back down and looked at John. He'd slumped against the window. "Boss, you get hit?"

"It's nothing," John said, pulling himself up and firing his gun out the window. Mel watched the blood trail down John's normally pristine white shirt. John ducked down again. "I'm almost out of bullets," he said.

"Me too," Mel said, checking his gun. Bullets continued to fly into the room. "We ain't getting out of this, are we?"

"No, I don't think we are," John admitted.

"At least you got Jemma and Ben out before all of this started. Did you know this would happen?"

"I knew there was a high probability," John admitted. "Those two, they deserve a future."

"You made them think it was their idea."

"It was the only way." John smiled. He coughed, covering his mouth with his hand. He rubbed it on his shirt; the blood made a smeared trail.

They both rose and emptied their guns out of the window. The return fire knocked them back onto the floor.

"Boss?" Mel gasped looking at him. John's head was turned away from him. "Boss?" He placed a hand on John's chin and turned his head toward him. John's eyes were wide open and empty. John Harden was dead.

"JOHN!!!" Mel screamed out in agony and loss.

alifornia

Marisol was driving, and Ben said, "Slow down when we go through towns. We don't want to draw attention from the cops."

"That went surprisingly well," she commented.

"What went well?"

"Papa. He didn't scream or yell when I said I was going with you."

"No," he mumbled, "he didn't."

"What was that you gave him before we left?"

"Did I give him something?"

She frowned. "It was an envelope."

"Oh, that. It was just contact numbers, in case they need anything."

They drove for a while. "How long do you figure?" she asked.

"About two days with the slowdowns."

"And if the police try to stop us?"

"Given the inventory you wanted to bring with us?"

"Yes."

"We outrun them." She gripped the wheel and grinned at him. "For now, keep it reasonable," he cautioned.

"Ben, I think we need to change out drivers."

"Tired?" he asked, stretching his arms.

"Getting there," she admitted.

"Pull over."

She pulled the car off the side of the road and got out. He held the door for her and waited for her to get in, then walked around the car and got behind the wheel.

"There's a car coming up fast," she said, looking back. He got the car onto the road and gunned the engine. "Do you think it's the police?" she asked, hanging onto her seat.

"Maybe. It's more likely that other bootleggers are trying to get our goods or even take the car." He pushed the gas pedal further down.

"They're still there!"

"They must be bootleggers!"

She shouted, "They're catching up to us!"

"Not for long," He pushed the pedal down to the floorboard, and they took off like a shot.

She turned and saw lights coming closer. "They're back."

"We're going to change tactics. Grab your gun and get in the backseat." He kept the car at the same speed. Marisol climbed in the backseat, reached back for her shotgun, and loaded both barrels. "Wait for me to run them off the road!" he shouted. Ben slowed down and let the car pull up beside him.

He turned the wheel abruptly, hitting them hard, shoving them off the road. He slowed the car. As they went by, Marisol steadied the gun on her shoulder and shot both barrels. "Did you get them?" he asked as she climbed back into the front seat.

"I got their engine. I don't think they'll be following anytime soon."

"Good thing I decided to bring you along." He grinned at her.

"Oh, *you* decided." She grinned back. "Told you I could be helpful," she said, kissing Ben's cheek.

CHAPTER 69

s they drove along, Marisol asked, "What's he like?"

"John?" He stared ahead, gathering his thoughts. "Tough," he finally said.

"Do you call him grandfather?"

He laughed. "No. Jemma's the only one brave enough to do that. His only soft spot is for Jemma."

"Not his daughter?"

"He's protective of her, but Jemma's like a female version of him."

"What about you, are you like him?"

"I haven't had to be," he admitted. "Jemma's always been the leader."

"Why's that?"

"Family dynamics," he said simply.

"You're in charge of the California branch," she pointed out.

"Yeah, I'm wondering about the future, after Prohibition."

"You think the wine bricks will no longer be popular."

His mouth twisted. "Your father's right about that. The wine made from bricks or our grapes is okay if you're desperate, but not when the good stuff's legal."

"What're you thinking about for the future of the two brick vineyards?"

"You said it takes up to eight years to plant and get the good vines going."

"I did. Are you thinking about converting some of your grapes to Papa's?"

"We're making plenty of money, and I can separate acreage to begin thinking of the future."

"A legal future?" she asked. Marisol was aware of Ben's family and their business in Chicago and New York.

"That's the plan."

"And Jemma? Does she have a plan?"

"We haven't talked about it," he admitted.

"Maybe that should happen."

"Maybe."

"Have you told them about me?"

"Jemma knows."

"And John?"

He shook his head. "The time hasn't been right. He's fighting for everything he's built."

"He sent all of his employees and their families to California and to New York City. Does he have anyone there with him?"

"He has Mel. He's always been with John."

She settled back and waited to meet this complicated man.

hicago

"Wake up, Marisol." She felt someone push on her shoulder. "I'm awake," she said, opening her eyes. "Are we here?"

"Yeah," he said and pounded the steering wheel.

"What's wrong?" He pointed. She followed his finger. Police cars and policemen were lining the street. "What's going on?"

"That's where John's office is located."

"Ben, I think we need to see what's going on."

"I agree." He got out and met her around the front of the car. She took his hand; he gripped it hard. He didn't want to face this.

They walked over and tried to break through the line of policemen. An officer held his gun in front of him. "No one's allowed through."

"We're family."

The officer looked confused. "Wait here." He ran over to a

detective in a suit and whispered in his ear. The detective nodded and they walked over to Ben.

"I'm Detective Johnson. You're related to John Harden?"

"I'm his grandson."

"I believe he also had a daughter?"

"She's overseas with my father." It took a moment for Ben to realize what the man had said. "*HAD?*" Ben asked, his voice strained. Marisol gripped his hand tighter.

"There was a shootout here last night. Mr. Harden didn't survive."

"Was he alone?" he asked.

"We didn't find anyone with him."

Where's Mel? thought Ben. *He's always with John.*

Suddenly, they heard a loud **Boom!**

They looked toward the sound. "What was that?" Johnson yelled.

Another boom sounded closer to them.

"Sounds like bombs!" shouted a nearby officer. It finally quit, and they waited.

"Let's check it out, men." Johnson pointed toward the rising smoke.

In the confusion, Ben pulled Marisol back toward the gun-riddled establishment that used to be John's office.

"What's happening?" she asked as she carefully stepped over the piles of glass.

"I think it's Mel. He's getting payback."

"Do you think you should tell them?"

He shook his head. "This is how the business works. One side attacks; the other responds." He put his hands to his face. "I wonder where Jemma is? She should be here by now."

"Is there someone you can check with?"

He lifted his head. "Lottie. I don't want to call the club. Jemma had mentioned her assistant manager Charlie's behavior had gotten worse." He looked around and said, "Let's find a phone." She nodded and followed. He said, "There's several of the family's businesses near here." They went from one doorway to another. "I don't understand; everything's closed. He's shut everything down."

"Should we go somewhere else?"

"No, I can get in. Wait here." Ben went around the side of the building. After a few minutes, he appeared at the door and opened it for her. "There's a side window with a broken lock," he explained.

She went into the dark space. Ben hit the lights, and once it was illuminated, she could see the long bar and tables along the walls. "This is nice."

"I bought several places for John and had them set up before I left." He went behind the bar and picked up the phone. He dialed quickly. "Chris?"

"Yes. This is Ben. Is Lottie in?" He listened intently. "Jemma! Oh god, when? Is she okay?" He paused, waiting to deliver his news.

"John's been killed." Another pause, then, "All right, I'll wait here for her." He slowly put down the phone.

"What is it?" demanded Marisol.

"Jemma was shot last night during a raid." The color had drained out of his face.

"Shot! Is she okay?"

"They said it was a shoulder wound, and she'll be on her way here tomorrow. That's the earliest her doctor would release her."

"Was she arrested?"

"Yeah. Lottie has an appointment with the judge, she will try to get him to allow her to come due to the family death."

CHAPTER 71

ew York

Jemma slowly opened her eyes and blinked. "Where am I?" She turned to her left and saw Lauren asleep, curled up in a chair next to her. Someone squeezed her right hand; she looked to her right and saw Lottie. She was holding the doll they had fought over years before.

"Lottie?" she said, her voice husky.

Lottie leaned toward her. "Good, you're awake. I think this belongs to you." She tucked the doll in the bed next to her.

"You bitch. You had her all along," she said, touching the doll's face.

"Yeah, not my best moment." Lottie smiled. "She's yours now."

"She always was," murmured Jemma, looking at her. She tried to sit up.

"No, don't get up," Lauren warned her, straightening in her chair.

"Ow, shit!" Suddenly, she remembered. "I was shot," she exclaimed.

"You were."

"Why did they do that? I wasn't resisting."

"Someone yelled fire, and the officers did," Lauren told her.

"You were lucky it was just your shoulder," Lottie said.

"I don't feel lucky," Jemma complained, feeling the bandage on her shoulder. Her thoughts were getting cleaner. "Our stock!"

"Yeah, that's all gone," said Lottie.

"It could've been worse," Lauren told her. "You were right about keeping the inventory limited."

"We did lose some good bottles." Jemma grimaced. "In fact, they blew one right out of my hand," she remembered.

"Just before they shot you," Lauren confirmed.

"Oh no, I was supposed to be on a train to go to John. He needs me." Lottie looked over at Lauren, and she nodded. Jemma watched them. "What's going on?"

Lottie sighed and sat on the bed next to her. "There was another shoot-out last night. John was taken down."

She dropped back, and tears started down her face. "What about Ben?"

"He's there; he called this morning."

"What about Mel? He never leaves John's side."

"Ben's trying to locate him."

"Lauren," she said, reaching out her hand.

She grasped it and asked, "Yes, Jemma?"

"I need you to contact Agent Danny Nolan; he'll need to know."

"He helped me bring you here last night. He told me he was your informant. Is that true?"

"Yes. But he needs to know what happened to John."

"Why does he need to know that?" Lottie asked.

"Mel is his father."

"What?" Lottie was stupefied. "I didn't know Mel had a son."

"No one really does. John sent me to him. He's kept us out of trouble for years."

Jemma started struggling to get out of bed. "I need to get to Chicago."

Lauren and Lottie pressed her back. "No, you need to rest," Lauren told her.

"But you said it wasn't bad," she protested.

"In case you don't remember," Lauren stressed, "you had a bullet in you, and you had surgery. You will need to stay in bed."

"How long?"

Doc Kelly appeared in the doorway. "I won't approve any movement for two days."

"But, doc," she protested.

He shook his head and approached the bed. Lottie stood and got out of his way. "Lay back and let me take a look," he said. She followed directions, and he pulled back the bandage. "It'll take time to heal. Movement at this time will cause bleeding. Be patient."

"A family member died, and I need to go to Chicago."

He sat back and considered that. "By train?"

"Yes."

"In that case, I'll approve tomorrow, if you rest all today. I'll need to see you one more time." He left the room.

"Am I under arrest?" asked Jemma.

"Technically, you were," Lottie admitted. "I got with a sympathetic judge after I talked to Ben. He will allow you to travel as soon as possible."

She frowned. "Why was he so workable?"

"There's hundreds of people who were arrested in raids in the last few weeks," Lottie explained, "and they just don't have the space to keep them. There's also the fact that you were fired upon without reason."

"What happens then?"

"We prepare for court."

CHAPTER 72

"I packed your bag," said Lauren.

"Did you remember to add a funeral dress?" Jemma asked as Lisette pulled up her dress to fasten it in the back.

"I did; I packed some of everything in case you're there longer than expected."

"Thank you."

"All done," Lissette said.

"Look, Jemma," Lottie said, "you'll need to contact me as soon as you get there and when you figure out how long you're going to stay."

"I will." She looked over at the doll on the bed. She picked it up and handed it to Lottie.

"But I gave this back to you," she protested.

"She's on loan to you. Keep her safe for me."

Lottie hugged the doll to her. "She'll be waiting for you."

"Ugh," Lissette groaned, "she's so creepy."

Jemma laughed and hugged her friends goodbye.

CHAPTER 73

The train chugged away toward Chicago. *John's dead. What's going to happen now? Will the operations stay in Chicago? Who's in charge of the family? Will Ben and I have to relocate? What about their business in New York and California?* Jemma had all of these questions and so many more running through her mind.

"You're quiet," Danny said. He had shown up at the train station just before the train left. He told Jemma that he had quit his job and wanted to go with her to Chicago. She'd reluctantly agreed.

"Yes," she said, looking out the window; the scenery was rushing by. "So many decisions will have to be made."

"Have you talked to Ben?"

"Before we left, he was looking for Mel."

"Pop's going after Capone." He'd heard about the bombs. He had no doubt; it was his father. "He's hitting him where it hurts, blowing up his bars."

"That won't fix anything."

"No, it won't. It might make things worse." He stopped and sighed. "We need to talk."

She nodded and looked him in the eye. "Did you lead the raid?"

"Yes, I volunteered. My goal was to get you out safely."

"Well, that didn't work out," she said, absently rubbing her shoulder.

He watched her movement and his mouth twisted. "No, it didn't. When we got there and got ready to go in, Bonner took charge and led the raid."

"Any idea who gave the order to shoot me?"

"I questioned my guys and the officers who were there; we don't know who gave the order. Several young officers made a mistake."

"Some mistake," she muttered. She looked at him. "You quit your job."

"I did. After I found out you were going to be okay."

"Are you sure it was the right time for you to leave it?"

"Are you asking for me or for you?"

"A little of both," she said honestly.

"When I saw that you had been shot, I just couldn't deal with you being hurt and me not being able to be there with you."

"When did you get so emotional?"

"When did you get so cold?" he countered.

She smiled and sat back. "I'd say there were times I wasn't cold to you."

He barked a laugh. "You have a point there." He reached over for her hand. She didn't pull away. "I didn't give you away and I want to help find out who did."

"What're your plans from here?"

"You mean for work?"

"I do."

"I don't know," he admitted.

"I do," she said thoughtfully.

hicago

The train stopped. Jemma stood and pulled on her hat. She started to pull her bag from the overhead rack.

"Stop." Danny reached up and took her bag for her. "Take it slow. You haven't fully recovered." They followed other passengers down the hall and out onto the train station platform.

"Jemma!"

She looked over and saw Ben. Emma and Jeremy were with him, and a young woman she didn't know. She hurried over to them. "Slowly, please," Danny told her. He had to run to keep up with her. They reached the group, and each person hugged her lightly.

Ben asked with a frown, "Who's this?"

She stepped back and took Danny's free hand. Emma and Jeremy looked at each other when they saw this. "This is Danny Nolan; he's Mel's son."

Everyone was shocked at that. As many years as they had known Mel, they'd never known he'd had a son.

Jeremy spoke first. "Jeremy Tilden," he held out his hand, "and this is Emma Evans."

"*The* Emma Evans?" Danny asked. "Pop's told me stories about you. It's nice to meet you." They shook hands. Emma smiled at him.

"Welcome and thanks for accompanying Jemma," Jeremy said.

"I'm glad Jemma allowed me to," he said simply. He looked at Ben. "Have you found Pop?"

"Not yet. We'll talk later."

Jemma looked at the girl standing by Ben and asked, "Are you Marisol?"

"I am," she said, stepping forward.

"It's lovely to meet you."

"Thank you; you too. I wish it were under better circumstances."

She stepped back. "What next?"

"We're going back to the house," Ben told her.

She looked at Emma and Jeremy. "Will you both be there?"

"We'll be there," Emma said. "We need to discuss how to find Mel."

"Have Mama and Papa been notified?" Jemma asked Ben as they walked to the cabs.

"Yes, it'll be some time before they can get home." She nodded. This wasn't how she wanted to come back.

The mood was somber in the cab. Jeremy took her hand in his and held it tightly. She leaned into him. The group arrived and entered the great ornate house where John had lived. Danny noticed Jemma's face had lost all of its color. "I think you should sit."

She put a hand to her head. "I wouldn't mind that."

Jeremy said, "Let's move to the sitting room."

They headed into the sitting room and sat down. "How're you feeling?" Emma asked her.

"A bit sore," Jemma admitted.

A maid walked in and asked, "Can I bring tea and cakes?"

"Yes, please, Ruth," Ben said.

As they were eating, Emma got to business. "First things first. We need to discuss Mel." She pulled out a notebook and a pencil to take notes and observations.

Jemma asked, "What's the damage so far?"

"Five of Torrio's bars have been blown up. Three in the first day and two more in the next two days," Jeremy said.

"Has anyone been killed?" Danny asked her, his voice strained.

"Not so far," Emma said.

"You know Capone's going to respond," Jeremy said, looking at Ben and Jemma. "You won't be safe here."

"We need to stop Mel," Jemma told them.

Danny looked at his hands. "I might know where he is."

"Where?" Ben and Jemma demanded.

"My grandmother had a house in the area. Pop kept it after she died."

"Are you sure?" Emma asked him. "We don't have records for that."

"No, you wouldn't. Pop paid people off to keep it in her name."

Ben stood up. "We don't need to be involved in a gang war! Chicago's a mess of gangs and crime."

"John fought to the end to keep the family here," Jemma told him.

"You aren't John," Danny said.

"No, you're right. We've never wanted to continue operations here," she said.

Ben nodded. "We have plans to move the business forward, in a mostly legal way."

Emma quirked an eyebrow at him. "Mostly legal?"

Jemma smiled at her. "Yes, mostly legal. But Prohibition has to end first." She stood and pulled out a cigarette; she tapped one on her case and lit it. "When do we go look for Mel?"

"You don't," Danny told her.

"Then who?" she asked.

"Me. He's my father and my responsibility."

Ben said, "No, we can't allow you to go on your own."

"Why? Do you think he'll hurt me?"

"I think he's a bit unstable due to his grief. Let Ben go with you," Jemma pleaded.

"All right, but let me take the lead."

Jeremy said, "Give us about an hour, and we'll set up transportation for you."

"Thank you," Danny said.

"We'll wait for you here, Jeremy," said Ben. "I need to get something upstairs. Marisol, would you like to join me?" She nodded and followed him up the ornate staircase to their room. He pulled on his jacket and grabbed a gun out of the top desk drawer. He checked to make sure it was loaded before he stuck it in his belt.

"Do you think you'll need to use that?" she asked, pressing her lips together in a firm line.

"I hope not, but I don't want to be unprepared."

"Ben, maybe you shouldn't go," she said hesitatingly. "He's Danny's father."

"Marisol, Mel's family. I'm as close to him as I was to John, closer than my own father. I'll be there for him. Can you understand that?"

"Yes, but I'll still worry."

"Come here." He pulled her to him. "Stay here with Jemma."

"I will."

He lowered his head and kissed her softly. A knock sounded on the door. He let her go reluctantly and went to open it.

"You ready?" asked Danny, his voice low.

"Yes."

Dan looked over at Marisol. "Jemma asked if you could join her downstairs."

Marisol picked up a book. "I'll walk you down."

The three moved downstairs. "Did you get Jemma to rest at all on the way here?" Ben asked.

Danny looked over at Ben. "Have you ever told Jemma what to do?"

Ben laughed suddenly. "You are right about that."

Jemma heard them coming down and met them in the entry-way. "What's so funny?"

Danny kissed her head and said, "Nothing."

There was a knock on the door. "I'll get it," said Ben. He came back to the sitting room with Emma and Jeremy following behind.

Jeremy said, "We have the route mapped out."

Emma laid out the map. "We have a car parked a few blocks away. You two will take that one. Jeremy and I'll be the decoy."

"Find him," Jemma told them.

"We will," Danny promised.

"Can we convince him to go to California or New York?" she asked.

"We'll have to leave that to him. He'll feel out of control as it is."

"Agreed," Jemma said. Ben nodded. Marisol moved beside Jemma.

Jeremy said, "I need to borrow your coat, Ben." Ben retrieved it for him. He put it on and raised the collar. "Ready?" he asked Emma. She nodded, pulled on her coat, and wrapped a scarf around her face.

"You two head out now," Emma told them. "Here are the keys." She handed them to Danny.

Ben and Dan went out the back, and Emma and Jeremy went out the front.

"You think they'll be followed?" Marisol asked Jemma.

"I bet we're being watched," she commented.

"We are? Where?" Marisol started to go to the window.

"Don't go to the window."

Marisol stopped. "What now?"

"We wait."

CHAPTER 75

Ben and Danny crouched down and stayed in the shadows. "Over there," Ben pointed.

Danny followed him, and they got into the car. Danny would drive them to his grandmother's house. The planned route was far longer than it should've been, but it'd be safer.

"How long since you've seen Mel?" Ben asked.

"A few months. He'd been able to get to New York to see me occasionally."

"I didn't know. I'm glad you've been able to see him."

"Yeah, me too."

"What're you planning to do once we get there?"

"Initially, try not to get shot."

Ben laughed. "Sounds like a plan."

They drove deep into the country, and the trees became more and more dense. "You know this area?" Ben asked him.

"I was raised here by my grandmother. Pop said it was safer."

"What about your mother?"

"She died when I was born."

"I'm sorry."

"It was a long time ago."

They pulled up and looked at the house. "He'll be watching."

"From the house?"

"Not likely. Just get out slowly with your hands in the air."

Ben followed his instructions and got out.

"Pop!" Danny called.

"Mel," added Ben, "we're here to see you."

A voice came from behind them. "Danny, Ben."

They whipped around. Danny had been right; Mel was definitely not in the house.

"Pop, we need to talk," Danny said.

"I assumed as much." Mel carried his gun loosely in his hand. "Come into the house." In the kitchen, Mel poured them coffee. "What do you want?" he asked them.

"We want to know what happened," said Ben.

"Torrio's stooge, Capone, is what happened. He started taking over our businesses. He initially acted like he would just come in as a silent partner."

"Can't imagine John liking that," observed Ben.

"No, he knew we were going under; he wanted to go out fighting."

"I'm glad you got out, Pop."

"No, I survived, no thanks to that rat Capone. John wasn't so lucky."

"When did all of this start?" Ben asked him. Jemma had wanted to know if John had had this in mind from the beginning of Prohibition.

"It was going on when you and Jemma first left."

"Jemma called that," said Ben.

"Yeah, she's a lot like him. He made it look like it was your idea to get away from Chicago."

"Protecting the family until the end."

Danny asked, "Pop, did you know the attack was coming?"

"We had word that Capone wanted to meet. We started shifting people out of town; we wanted to limit who could be hurt. That's why he sent his people to you and Jemma. He knew you'd take care of them."

"What's left of the business?" Ben asked.

"We still have all the bars; the gambling establishments were overridden by Capone's men."

"What about the money?" asked Ben. He and Jemma had been sending a cut of their profits. It should've been a significant amount.

"It's here with me." Mel left the room and returned with a bag stuffed with cash. "He wanted you to take it and make sure that it helps the other families and sets them up for their new lives."

"Pop, you planning to blow anything else up?" Danny asked him.

"I'm done. That last one, I waited a little too long."

"What happened?"

"There was someone in the building. I got them out before the building blew. Next time, I might not be so lucky."

"It's time to get you out of Chicago," Dan said.

"What are you both thinking?"

"Your choice, California or New York."

"Capone was born in New York, and he still has contacts there; it might be too hot for me there. California."

"California, it is," said Ben. "I have an idea, if you're open to it."

"I am."

CHAPTER 76

"Will Mel stay put until we move him?" Ben asked Danny as they drove back.

"He will. He could jeopardize the family if he continues; he knows John wouldn't want that."

Ben thought about that all the way home. They dropped off the car where they'd picked it up and snuck back to the house. The sun was setting, offering them the cover they needed.

They went through the back door. Ruth turned the corner and screamed when she saw them. "It's okay, Ruth," Ben said.

"Sorry, you scared me to death," she said with a hand to her chest. "Go wash up. Dinner will be on the table soon."

"Thanks. Where's Marisol and Jemma?"

"We're here," Jemma said from the doorway. "We heard the scream."

Ben walked over and kissed Marisol. Dan held out his hand to Jemma. She took it. "Are you okay?" she asked him.

"Yeah, it was good to see him in one piece."

"Come into the sitting room and tell us what happened."

They followed and shared Mel's plans. "California, how do we get him there?" Marisol asked.

"I have an idea," said Ben. "I need to make a phone call." He excused himself and went to the study.

"Any idea what he is thinking?" Danny asked Jemma.

"Yes, I think so."

He came back. "I've worked it out."

"Let me guess?" asked Jemma.

Ben smiled at her. "Sure."

"Jean?"

"Yes." He laughed. "We'll fly him out of here."

"How?" Marisol asked.

"We basically need an empty field so she can land and then take off."

Dan said, "There's a place near grandmother's house."

"Get me the coordinates, and we'll set it up."

Dan provided them, and Ben called Jean back. When he returned to the group, he told them that she'd be on her way in a few days.

Dan said, "I'd like to go spend some time with Pop before you get him out of town."

"Emma and Jeremy said the car is yours for however long you need it," said Jemma. "When will you leave?"

"Tonight. I want to tell him the plan and have him ready to go."

She nodded and walked over to him. She brushed his hair back on his forehead. "Come back to me after you see him off."

"I will," he said in a low voice.

He took his bag and made his way to the car. The path was familiar, even in the dark. He drove back to his grandmother's and waited. "Pop, it's Danny."

"Come on up," Mel called. He met his son on the porch. He grabbed him in a bear hug, and they stood together for a few minutes. "I'm glad you came back."

"Me too, Pop. Me too."

Later, Danny told him the plan over dinner. "An airplane!"

"Jean, Patrick's wife, is a pilot and is on her way here."

"Flying? Who woulda thought at my age." Mel shook his head in wonderment.

CHAPTER 77

After dinner that evening, Jemma, Ben, and Marisol had gone back to the sitting room to wait for Danny.

"I was able to get a telegram to Mom and Dad," Ben said.

"And?"

"They'll be here in another week."

"And when they get here?" Ben asked.

"You know they aren't involved in the business," Jemma pointed out.

"Are they safe, though? I'm worried they could be used as leverage against us."

"Do you think they'd relocate to New York or California?" Marisol asked.

"Hmmm. That won't go well," muttered Ben.

"Okay, we'll wait for Mom and Dad to get here, we'll bury John, and then we'll make some decisions," Jemma said.

"Will they be safe here? If we can't convince them to leave?" he asked.

She tapped her cigarette. "We have to make sure they're safe, no matter where they call home."

"And how do we do that?"

"Let me think about it."

Marisol took the hint and said, "I'll notify Papa that we'll be a few more weeks."

"Tell him to call if anything comes up," said Ben.

"I will." She leaned down and kissed him, then walked out and shut the door behind her.

"Jemma, what're you thinking? Something dangerous?" he guessed.

"You know me so well," she murmured. "It's time for us to meet with Capone."

"Meet Capone! Who?"

"Me." He looked at her nonplussed. "It'd be a surprise," she said, "something he wouldn't expect. A woman who wants to talk business."

"Doesn't he have women working as managers?"

"I've heard that he used to have women run some of his brothels," she commented.

Ben frowned. "Has that changed?"

"Prohibition's taking all levels of leadership from women," she said. "Most of us are being phased out."

"Are you strong enough to do this?" he asked.

She moved her shoulder and grimaced a bit. "It's getting better, and I should be good to go to the meeting."

"When?"

"Our timetable is Mom and Dad's arrival in a week, then we hold the funeral the day after. Then we schedule the meeting with Capone."

Marisol knocked, and Jemma called, "Come in." She sat with them on the couch. "We'll keep the funeral small. Just family, no outsiders."

"Will your mother be unhappy that you're planning this without her?" asked Marisol.

Ben laughed, and Jemma joined him. "No, Mama has no interest in planning anything. She's usually taken care of.

John was overprotective of her and didn't want her worried."

"So, nothing like you or Ben, I'm guessing."

"No, nothing like us," Ben said. Jemma nodded in agreement.

Jemma glanced at the phone. "Now that we have a date, I need to let Lottie and Lauren know when I'll be back."

Jemma excused herself, and Marisol sat talking quietly to Ben.

She made the first call to Lottie. Then she called the club. She frowned, hung up, and dialed again. Frustrated, she slammed the phone down.

"What's wrong?" asked Ben. He and Marisol stood in the doorway of the study.

"I can't get through to the club."

"Why not try Charlie?"

"I'd rather talk to Lauren."

"Is Lottie able to go by and check on things?"

"She said she was going to court with another client; I didn't want to bother her. The club's closed until after my trial. It should be fine." She kept frowning at the phone.

"Call Charlie," Ben urged her.

"I don't want him to know my schedule. He tries to run my business too much as it is."

"Why not let him go?"

"Lauren's ready, and that'd leave me with an open spot."

"I heard Dan's unemployed."

"So he is."

All four of them were there when the plane landed. "Okay, Mel, it's time for you to go," called Jemma.

Jean had the requested gasoline; Ben went to help her get it fueled up. When they were done, she walked over to them.

Mel's eyes widened. "I've seen your movies," he said, starstruck.

"Aw, thank you. You must come to the set and watch one being made," Jean said.

"I… I'd like that," he replied, grinning and continuing to stare at her.

Jemma leaned to whisper in Danny's ear, "I think he's a fan."

"Boggles the mind. I didn't know he had any outside interests."

Mel hugged Ben, Danny, and Marisol. He looked at Jemma. "You're the boss now. Take care of our family."

"You know I will." She hugged him. "Thank you for looking out for John all these years."

Mel stood back and wiped his eyes. "Bye, boss."

Jean led him easily to the cockpit. They both climbed in and started the plane. "Out of the way!" she called. They stood back and watched them take off.

"One less problem," Ben said.

"Now to go pick up the other one," Jemma replied.

"Which is that?" asked Dan.

"Our parents. You and Marisol head back to the house. We'll meet you there," she said.

Marisol and Dan took one car. Ben and Jemma took the other.

As he drove, Ben looked at her. "I'm not looking forward to this."

"Me either."

The train station was their next stop. They arrived and parked. "Deep breath," Ben told her.

"You too," she said. "There they are."

Ben looked toward a woman and a man descending the train. Jemma and Ben rushed over to them. The woman was balancing a large box and trying to keep her wide hat on her head.

"Catherine, move forward. People want off the train."

"I'm trying, Sam," she dithered, moving the box and trying to see around her hat.

Ben grabbed her box, Emma took her mother's arm, and they guided her off the train.

She lifted her hat; it'd slid over her eyes. "Oh, Jemma." She looked at her daughter and wrinkled her nose. "That's what you choose to wear when you come to pick us up? And what happened to your hair? Your neck is all wrong for that haircut." She looked around. "Now, where is…" She saw Ben. "Oh, Benji, I missed you."

He waved back at her and said, "Dad! Welcome home." He ran over to help him with bags and wrapped canvases.

"Oh, thank you." Sam handed them over. "How're things here?"

Ben knew it wasn't a question he wanted the answer to, so he said, "Good. We have set up everything, and the house is organized for you."

He nodded and said, "Mom was concerned she'd have to plan the events."

"Everything's already organized."

They joined Jemma, and she kissed her father on the cheek. "It's good to see you both."

"We're blocking traffic," Ben said. "Why don't we go home and talk there?"

"How far is it to the car?" Catherine asked. "Can I just wait here and you come pick me up?"

"Ben parked close, Mom," Jemma told her.

"Oh, all right, but if I break a heel, I'm going to be upset."

They followed Ben to the car, and once they were loaded in, the conversation turned to all about their travels. Sam and Catherine never asked about John. When they got back, Ben and Jemma were left at the car with a mountain of luggage and canvases. Ben said, "They haven't changed."

"Mom's changed," she said.

"How so?"

"Let's see, she only complained about my clothes and my hair. She didn't say anything about my weight."

Ben sighed. "I expect they'll be planning their next trip for the day after the funeral."

"It'll be easier for us if they do."

Dan and Marisol came out of the back of the house and walked down the driveway. Dan asked, "Can I help?"

"Please," said Jemma. They all picked up bags and canvases and moved them inside. Jemma saw Ruth. "Mom and Dad are here. Please bring out the coffee and cakes. And, Ruth," Ruth turned back to her, "please make sure the coffee and cakes are fresh. You know how Mom is."

Ruth grimaced, "Yes, ma'am," and headed back to the kitchen. She knew exactly how Jemma's mom was.

The group trudged upstairs to their parents' room. "How much do you think we should tell them about John?" Jemma asked Ben.

Ben plopped on the bed. "They won't want to hear about anything to do with the business or about John."

"Why not?" Marisol asked. Her parents were key to their business. She couldn't imagine them not being actively involved.

"Mom distanced herself from John's world a long time ago," said Jemma.

Ben continued with, "Jemma was abducted when she was a few months old. Mama never recovered; she blamed John and his profession."

"John did what he could for her. He downsized his operations to just Chicago. He wanted her happy."

"How were you found?" Dan asked Jemma.

"Jeremy and Emma are Pinkerton detectives; they went undercover in a brothel and found a kidnapping ring. I was found left alone in a closet."

"Oh my," said Marisol, looking at her with wide eyes. "Did they get the bad guys?"

"The other children and I were returned to their homes."

"Some of them didn't go home," Ben reminded her.

"Why not?" asked Marisol, thinking of their baby.

"Some of the families didn't want the damaged children back."

"That's horrible; they're awful people."

"Yes. Emma and Jeremy helped them get settled with families who wanted them. They still see them occasionally."

"When Emma and Jeremy took me to John, he got me back to Mom and Dad."

"And your relationship with Emma and Jeremy?" asked Dan. "You seem close."

"They're our godparents. They've been in our lives ever since and have treated us like their own family."

Marisol clapped her hands. "I get it now! Jemma—Jeremy and Emma." She laughed.

"From what I hear, John's face was a sight when he was told about my name change."

"We might as well go down," said Ben. The four made their way downstairs.

Catherine could be heard laughing.

"That's just odd," murmured Marisol to Dan.

"I agree."

They went in, and Catherine called out, "Jemma, Benji, introduce us to your friends."

"Mom, this is Marisol," Ben introduced his girlfriend.

"Are you Mexican, dear?" Catherine asked.

"Mom!" Ben warned his mother.

"Uh, yes. My family's from Mexico. Is that a problem?"

"Oh, no. It's fine." Catherine looked at her and wrinkled her nose. "Putting on some weight, haven't you, dear?"

"MOM!" Jemma and Ben yelled at the same time.

"What? I was just curious." She looked at Dan. "And who are you?"

"This is Dan," Jemma said.

"And what do you do?" Catherine asked.

"I used to be a federal agent."

"A copper? Jemma, you brought a copper home?" She laughed. "Oh, your grandfather must have been *so* happy." Ben had to restrain Jemma from attacking her. "Sit, sit. I'm Catherine, and this is my husband, Sam. Have you been here long?" she asked Marisol.

Marisol frowned, and Jemma answered for her. "They're here to accompany us to the funeral."

"Oh yes, I suppose that's coming up," Catherine said, waving her handkerchief around.

Sam asked, "Will it be, um, crowded?" What he meant was, would John's associates be there?

"No," Jemma said. "John sent everyone to me and Ben. It'll only be us, Emma, and Jeremy."

"Oh, that's nice. I'd like to see them again." Catherine clapped her hands. "It'll be a little party. I'll have Ruth get something together for them."

Ruth walked in and set out the coffee and cakes. Everyone picked up one of each and started eating and drinking.

"Ruth, dear, we're going to be having some guests after the funeral. Please make sure we have plenty of everything. And make sure it's fresh, will you? You're a dear. Mwa!" Catherine kissed the air in Ruth's direction as the woman left the room.

"Mom, aren't you sad John's gone?" Jemma asked.

"Now, Jemma..." Sam started.

"No, Dad," said Ben. "I'd like to know the answer to that question."

"Well," Catherine said huffily, "I don't know why you put me on the spot like this. Can't we just be pleasant? "

"Pleasant, Mom? *PLEASANT!* John was shot, so many times. So many it was hard to identify him," Jemma fumed.

Sam grimaced and sat back. He looked like he was going to be sick. "Well, I didn't need to know that," Catherine argued.

"Yes," Ben said, "I think you do. What do you think pays for all of your expenses?"

"Well, I..." She looked at Sam.

"And who'll be expected to pay in the future?" asked Jemma.

"This is *not* what I expected," Marisol whispered to Dan.

"It has taken a turn," he responded.

"And we have a front row seat," she said, gleefully taking a large bite of cake.

"Oh, you and Ben will take care of things, I'm sure," Catherine said, waving her handkerchief at them.

"If you remember, John downsized the operations because of your preferences."

"But you and Ben are making money."

"We have employees to be paid and businesses to run."

"Surely there's money left for me from John?" she said.

Jemma nodded. "There is some."

"Good, that's all settled then," Catherine said, relieved.

"It won't be enough to pay for your extensive travels," Ben pointed out.

"Then what'll we do?" Catherine moaned.

"Think she'll swoon?" whispered Marisol, taking a sip of her tea.

"Five bucks says yes," Danny whispered back.

"You're on." Marisol nodded and turned back to the show.

Catherine sat gracefully on the settee and rested her head, eyes closed breathing deep.

"Dammit." Marisol reached into her pocket and gave Danny the money. She caught Ben's eye, and he winked.

"You'll have a home either in New York or California," Jemma told her. "We'll sell the one here, along with the businesses."

"Sell our home?"

"Mom, you and Dad are hardly ever here."

"Yes, but it's always home. It's where they finally brought you back to me, Jemma."

"Oh, there it is," Jemma said, disgusted.

"There what is?" her mother asked.

"The manipulation to get your way. John fell for it every time. Well, guess what, that doesn't work on me. It's time to let those things go."

"You don't have to be so nasty about it," Catherine whined.

"I think we'll go to California," Sam said with a firm voice. "It'll be good for painting."

"You think so?" Catherine asked. "Will I be able to take things from the house?"

"Mark the items you want, and we'll have them shipped to you," said Ben.

"Fine," Catherine said. "Let's go, Sam. Tear some paper for me."

They left the room. Ben looked at Jemma. "Well, that went better than I expected." Jemma laughed and punched him in the arm. "What made you tell her you were selling the house?"

"We have to get them to a safe location, and I don't think they'd survive for long in Chicago. Plus, I think we do need to sell all of this. Capone's going to be a thorn in everyone's side, and the sooner we get out, the better."

The four sat enjoying their cakes, watching Sam and Catherine run from room to room. "Betting on our family?" Ben asked Marisol and Danny, his expression neutral.

"Really?" asked Jemma. "What were the stakes?"

"Five dollars," volunteered Danny.

"And what was the bet?" she demanded.

"That your mom would swoon."

Jemma cackled. "That was a guaranteed win. You were a patsy, Marisol."

"Yeah, I'll know better next time."

he Funeral

"What's with all the flowers?" Danny asked, walking around. "I thought you were keeping this simple."

"Capone sent them." Jemma's mouth twisted. "Mom will love it; she'll think they're for her."

"Will you or Ben say anything?"

"No, I don't think so. Father Casey will give us some nice words. John always made sure he donated to the church."

She heard a noise at the door, and she turned around. Emma and Jeremy walked in. Behind them came Tim and Dora, Jake and Ethyl, Ethan and Savannah, Thomas, Clair and their daughter, Tony, Peggy and their daughter. Jemma even saw some of Emma's uncles from her family's bakery. Bringing up the rear were Ellis, Abigail, Cole, and Amy.

Jemma ran to them, crying and hugging everyone she could reach. She was so happy; they were her family. When Ben and Marisol entered, he joined the hugging party, too.

After everyone finished, they took their seats. At that moment, Catherine and Sam walked in. Catherine held a handkerchief to her face and was loudly snuffling. As she walked down the aisle, she greeted Emma's family. Jemma just rolled her eyes.

"I won a bet this morning," Marisol whispered in her ear.

"What was it?"

"That Catherine would be head to toe black."

"Yeah, the veil really capped things off," Jemma said with a shake of her head. "How much did you win?"

"Ten, this time." Marisol smiled.

"Danny, really? I'm disappointed in you."

He hung his head and said, "I thought she might wear a bright color."

Father Casey made his way up and said nice things about the money that'd been paid and what it'd been used for.

"Expect a pinch on the way out," Ben warned Jemma and Marisol.

"Yeah, he tried to corner me on the way in," Jemma replied. "I'll give him a final payment when John's buried."

After the ceremony, they said their goodbyes to Emma, Jeremy, and her family. They wouldn't be going to the graveside service.

The casket was moved by the men of the church, and the small group followed to the carriage. The graveyard was nearby, and the family followed slowly in two cars. A small service was held there. Catherine was chattering away about who was at the funeral and who wasn't and other inconsequential things as she got in the car.

"You know," Jemma stated, "I think I'll stay behind and confirm some things with the priest."

"Me too," Ben said.

"Count us in," said Marisol for her and Dan.

"Oh well, more for us. Come home when you can. Oh, Jemma, be careful. You know what the weather can do to your complexion. Especially at your age. Ta-ta," Catherine said.

Ben had to restrain Jemma from attacking her. Again.

He looked searchingly at Jemma. "What would you like to do now?"

"I'd like to sit around and talk about John and what he meant to us." He nodded. They looked at Marisol and Dan.

"I'd like to stay," Marisol replied.

"Me too," Dan said.

Marisol said, "I'd like to hear more about him."

They walked back over to where John's coffin had yet to be lowered into the ground. They sat in the chairs, and Dan asked, "What was he like?"

"He was a gangster in every sense of the word," said Jemma.

"Yeah, he'd slowed down after we came along," Ben said. "He reduced his operations. I think he planned to eventually dissolve everything."

"Until we started to show an interest in the business," Jemma reminded him.

"And Mom and Dad had started traveling."

"Mom disconnected from him after I was brought back home. She didn't want anything to do with him. She wanted his money but nothing else. She thought she deserved it after what happened to me. Ben and I loved the business. We worked for John in the joints, even when we were little."

"Well, there were times when Jeremy and Emma stepped in," Ben added, "and we'd stay with their family for long stretches. They wanted balance for us."

"Emma and John," Jemma murmured, "now that was a complicated relationship."

"You mentioned they rescued you after you were kidnapped."

"Yeah," Ben said, "but their relationship began much earlier than that."

"John was involved in the death of Emma's mother," Jemma explained.

That shocked Marisol and Dan into silence.

"After that, he went to prison," Ben told them. "Emma was the one who actually got him sent to prison the first time."

"John was able to run his business from jail, even better than before," said Jemma. "Everyone thought locking him up would stop him; it only made him stronger."

"That's when Pop became his assistant," Dan put in.

"His most trusted man." Jemma smiled at him.

"What kind of enterprises was he involved in?" Marisol asked.

"You name it, John was involved in it. Gambling became his number one thing. Like I said, he downsized after the kidnapping," Jemma explained.

"Was he happy?" Marisol said.

Ben smiled. "I like to think so; he seemed settled."

"Until Capone," Jemma snarled.

"Capone wrecked John's world. He wasn't used to competition. When he was in his prime, Capone would never have taken him down," Ben said proudly.

Jemma stood and glared at his casket. "He should've called us; he should've involved us in the takedown."

"No, he wanted us gone. Mel told me that when we found him," Ben told her.

"He knew all the way back then," she murmured.

"He knew that it was a possibility, and he wanted us to start our own businesses."

"Does that make you the boss?" Ben teased her.

Jemma watched the casket being lowered. "Mel said I'm boss now, so I guess I am," she said and dropped the flower she was holding into the grave.

"It's time to go back," said Ben.

"To the house," she muttered.

"No, back to our businesses. We have a family to support now."

CHAPTER 80

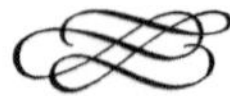

"Give it to me," Danny demanded.

"What? I don't have anything," Jemma said, her hands on her hips. He just held out his hand and waited. Ben hid his grin; not many people could call out his sister. She glared at him and finally pulled a pistol out of the back of her skirt.

Danny took the gun from her. "And?" She sighed and reached down to pull out the knife strapped to her thigh. "Is that all?" She picked up her purse and handed it to him. He took out a small handgun.

"I'll drive you over and wait out front."

"Hey, sis," Ben said.

"Yes?" she said, absently pulling on her hat.

"Don't call him Scarface. He doesn't like it."

"Interesting."

CHAPTER 81

"**D**o you have any weapons?" Capone asked her.

"You want to search me?" she asked. He didn't get up; she continued to stand. "We need this war to end," she stated.

"That's easy; give him to me."

"We've taken care of that problem for you."

Capone took a sip of his drink and set it down carefully. "Permanently?"

"Yes."

"What do you want in exchange?"

"We want assurances that the family we have here won't be dragged into this war."

"You'll close out all of the business?"

"For a price. We also want to be reimbursed for the business you've already taken."

He nodded. "And that'll put an end to the hostilities?"

"Yes."

"Sure, you don't want to stick around and run them for me?"

"I have other interests."

"If you're sure."

"I am."

Capone waved to Frank at the door. "Bring the box, Frank." Frank picked it up and took it to the table and placed it in front of Capone. Capone opened the box and pulled out stacks of cash. "I think you'll find that sufficient."

Jemma picked up a stack and flipped quickly through it. She opened her purse and dropped it and the other stack inside. She started toward the door, then stopped and turned to him. "Oh, and if you try to stop us from leaving, we'll detonate the four bombs that were placed in strategic locations."

"What!" he yelled.

"Someone we know planted four bombs somewhere they can't be found. He wouldn't tell us where they are. He did say they would cause you maximum pain. They could be anywhere in the city. One could be at one of your bars, or one could be at your house. One could be here. I don't know. I do know that, if I don't leave here, one or all of them will be set off."

Capone stood and flipped the table over. "You bitch. Stop her!" he told Frank.

"I wouldn't do that if I were you," she warned him. She looked at Capone. "That's part of the deal."

"How can I trust they won't blow them up?"

"I have someone ready to hand deliver a letter to you once we're safely gone."

"I seem to have no choice."

"No, you don't. We're on our way out of town as soon as I leave here."

"So, we just wait."

"Yeah. You get to feel the terror we felt when we knew John was in jeopardy." She reached for the door. Frank blocked her exit.

"Let her go," Capone said.

She went out of the room onto the street. A car pulled up, and she jumped in. "Go!"

Danny drove quickly to the train station. Ben and Marisol were waiting for them. They'd drive their car home. Danny and Jemma ran up. "It worked! We're out," she exclaimed

"Mom and Dad are on the train to California," Ben said. "Capone won't come after us?"

"He says no."

"And we're taking Capone's word," Ben scoffed. "Torrio's stooge?"

"I think he'll be more than that; we should be getting out of Chicago. I also got what I went for." She patted her heavy purse.

"Good. We have our money to get everyone settled and expand our businesses."

"Yes."

"Will you be okay? Should I come for your court case?"

"Lottie says she has it under control," she said quietly.

He grabbed her by the chin. "Hey, call me if you need me. I'll be there, in gangster mode if necessary," he teased.

"Didn't we say I was the boss now that John's gone?" she teased back. Her eyes filled with tears. "Oh, Ben, I miss him so much!"

"Me too. There's a hole without him."

"Will you be able to handle Mom?"

"Dad's stronger than you think. I heard him put his foot down last night and tell her that the decision was final. I think he's tired of traveling and would like more control of his life."

"Who woulda thought."

"I know."

Marisol called to him, "We should be going if we want to get to Los Angeles before your parents."

"Okay," he responded, "I'm on my way."

"What'll we do with John's house?" he asked. "Will we keep it?"

"Yes, for a while."

"Think we might come back some day?"

"It might be something that happens after Prohibition's ended. Some place where we could have our kids hang out."

"Kids!"

"Hmmm," she said, "you and Marisol?"

"Hmm," he mocked, "you and Danny?"

"I think you've gotten the jump on us."

"How did you know?"

"I just know. Congratulations, brother."

"Thanks! Call us when you get back to New York."

CHAPTER 82

A couple of days later, a knock sounded on Capone's door. "Al, there's a man here with a letter," Frank said.

"Get it and bring the man in here." A tall, slim man in a black suit walked into the room. His gray hair shone silver in the light.

"I understand you want this," the man said, holding up an envelope.

"Hand it over!" Capone demanded.

The man did as asked and handed the envelope to him. Capone ripped it open and found a note. *There are no bombs.* He smashed the note and looked at the man menacingly. "Who the hell are you?" he demanded

"Me? I'm Cole Tilden with the Pinkertons. We have the place surrounded and will report on everything we've seen. So, if you make any moves toward Jemma or any of John's family, we'll make sure there'll be trouble for you."

"Fine, whatever! Just get out."

"See you later, Scarface." Cole turned and strolled out.

CHAPTER 83

Marisol was driving and watching for cars behind them.

"Be careful, we still have the alcohol with us."

"Yes, no drop off on this trip." She glanced over at him. "Your parents chose to live near us."

"Well, we basically live with yours," he reminded her. He tapped the dashboard. "We need to get them something to do."

"Any ideas?"

"Maybe, I'll have to think about that."

CHAPTER 84

alifornia

The return trip home took much longer. They stopped and rested at the halfway point. "It's good to be home," Marisol said, looking around the vines as they drove by. "That's odd," she mumbled.

"Is something wrong?"

"Stop the car."

"What do you see?" Ben asked, looking around them.

"It's what I'm not seeing; we should be seeing men in the field at this time of day."

He resumed driving and headed toward the house. They stopped, and he said, "Let's just take it easy. There's nothing to worry about."

She took a breath and said, "You're right. There's probably a good reason they're not in the fields."

Ben took her hand, and they entered the house together.

They went room to room, but the house was empty. "Where do you want to check next?"

"The main building." They walked out, and Marisol stopped and pointed at something. "What are those?"

Ben walked over and looked. "Gas cans. And they're empty," he said grimly. "I need to make a call." He ran back into the house with her following closely behind. He dialed quickly and made his request.

"Will that be needed?" asked Marisol.

"I'm afraid it might."

"We'll need the guns from the car."

They walked back to the car. He retrieved his pistol and her shotgun. They carried the weapons in case they were needed. The quiet was eerie; all the time he'd been there, there'd always been people around.

As they got closer to the building, they could hear a man shouting. Ben held up his finger to his mouth and pointed to the side window. They went over and looked in; the man's back was to them. "It's RL," she mouthed. He nodded and listened to what the man was saying.

"Where is she?" RL demanded.

"She isn't here," Angelo said. "RL, you need to let the men go. They haven't done anything to you."

"No! I'm in charge here and they'll stay!" He paced up and down, crying, "Why is he family and I'm not? He's a stranger; I was raised here. Why him and not me!" he screamed. The people in the room were quiet. Bella spotted Marisol and Ben at the window.

RL whirled on her. "What're you looking at?" he snarled.

"I have to start making dinner. I was just looking toward the house," she said, trying to distract him. It seemed to work as RL quieted for a moment.

"What do we do?" Marisol whispered.

"I'm afraid I might hurt someone if I try to shoot him through the window," Ben said.

"I have an idea." She reviewed it with him.

He frowned. "It might work, but don't get too close to him."

She stood and walked to the door. She pushed it open and called, "Mama! Papa! I'm home!"

"Marisol," RL said and started toward her.

Ben stepped out from behind her, his pistol in his hand. "Stop right there."

"I have a gun also," he said with false bravado.

"RL, I don't think you want to see who's the better shot. What was your plan here?"

"Kidnap Marisol." He looked at her. "I'll keep you with me, and then you'll have to marry me."

"It won't work," she said.

"Yes, it will! Your father will make you marry me."

"You're not listening. I AM ALREADY MARRIED!"

"What?" he asked, looking dazed.

"You heard me. I'm married."

"To that man?" He used his gun to point at Ben.

"Yes, to Ben."

"No," he scoffed, "there's been no wedding. I would've heard about it."

"They're married; there's nothing you can do about it," Angelo told him.

"Papa, you knew?"

"Of course. Would I let my daughter travel with a man and not be married?"

RL shook his head, dropped his gun, and ran toward the vines.

"Is everyone okay?" Ben asked them.

Angelo stood and helped Bella stand. "I think so."

"The envelope," asked Marisol.

"Marriage license," confirmed Ben.

"It is framed and hung in my office," said Angelo.

"Is he gone?" Bella asked, walking over to look out the door.

"I wouldn't count on it," Ben replied. The workers stood and started to file outside.

"What is that?" someone called.

"Smoke!" Angelo bellowed.

"He's trying to burn us down!" Marisol screamed.

The group raced toward the fire. They saw RL running toward them down the middle of the vines with a fire torch. "This shit's gone on long enough," Ben said and drew his gun. He got RL in the sights and pulled the trigger. He fell, and the torch landed on the ground beside him.

"The fire's spreading!" called Bella.

The workers retrieved blankets to start suffocating out the fires. Ben called, "Marisol, go into the house. Bella, come get her."

"But I want to help."

Bella gathered her up. "Marisol, we need to protect the baby." She nodded and turned to go to the house. A horn sounded in the distance. "Who's that?"

Ben yelled, "Reinforcements!"

Trucks rolled up and men began jumping out. Patrick led them. "Tell us what to do," he said. Angelo directed them; they used blankets and any available water to try to stop the fire.

"I don't think we can stop it from spreading!" yelled Angelo.

A plane buzzed overhead. "That should help. Everyone back," Patrick called. The plane came lower and released water on the vineyard. "Stay back. She'll be coming by again." The plane came lower again and released additional water on the vineyard.

"How is that possible?" said Angelo.

"Modified crop-dusters," explained Patrick. "Jean has a group of pilots who are always experimenting with new devices. This is their latest firefighting efforts."

"The fires are out!" Angelo whooped.

Their small group cheered. They waved at the plane as it tilted a greeting and flew off.

"Brother," Ben walked over to Patrick and hugged him. "Thanks!"

"Got to protect the family business."

ew York

Jemma knocked on the door and waited. Their train had arrived, and she went straight to the club. The slot on the door slid open. "We're not open." The slot closed quickly. She frowned and knocked again. The slot opened again. "Lady, I told you…"

She had her gun aimed at the space between his eyes. "I'm the owner, and you WILL open the door."

"Boss!" he screamed. He was yanked from the door, and another set of eyes was there. They widened in surprise and the door opened. It was Charlie. "Sorry about that, Jemma. We had some staffing changes since you left."

She put the gun back into her purse. "You'll have to explain that to me, Charlie." She walked into the main room and looked around. It looked much the same, and she headed to her office. "Bring me a beer," she called to the bartender.

He wasn't someone she recognized. "Right away," he called.

He met her before she crossed the room. She took a long drink and stopped. She turned and spit it back into the glass. "What the hell is this?" she demanded.

"Uh, beer," the bartender said. "Isn't that what you asked for?"

"That is not our beer."

"It is our beer," Charlie said. "We just watered it down a little."

"So, customers drink twice as much?"

"That's the idea."

"And who approved that?" she asked slowly.

"I did. You weren't here. I had to make an executive decision."

"I see. My office, Charlie. NOW!"

Charlie followed her. "What's this?" she asked, looking at the items on her desk.

"I'll take care of it," he said and dumped all of the contents into a bag beside the desk.

"Where's Lauren?"

"I got rid of her," he said gruffly.

She studied him. "Excuse me?"

"You heard me."

"You don't have the authority to let go of any of my personnel."

"You weren't here," he said defensively.

She looked at him incredulously. "Where is she?"

"How should I know?"

Her eyes narrowed. "You know where she is," she accused.

"She's trying to get money to pay us back," he admitted.

"Us?"

"You," he corrected.

"She doesn't owe me anything." He mumbled something. "Speak up."

"I told her she was also responsible for her brother's debt."

"That's a lie; they owe me nothing. That debt's been settled. I told you that." He stared at her stonily. "Charlie, I have a few questions for you."

"Go ahead, I got nothing to hide."

"Did you send Dolly in here to make trouble?"

"It would've made us more money to use the girls like that."

"Did you rat me out and get me shot by yelling fire?"

"You can't accuse me of that!"

"I don't have to accuse; all the things that've happened are adding up to you."

"So, what're you going to do about it?"

"Oh, I plan to do a lot." The boss knew when to make hard decisions, and she was about to make them.

He didn't like that and started to storm out. "Charlie, you're fired. Gather your things and get out."

"You can't do that."

"I'm the owner; you're an employee. You haven't met my expectations and are released from your job here. You're not welcome at any time."

"Oh yeah? And who's going to make me? You, you dumb broad?"

"That would be me," Mouse said from the door.

Charlie laughed loudly at that.

Jemma nodded at Mouse. Mouse swung his fist and hit Charlie in the stomach. As Charlie started to double up in pain, Mouse swung his fist into his face. He went down hard to the floor. "I'll get this cleaned up for you, boss," he said.

"Dump him far away from here, if you please."

Mouse went out to the main floor and waved to the bartender. He came over, and they pulled the man out of the room.

When he came back, Mouse said, "Boss, Lauren's at a dance contest."

She frowned. "That doesn't sound too bad." She hesitated,

thinking of his statement. "It's not a marathon dance contest, is it?"

"Yeah, the one at the Renaissance Ballroom."

She stopped. "Mouse, get everyone back. I want all of my original employees."

"Yes, boss, right after I get rid of this lump."

"I'm going to get Lauren." She headed out the back and saw Jojo sitting on the curb by her car.

"Jojo."

"You're back, a little late," he said looking dejected.

"I'm back now. We need to go get Lauren."

"She doesn't want to see me."

She kicked his leg. He looked up at her in surprise. "Get over it, you jackass. We need to go help her."

He stood and followed her to the car. The driver got out and opened the door for them.

"You're not Rocky. Who're you?" she demanded.

"I'm the driver. Charlie hired me."

"I'm the boss," she told him. "You're fired. Get out of the way. Jojo, get in."

Jemma jumped behind the wheel and Jojo got in on the other side. "Where're we going?" he asked.

"Mouse said she was at the Renaissance Ballroom in Harlem."

"I know that place," Jojo said as Jemma pulled into traffic. "Is that where Lauren is? But that's one of those marathon dances. And she's..."

"I know what she is," she interrupted. "Which is why a dance contest that has a risk of exhaustion and dehydration is danger- ous." She turned to face him. "Why didn't you know where she was?"

"She doesn't want to see me," he said, hanging his head low.

"Suck it up, Jojo. We'll deal with that later. God, I'm gone a couple of weeks, and everything goes to hell," Jemma fumed under her breath.

They stopped a block away from the ballroom. "Why're you stopping here?" Jojo asked.

"We can't get closer. Look, the crowds took over the streets all around the place."

They got out of the car and walked to the entrance. Jemma looked at the crowds in the street in front of them. It was packed.

An officer walking the area said, "You can't park here. That dance is already causing havoc."

"How long has it been going on?" Jemma asked him.

"This one? At least twenty-four hours."

"That means Lauren has been on her feet all that time?" Jojo said.

"That means we need to get in there and get her out."

"Sorry, folks, no can do," said an officer, walking his beat.

"Look," Jemma said, "we're looking for a friend. I'll give you a hundred dollars to let us park here."

He looked around. "Be quick about it."

"We will be," she promised and handed him fifty dollars.

"Hey!"

"Fifty now and fifty when we return."

He nodded and pocketed the money.

When they reached the club, she turned to Jojo. "Do you know who she's with?"

"Darren, probably. She kept saying she had to pay you back some money."

"Did she ask you for it?" He was quiet. She stopped and felt him run into her. "Well?" she asked.

"I offered and asked her to marry me. She said she'd find a way to pay her own debt."

She sighed. "Let's go." She pushed their way to the front of the line. A large man stood in the shadows, blocking her way.

"We need to get in," she said.

A deep voice from the man in front of her asked, "Boss?" The large man stepped out where they could see him.

Jemma stared up at him. "Casper, what're you doing here? Why aren't you at the club?"

"When they shut the club down, I had to work."

"Well, we're going to open again soon."

"Yeah?" he asked hopefully.

"Come back tomorrow."

"I'll be there."

"Casper, we need to get in. Lauren is in the contest."

"I saw her enter with Darren."

"Is she still dancing?" Jojo asked him.

"As far as I know. This thing is a real mess; it has been going on for twenty-four hours. Several people have been carried out."

"Oh no," said Jojo.

He opened the door for her, stepped aside, and people started yelling behind them. "Shut up," he called, "or you won't get in at all." That quieted them down.

Jemma stopped at the door and looked at him. "Casper, we may need help getting them out. Can you assist us?"

"Yes, boss. You'll need to buy a ticket to get on the dance floor."

"They look full up," observed Jojo.

"They just tell me to keep letting people in." Jojo and Jemma pushed their way to the ticket table. They paid twenty-five cents to enter. "Twenty-five cents for this?" asked Jemma.

"People like to watch human misery," Jojo commented.

"It is that. This should be banned. And they go after me for alcohol," she said, her mouth tight.

Jojo didn't respond. The smell of sweating bodies was overwhelming. People were in all states of dress; men were in their undershirts, and women had their dresses unbuttoned lower than was accepted. The crowds got denser as they got closer to the dance floor. Jojo was tall enough to see above the horde. "Do you see them?" asked Jemma.

"Not yet. No, wait, there they are," he said, waving to his left.

"Let's go. Casper! Over here," she called to the bouncer. He nodded and started moving in their direction. She and Jojo pushed people around them to get to the wall that separated the spectators from the dancers. They climbed over it and raced through the dancers to Lauren and Darren. "Hey! You can't be on the dance floor," called several men in suits, running toward them.

Lauren and Darren held each other, swaying. "We have to get them out of here," Jemma told Jojo. "Lauren!" She shook her shoulder. "Look at me. We need to get you out of here now!"

"No," she mumbled into her brother's shoulder, "no, we have to pay the money back."

"Have to pay you back," Darren said, barely coherent.

Jemma saw the men had gotten reinforcements and were barreling their way. She moved to stand in front of the couple.

The man in the lead said, "You can't be on the dance floor; this is for the contest only. You can't interfere with dancing couples."

"Oh, I think we can," said Jemma. "They're coming with us."

"They're committed to the contest. Why would they want to leave?"

Casper walked up to them and asked, "You ready, boss?"

"You work at the gate; get back to work," the man said.

"I don't work here anymore." He grabbed Darren and said to Jojo, "Get Lauren." Jojo didn't listen to Lauren's mumbled arguments and picked her up.

"Any questions now?" Jemma asked the group of men.

"No, I guess not." The crowds were booing as they moved the couple off the ballroom floor.

"This place is like a zoo," she said, looking around.

"They're here to see people collapse," said Casper. He picked up Darren and threw him over his shoulder. "Let's get out of here."

"Where to?" Jojo asked.

"My home. I have something to take care of at the club. And these two need to rest."

They made their way down the block to Jemma's car. They put them inside and crawled in together, Casper getting behind the wheel. As they drove away, Jemma said, "Roll the windows down." They cranked them down, and the cool air blew into the car. Once the air hit Darren and Lauren in the face, they started to be aware of their surroundings.

Darren was the first to react. "What? No! We have to finish the dance."

"Dance," commented Lauren groggily. "Have to keep dancing. Have to pay back the boss." Her feet started to move.

"Shhh, baby," said Jojo. "It's okay." She settled down but didn't open her eyes.

"But he'll kill us if we don't pay back the money," said Darren wildly.

"Who'll kill you?" Jemma asked. He collapsed on the seat, not answering. Jemma sat back; she didn't need the answer. She already knew.

CHAPTER 86

"Casper, put Darren in the room over there; Jojo, put Lauren in that room."

Jojo and Casper followed her directions and put them in beds. Jemma pulled the covers over both.

"What now?" asked Jojo, watching Lauren closely.

"Let them rest. Let's go into the living room." They followed her and sat down. "I need the full story. What's happened since I've been gone?"

Casper started. "You'd been gone for a few days, and Charlie said you weren't coming back. He said he now owned the club and would be making all decisions from then on."

"Did everyone accept that?"

"I didn't," said Casper. "I questioned it, and he told me to find someplace else to work."

"Jojo, you were still there?" she asked him.

"Me, Mouse, and Chef stayed. There were still a lot of us there at that time. We thought we'd just wait for you."

"What happened? I didn't recognize anyone when I went this evening."

"Charlie got rid of anyone who questioned him; they went one at a time."

"Why did Darren and Lauren think they owed me money?"

"Charlie cornered Darren and told him that the debt for the barrels was still there. Darren tried to explain that the debt had been worked out. Charlie said that was under your management, not his."

Darren spoke from the door. "He threatened to kill Lauren if we didn't come up with the money. He also fired us from the club." He leaned on the door, trying to stay upright.

Jemma said, "I'm sorry you had to go through that. There's no debt. Go back and rest." He nodded and dragged himself back to bed. She looked at her watch, "It's late." Casper stood. "Please be at the club on your normal schedule."

"I'll be there, boss." He smiled and left.

"Jojo," she asked, sitting back on the couch, "what's going on with you and Lauren?"

"I love her."

"And does she love you?"

"Jojo," called a soft voice.

"Lauren, you shouldn't be up," Jojo said and rushed over to her.

"I love you, too."

Jemma excused herself and went to her bedroom, giving them their privacy.

CHAPTER 87

The next morning, the sun shown into her room. She stretched and thought, *Today's going to be a good day. Charlie's gone, and things should be back to normal.* The only thing in her way right now was her court case. That had to be resolved before the club could be reopened. She pulled on a robe and went into the kitchen.

She stopped in surprise at the door. Lauren sat at the table in the same dress as the night before.

"You keep having to rescue me," she said, staring down at her juice glass.

"Friends do that," Jemma commented, putting together the coffee pot.

Lauren started to cry. Jemma went over to her and put her arms around her. "I'll make you a deal. Next time I am in trouble, I will expect you to help me."

She sniffed and said, "Deal."

"You good now?"

"Yes."

"Where's Jojo?"

"He went home to shower and change. He said he'd meet you at the club."

"Did the two of you settle things last night?"

"We're getting married."

"I'm glad."

"Me too."

"I need to get dressed; there's a lot of work at the club this morning."

"I heard you ran Charlie off."

"Yes, but I think he's still a threat."

"I might have something you'll need if he shows up again."

"What is it?"

Lauren got up and moved into the living room. Jemma followed. She reached under the desk and moved a hidden shelf. "I put this here when you were gone, figured it'd be a more secure location." She handed her the book.

Jemma opened it. "Hmm, this will be useful."

CHAPTER 88

Jemma walked down the steps and around the building. A large group of people were gathered around the door. As she got closer, she saw that it was all of her employees. She spotted Casper and waved. "Boss!" The group turned to her. Everyone greeted with choruses of, "Welcome back," and "We are so happy you've returned!"

"Thank you all. Why're you standing out here?"

Mouse walked up to her. "Charlie barricaded himself in."

"I thought you took care of him," she said.

"Guess I didn't do a good enough job."

"Is there anyone with him?"

"I emptied the place of Charlie's employees after you left; he should be alone."

"What about Bob?" she asked. "They were always together."

"Yeah, well, Bob thought he was a part owner once Charlie took over. He shut that down and fired him."

Casper joined them and asked, "What's the plan?"

"Well, I can't call the police," she said drolly.

Jojo joined them. "How's Lauren?" asked Jemma.

"Still tired. I told her to stay in bed. What's going on here?"

"Charlie barricaded himself in my club."

"Has he?" he said and studied the building.

"You have an idea?" she asked.

"I do; we'll need some things from my workshop." He looked around, "Everyone who wants to help, follow me." Everyone moved to follow Jojo. At the workshop, Jemma asked, "What're you thinking?"

"Here, here, and here." He pointed to the drawings in front of him. "These are places where we could use rams to enter."

"I'm not sure." She hesitated. "We don't want a gun fight." She studied the drawings. "Have you fixed the door to my secret space?"

"No, we waited for you to return."

"I want to go in that way."

"You, alone?" asked Jojo.

She looked around at the people stuffed in the workroom. "Yes, I created this situation, I need to see it through."

"Please take someone with you."

She shook her head and said, "Keep everyone here. Wait for me to send word."

And if you don't? thought Jojo.

She headed out and Casper and Mouse followed her. She stopped and said, "Stay here."

"No, John sent us for this reason," Mouse said. Casper nodded.

She relented. "Don't put yourself at risk."

The three headed back to the club. She stopped and said, "We'll do this three ways. Casper, you'll go create a ruckus at the front door, demanding to get into the building."

"Do you mind if I damage the door?" he asked.

"Demolish it, if you want."

"And me?" asked Mouse.

"There are windows at the top of the backroom."

"I haven't seen any?"

"They're covered, but you should be able to kick one out."

"And you?" asked Mouse.

"Me? I'm going through the secret back door through my wine room. Guns?" asked Jemma. Both nodded. "Don't use them unless there's no other way."

They each went to their destinations. Jemma pushed the door and entered the small room. The glass had been cleaned up, and the floors were stained red with wine. The door had been leaned back up, but there was a large enough gap for her to get through. She waited and watched; she couldn't see Charlie. She jumped in surprise when the banging started at the club entrance.

She wasn't the only one. Mouse had gotten through the window and was sliding down the wall when the banging started. He dropped faster than he expected to the floor. He eased out to the entryway of the kitchen. He saw Jemma, and he nodded to her.

Charlie ran to the door. "Stop, you're damaging the door. Who is it?" He tried to open the peep hole, but it seemed jammed. **Bang bang bang**. "Stop! I said stop!" he screamed. "The door's coming off the hinges."

Jemma moved out of her space and waved to Mouse. Each had their guns drawn. "You might want to back away from there," she suggested. "I think the door's about to give."

Charlie spun, his gun drawn, and pointed at her. "This is my club, get out."

"Oh, Charlie, I could say the same thing."

The door broke. A large piece hit him on the back, pushing him forward to the floor. Mouse kicked the gun out of his hand.

It wasn't just Casper who charged in; it was all of her employees. "Good plan, boss," he said. The group surrounded Charlie.

"Drag him into my office. This isn't over yet," said Jemma.

They moved him and waited for him to wake. "It's about time," she said. "Ready to talk now?"

Charlie pulled himself up to his knees.

"Watch yourself," said Casper. He was close enough to grab him if needed.

Charlie watched Jemma begin to clean her small handgun. "We need to talk about betrayals, Charlie."

"I didn't betray you. I've supported you since the beginning."

Jemma finished cleaning the gun, picked it up slowly, and pointed it at him. "You'd know about betrayal, wouldn't you, Charlie?"

He held up his hands. "Now, look, I'm on your side. I always have been."

"Are you, though?" She reached over and opened the bag sitting next to her. She threw the book Lauren had given to her onto the table.

His face turned white. "Where'd you get that?"

"Let's just say I have someone looking out for me who *is* loyal."

She still held the gun on him. He laughed. "So, what, you're going to kill me? Who do you think you are? A gangster?"

She laughed, a low one that came from her belly. She stopped abruptly and said, "Funny you say that. I have a family full of them. Ever heard the name John Harden? I'm his grand-daughter."

He paled. "No one told me that."

Before he could react, the office door swung open, and three men strode in. "Grab him," directed Clay.

The other two men moved toward Charlie. He backed into the wall, trying to get away. When he had nowhere to go, each man took an arm.

"You can't do this!" he protested.

"You stole from me, Charlie, skimmed off all of my accounts. Very detailed accounts, by the way."

"It's my money! I'm a partner here."

She laughed again. "You were a worker, never a partner. There was never an agreement."

"I only took what was mine."

"No, what you took was mine, and I got it back."

"How? How could you know where I put it?"

"That doesn't matter now," Clay said. "You're coming with us. Back door?" he asked.

"No," she said, staring at Charlie, "drag him through the club, set an example."

He nodded and motioned at them to take him out. Once they were out of the office, Clay said, "Good to see you, Jemma. Thanks for taking care of Edna for me."

"Not a problem. I expect you'll come to work for me full-time."

"I will."

He tipped his hat at her and headed out.

Jemma put her gun and book back into her desk and strolled toward the large open room. Everyone stood watching as Charlie was dragged through, crying out for help. Once he was pulled out the front door, the employees went right back to work.

Jemma went and sat down at a large corner table. An arm came around her. "You got the money?"

"It's here," Danny said and patted the bag sitting next to him.

"I'll have to find a position for you."

He lowered his head to hers, and just before their lips touched, he said, "I can't wait."

CHAPTER 89

Jemma hurried into the courthouse. "You're late," Lottie scolded, meeting her at the entrance.

"Isn't this just a technicality? Won't I just get off with a slap on the hand?"

"I'm not sure how this will go. There haven't been enough cases."

"But the jury's usually on our side, right?" Jemma asked.

"The judge could overrule the jury; we still have to be careful."

She nodded. The court doors opened, allowing them in. They sat, waiting for their trial time.

"Is Charlie gone?" Lottie asked in a low voice.

"He hasn't been seen in the last few weeks," Jemma said noncommittally. It was best that Lottie didn't know how Charlie ended up.

"He's a threat."

Not anymore, she thought.

"How's Lauren?"

"She's fully recovered and is now our manager, having replaced Charlie."

"Who took over for her?"

"Danny stepped in and will assist Lauren more as she gets further along in her pregnancy."

"The wedding was wonderful."

"It was." They'd held it at the club as a private party.

"All rise," the bailiff called.

The judge entered. Jemma recognized him, but didn't show it.

"Smile for the jurors," muttered Lottie.

"Why?"

"Because they're going to keep you out of jail."

Jemma smiled and glanced toward the men who were being selected for trial. Most smiled back. She recognized some from her club.

They started the questions, and over and over, men were dismissed for declaring their opposition to the dry laws.

"Unpopular law," Lottie whispered.

"Yeah, it is."

At the end of the day, not one man had been empaneled. "How many more days of this?" Jemma asked.

"Until they realize this won't work."

The judge banged his gavel and said, "We'll start again tomorrow."

They exited the courtroom, and reporters stopped them, shouting, "Why didn't the case start today?"

"There was no jury selected," Lottie told them. "There has to be a jury." She took Jemma's hand, and they walked out through the crowd of reporters.

They went back to court every day the following week. By Friday afternoon, sixty-nine jurors had been interviewed, and fifty-seven had been dismissed. And they finally had a trial date.

"Rum courts, that's what they were being called," Lottie said.

"That wasn't rum that they shot out of my hand," Jemma said drolly.

CHAPTER 90

The following week, Jemma and Lottie left the courthouse. "I'm glad that's over," said Jemma, walking down the stoop. "You'll need to have a lower profile."

"What for? That was just a misdemeanor."

"For now. Jemma, should you continue this business?"

She paused. "What do you mean?"

"It might be time to shut down."

"That's the last thing I'd do; I have a lot of mouths to feed. Besides, I have friends in high places. Quite literally, in fact," she said, looking back at the courthouse.

Lottie raised her eyebrows in question.

"The judge has been a private party member." Jemma smiled.

Lottie's eyes widened, and she looked back toward the courthouse. "Do you think he recognized you?"

She laughed. "Oh, I know he did. I expect he wanted this over sooner rather than later, so that he could have his private stock back."

"I thought they broke all of your bottles."

"Whoever informed on me isn't aware of all of my secrets."

"Do we still need to worry they'll report you again?"

"No, that person's gone. Can we open now?" she asked Lottie.

She sighed. "The courts are so backed up that even if you get arrested again, I don't think it'll go through the system. I think we'll see Mullan-Gage shut down in the next two years."

"Thanks for the help."

"That's what you pay me for. Lissette wants a girls' night with you and Lauren sometime soon."

"Just let us know when. Teatime starts tomorrow, and the club will be open on Friday night."

"I'll let Lissette know to get the word out."

CHAPTER 91

Jemma knocked on the door, and the peephole opened. "Hey, boss." Casper grinned. She entered and gave him her coat and hat.

"Gather everyone up, Casper. I have an announcement."

He called out, "Everyone, gather in the main club! The boss has an announcement."

She went to the bandstand and picked up the mic. "Is everyone ready to get back to work?" A cheer went up from the crowd. "We want everything perfect, so get your uniforms cleaned and pressed. New hires, keep practicing carrying trays. We don't want any broken glass."

She started walking to her office. "What about the teatime?" Lauren asked as she caught up to her.

"Tomorrow. Lottie will get Lissette to let the ladies know."

Later in the day, flowers arrived. Casper put them in her office. "Who are they from?" she asked.

He pulled out the card and read it. "They're from the mayor; he's looking forward to a special event when it can be arranged."

She nodded, thinking. "Send Jojo in." He stepped out to find Jojo.

"You called for me."

"Is that grin permanent?" she teased.

"I think it might be; thanks for having the wedding here."

"I enjoyed it. I called to ask about our secret wine room."

He frowned. "I'm not sure we should use that space again. I think the secret's out?"

"Do you have any ideas for another space?"

"There's two inventory storage areas on the next block."

"You know," Jemma said thoughtfully, "Ben has a speakeasy behind a soda shop."

"We have a larger space; we could use it as a shop with a large back room and a back entrance."

"We could sell the bricks in the front and have the private parties in the back. We can make it more comfortable with tables and banquets."

He laughed. "I like that."

"Good, walk over with me later and show me your ideas."

"I will," he started out. "Oh yeah, I think I've come up with a solution for how to prevent you from getting caught with the bottles next time."

"How so?"

"A chute to the basement, similar to the system at the bar."

"What happens there?"

"Crash."

"Crash," she said incredulously. "Do you know the value of the bottles I keep here?" She thought about it. "Could the chute be made of cloth and caught at the bottom instead of crashing into the floor?"

"Well," he said, "we could work on the location and a spring on the door, closing on both ends to hide where the bottles went."

"Hmm," she said, "I like that."

"You'd have to schedule someone down there each night, just in case."

"I'll work on that."

CHAPTER 92

"*L*auren, are the cards ready?" Jemma asked.

"They are. I got the shipment in a few days ago."

"Bring them in here. I want to hand them out Friday night at the opening."

"I'll be right back."

Jemma worked on her books; she'd managed to put all of the employees back to work. Some were stationed in the club, some on Darren's teams, and others were managing inventory at various locations. She heard an argument outside her door. She went over and opened it.

"They're too heavy for you; you need to be more careful," Jojo was saying to Lauren. The two of them were in a tug of war with a large box in between them.

Jemma clapped her hands. "Children! Hand them over to me." They handed her the much contested box. "Jojo, I think you have work to get to?"

"Yes, boss," he mumbled and left them.

"He won't let me carry anything," Lauren groused.

"And you love it," Jemma teased her as she set down the box on the table.

"Yeah, I do, but don't tell him."

"Show me the cards."

Lauren reached into the box and pulled out the first set. She unwrapped them and handed the red and black cards to her.

Jemma read, "Club York. I love it. We'll need different colors every few weeks."

"Yes, I'd thought of that." Lauren handed her a stack of cards in multiple colors.

Jemma laughed. "You were right all along; you should've been my manager from the start."

"Exactly. You should listen to me in all things."

"We'll pass these out on Friday night to the regulars. Get Casper in here so we can review this with him."

Lauren left and came back a few moments later with Casper. "What's up, boss?" he asked.

"Lauren's come up with a way to hopefully make us more secure."

Lauren handed him a card. "Regulars will have these."

He looked at it. "Will we still use passwords?"

"At first, I think we will use both," Jemma replied.

"Just don't let Izzy in again," teased Lauren.

"Oh, boss," the big man seemed to shrink in front of her, "he had a barrel of pickles. How was I to know a fat man with pickles was an agent?"

"I heard his latest trick was a trombone," said Jemma.

"How would that work?" asked Lauren.

"He can plan the song 'How Dry I Am' on it; bartenders rush to give him a drink."

"It won't be me, boss. I promise. I won't let anyone in with a trombone."

"I believe you."

CHAPTER 93

It was like they'd never been closed. The band was playing, people were eating, drinking, and having a good time. Lauren and Jojo were milling with the customers, making sure they were having a good time. Casper was at the door making sure those with the ID cards were able to get in, and those who didn't, well...

Darren was behind the bar with Maeve and Nate. He was making sure there was plenty of liquor. Chris was sitting at the bar, catching eyes with Nate as often as he could. Mouse and Chef were checking the food to make sure it was being refreshed.

Jemma spotted both Mayor Hylan and Lois Long having a grand time. She waved at Lottie and Lisette dancing together, openly.

She smiled and waved at the judge from her hearing, and she saw a couple of the jurors, too.

Danny walked by, and she grabbed him and pulled him onto the dance floor. "C'mon, lover, it's time to celebrate."

"Wait, I don't dance!"

"You do now!" She laughed and pulled him close to her.

alifornia

Mel sat in his apartment with Ben. "I don't have anything to do here," he grumbled. "I feel useless. This is what it's come down to? I'm being left behind. John's gone now, and the whole business we ran no longer there. Maybe I should go back and face Capone."

"I've been thinking about that," Ben said. "I have five bars in town. Would you like to see them?"

"Might as well, I don't have anything else to do."

They went to the first bar and picked up Johnny, and they toured the bars and the soda shop. "You already got a manager." Mel pointed at Johnny. "There's nothing for me here out here."

"Mel, you can do whatever you want; the bars are yours."

"What? Mine!"

"Yes, yours. John left me and Jemma with instructions that you were to be taken care of, wherever you ended up. If you'd chosen to go to New York, Jemma would've given you the same deal. Mel, this is your pension, a thank you for a lifetime of support."

"But… but, this is yours."

"Just for a little time. It has been yours all along. I do trust you'll still buy the wine from us," Ben added.

Mel suddenly smiled. "You got a deal."

CHAPTER 95

ew York

It was early, and the sun was coming up as they walked back to Jemma's home arm in arm. "Successful night," Danny said, kissing her temple.

"It was. I think we made back what we lost when we were closed."

She unlocked the door and went inside. He grabbed her hand. "Now I have you all to myself." She laughed and allowed herself to be pulled into the bedroom.

She fell back on the bed, and he followed her down. His lips were close to hers when the phone rang. "Leave it," he murmured, kissing her.

"I can't, that might be Ben. I told him I'd tell him how the opening went."

"Ugh," he groaned and flopped down beside her. She moved to the bedside and picked up the phone. "Hello."

"Jemma, it's Ben."

"It's wonderful to hear from you."

"Says you," muttered Dan. Jemma swatted his arm as he stood and started to unbutton his shirt. She watched him closely.

"Jemma, are you there?" Ben asked.

"Yes, sorry about that." She turned away from Danny to concentrate on what Ben was saying.

"Mom and Dad got jobs."

"Jobs! Doing what?"

"Mom's working in the movies; Jean said she's a natural, go figure. And Dad's painting glass for special effects and painting backgrounds."

"They're making money? John would be shocked."

"I know. Maybe he should've pushed Mom to do more." He was silent for a long moment. "Jemma?"

"Yeah."

"Are you happy?"

She looked at a shirtless Dan and said, "Yeah. What about you?"

He looked over at a sleeping Marisol, her pregnant belly showing. "Yeah. Yeah, me too."

HISTORICAL NOTES FOR THE FAMILY BUSINESS

Prohibitions (the Volstead Act) lasted from 1920 to 1933 and opened up opportunities for gangsters to make a lot of money from the illegal production and distribution of alcohol. Al Capone made a name for himself during this time. He was known to have made 60 million annually during the years that alcohol was limited.

Isidor "Izzy" Einstein was responsible for shutting down speakeasies using unusual disguises. Izzy did show up at the door with a barrel of pickles and got let in. He also used the trombone to trick bartenders into giving him alcohol. His rotund figure and jovial manner got him in the door, even when he told them he was a prohibition agent.

To "86th" was a call to exit when the club was being raided. It is often attributed to the 86th Street in New York. It became part of the slang of the time, used by everyone from newspapers, books, and other media.

Mullan-Gage started in New York in 1921 and empowered law enforcement to enforce the Volstead Act. It was a confusing time, and most did not agree with the law. Eventually, it was determined to be largely ineffective and was repealed in 1923.

Capone and funeral flowers. Capone was known to send funeral flowers to the families of those who had been killed by his organization.

California's wine industry took a big hit during prohibition, and many vineyard owners pulled out their vines and planted orchids. Bricks to make wine saved the entire industry.

Airplanes and fire response. In 1921, women were pilots and were participating in the changes happening to airplanes. Though not used on a commercial basis yet, pilots were experimenting and looking for other uses for crop-dusting airplanes, such as firefighting.

K.R. MULLINS

Divided
Lives

ABOUT THE AUTHOR

Kimberly Mullins is the author of series of books titled "Notebook Mysteries", "1897 A Mark Sutherland Adventure", "Divided Lives" and "Lights, Camera, Murder!!!". Her stories are based on historical events occurring in the 1880s to 1920's. She holds a BS in Biology and a MBA in Business. She lives in Texas with her husband and son. When she is not writing she is working as a Process Safety Engineer at a large chemical company. You can connect with her on her website www.kimberlymullinsauthor.com.

Photo Credit: Blessings of Faith Photography

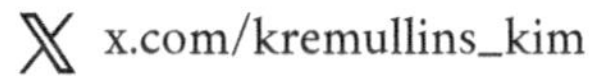 x.com/kremullins_kim